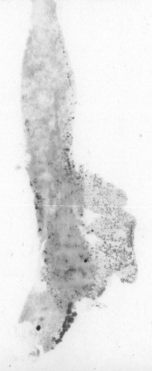

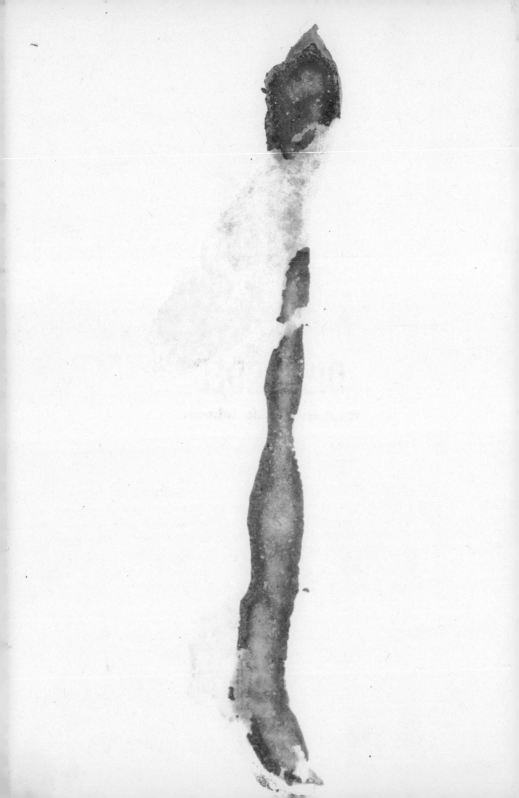

Aransas

ARANSAS

A Novel by
STEPHEN HARRIGAN

 Alfred A. Knopf   New York   1980

Fic
HAR

I am grateful to the Texas Institute of Letters and the University of
Texas at Austin for the Dobie-Paisano Fellowship that allowed me to
complete this novel. I would also like to thank Terry McCoy, Suse
Shame, Phillip Berry, and Robert Reyna for their assistance and hos-
pitality.

THIS IS A BORZOI BOOK
PUBLISHED BY ALFRED A. KNOPF, INC.

Grateful acknowledgment is made to the following for permission to
reprint previously published material:

The Ecco Press: "Messengers" by Louise Glück. Copyright © 1975
by Louise Glück. From The House on Marshland, published by the
Ecco Press, and reprinted by permission;

Irving Berlin Music Corporation: Excerpt from Easter Parade on
page vii by Irving Berlin. © Copyright 1933 Irving Berlin. © Copyright renewed 1960 Irving Berlin. Reprinted by permission of Irving
Berlin Music Corporation.

Library of Congress Cataloging in Publication Data

Harrigan, Stephen, [date]   Aransas.

    I. Title.
PZ4.H 297Ar   [PS 3558.A626]   813'.5'4   79-21983
ISBN 0-394-50624-3
Manufactured in the United States of America

FIRST EDITION

For Marjorie and Tom

You have only to let it happen:
that cry—release, release—like the moon
wrenched out of earth and rising
full in its circle of arrows

until they come before you
like dead things, saddled with flesh,
and you above them, wounded and dominant.

"Messengers"
—Louise Glück

Aransas

Chapter 1

We lay in ambush on the Laguna Madre, just below the lip of the great open basin of Corpus Christi Bay. There were two of us, in two small outboard skiffs, rented Boston Whalers. I was wearing my wetsuit top, which warmed the air around my torso but left the rest of my body vulnerable to the early morning chill. On the Gulf side of Padre Island the sun had begun to appear, backlighting the dune grass with a rose-colored band that followed the horizon to the ends of vision. The shallow inland water was as still as a glacier, though as I lay on my back in the boat, my feet slung in the steering wheel and my head resting on a hundred and fifty feet of carefully coiled net, I could feel a gentle, rhythmic swell beneath me, like the shallow breathing of a sleeping person. I thought of the porpoises ranging about somewhere in this water, gliding through it with concern and grace.

We were here to capture two of these porpoises and take them back to Port Aransas, where we would train them to perform tricks. This was my job, what I had come home for. I wish I could believe that the misgivings I felt that morning were more profound, or at least more emotional, than they actually were. In fact my misgivings were merely practical: I simply could not believe it was possible to extract a porpoise from this

water, and I was impatient for us to fail. The lagoon was as lus-
terless and tranquil as if it had never been visited by a living
thing. It seemed to me we would have better luck trying to
snare high-flying birds from the sky.

I had some feeling, of course, for the creatures themselves,
some notion of the general vulgarity of animal training, but I
was willing to lay these considerations aside in the improbable
event that we succeeded. I was not stupid—I did not believe
we were doing the porpoises a "favor," as Canales had told me,
by giving them the opportunity to refine their intelligence under our direction. But I did not want to take an extreme position the other way. I just wanted to live in the world again. So I
lay in the boat with my head on the net, which was studded
with the remains of long-dead sea creatures. The dry husk of a
crab scratched my cheek, and I breathed in the rich, pungent
smell of living things that have corroded in salt air.

When I closed my eyes, lulled by the almost imperceptible
movement of the boat, I encountered a disquieting image, so
sharp and insistent it must have come from memory, though I
did not "remember" it in the normal way. A man in a boat
skipper's hat was standing on a pier with an odd grin on his
face and an oversize rod and reel in one hand. The other hand
hovered tentatively above the dorsal fin of the creature hoisted upside down beside him—a porpoise, hanging by its flukes,
the carcass enmeshed in rope, bleeding from the spiracle and
from a gaff wound in the broad forehead. It was a still image,
as from a photograph, but the man's smile, though stationary,
grew grim and urgent the more I focused on it, and his hand
seemed to be trying to move away from the thing he had
killed.

"You asleep?" Canales said from the other boat.

"No," I muttered, though the image had been so vivid I
thought perhaps I was. I looked over at Canales, lifting my
head a little to clear the low gunwale of the skiff. The sun was
up now: it gleamed on the mounting of his solitary shark's
tooth necklace.

"I don't know what's keeping Dude," he said. "You might

as well go to sleep if you want. If he doesn't get here soon you might as well sleep all day. Damn porpoises'll be all the way up the channel."

"He'll show up," I answered, but Canales was not reassured. I had never known Mr. Granger to be on time, but he was never late enough for it to make a difference. In another person this sort of timing might have been calculated, but in his case I'm fairly certain it was not—some internal knowledge impelled him to show up, in all innocence, at that precise moment when his presence would be most appreciated.

Canales sat up in his tiny boat, impatiently picking bits of carapace from the net and dropping them into the water. His wetsuit—a pale blue custom model with yellow stripes along the arms—was unzipped to the sternum so that a sun-bleached tuft of hair was visible, and above it the necklace with its single serrated tooth. He had a trim black mustache and a glossy, well-tended head of hair that looked like a detachable shell; but his good grooming, set against this featureless land- and seascape, only made him seem conspicuous and uncomfortable.

I hardly knew him at all. Mr. Granger had introduced us as soon as I arrived two days earlier, but Canales had been so busy seeing to the construction of the pool, to the procurement of the equipment we needed, and to a last-minute bureaucratic snag with his permits from the Marine Mammal Commission that we had done little more than shake hands.

"You've never worked with porpoises before," he had said, "is that right?"

"That's right."

"You know something about them, though? You know they're mammals, for instance—that they breathe air?"

"Sure."

He looked relieved. "You'd be surprised how many people don't. I imagine you'll be all right. Anyway, Dude wants you in, and it's his money."

Canales' contribution to the project was his expertise. He had worked with porpoises before at Sea Park in California,

and after that had done "some free-lancing," and then had finally come down to Texas six months ago, casually looking for
investors for a modest oceanarium he had in mind—hardly
more than a subsistence operation to be built right on the water, eliminating the need for filtration systems and mammoth
infusions of salt. By and by he found Mr. Granger, who was as
usual looking for exotic ways to invest his corporate assets.

"What we've got here, Jeff," Mr. Granger had told me
about Canales, "is a man who knows his business. He's worked
with whales and seals and those—what do you call those, the
ones with the tusks?"

"Walruses."

"He's worked with walruses. At the biggest place in the
country. So I thought he just might know what he was talking
about."

I didn't doubt Canales' credentials, or his skill, but I sensed
that Mr. Granger's bankrolling of the project had been a lucky
break, one Canales hadn't really expected. He seemed constantly to be reining his energy in, not wanting to blow his
chance.

"You want to go over it again?" he asked me now. "I don't
think we'll have but one or two chances before the whole herd
catches on to what we're doing. Then we'll have to start all
over, way up the channel in Copano Bay or someplace."

"I've got it down," I said.

"Sure?"

"Don't worry." I was looking over the side of the boat,
bogged down in reverie, and did not want to be disturbed. A
cabbagehead pulsed along a few inches below the surface, suspended in the murky water like fruit in gelatin. A mullet
slipped into the air and slapped gracelessly back into the water. The sunlight was everywhere now, in force—the island,
the water, the desolate spoilbanks were all melded together
into one seamless mass that quavered beneath the heavy South
Texas air. The trapped air inside my wetsuit began to feel un-
comfortably warm, and I wondered if it would be worth the effort to pull the thing off.

"Finally," Canales said.

He was looking down the channel, watching Mr. Granger's pontoon boat idling toward us. Its broad beam plowed through the still water and left a gouge that took a hundred yards to heal itself. The boat's deck was as bare and flat as a dance floor, with a pulpitlike steering platform rising from the port side, behind which Mr. Granger sat like a prudent beginning driver. The three high-school kids he had hired to help out were standing at the bow railing, fighting over a pair of binoculars.

Mr. Granger pulled the boat out of the channel and brought it alongside the skiffs, nearly swamping us. One of the kids tossed me the bow line. I slipped a clove hitch around the rotten piling my own boat was tied to.

"How we doin'?" Mr. Granger asked from behind the steering platform. He was asking Canales, but he winked at me when he said it. As long as I had known him—and that was nearly all my life—he had always assumed some secret knowledge between us. When he had greeted me at the ferry landing two days before, there had been that same wink, but I had noticed right away that some of the old irony behind the gesture had vanished. The old man had broken into tears, sat down on the hood of his car and actually sobbed, then reached out blindly and gripped my forearm, telling me how much he had loved my parents, how he had missed them all these years. I didn't want to hear that, but for his sake I listened and didn't find it so unbearable.

In the past eleven years I had seen him only once. He had come to Santa Fe one spring, walked around with his hat in his hands, saying over and over in his high, womanish voice, "It's a damn pretty place, isn't it, Jeff?" Later he insisted on taking me and a half-dozen of my friends out to dinner. In the restaurant he had recited poems by Rudyard Kipling, and my friends had stared at him and smiled, charmed, like all good hippies, by any display of eccentricity. He stayed another day, tried to strike up conversations with the Indians on the plaza, then finally acceded to their silence and bought a grocery-bagful of expensive turquoise and silver trinkets to distribute among his friends on the coast. It was not until he was seated behind the wheel of his Seville, ready to go home, that I understood he had come all this way just to see me. I did not know what to say to him. He sat alone in his car and looked down the road, tapping the steering wheel with his fingers. He looked forward, he said, to seeing Billy the Kid's grave in Fort Sumner on the way home. I said it was not to be missed. We shook hands and he drove off.

In those eleven years he had not once forgotten my birthday, sending me each year an ant farm, or a pair of handmade cowboy boots, or a silver overlay for my telephone receiver engraved with my name; once even a Nehru suit, which I kept for years in a box under my bed, feeling guilty whenever I thought about it.

He looked no better this morning than he had two days ago. The last six years had aged him badly. He was over seventy now, and though nothing specific had gone wrong with him he seemed to have slackened, begun to play out. His glasses were now as thick as ice cubes, and from most angles his eyes were lost in refraction. Without them his face had a sweet, vacuous look.

He was wearing an authentic Panama hat, the kind with the ridge along the crown, and one of the white suits of his own design that were made for him by the closetload by a family of tailors in Refugio he kept on retainer. I remember those suits from my earliest childhood—the coat plunging straight to Mr. Granger's knees without benefit of style, stitched all the way down with odd, asymmetrical pockets from which he used to withdraw cheap little dime-store toys every time he came to visit.

"These three gentlemen," he said now, indicating the high-school boys he had brought along, "are going to be helping us out today." He introduced them more elaborately than the circumstances required, so that Canales and I were obliged to stand in our boats and reach up and shake hands with each of them over the railing.

Canales was impatient with the ceremony. "We'd better start looking now," he said. "They'll be coming up the channel, a pretty big group. There's a big old male porpoise with a strange fin, sort of chopped off close to his body. It's more triangular than your usual dorsal. Then there's about a dozen others that travel with him." He took a spiral notebook from a tackle box and studied it for a moment. "I'd say some time in the next twenty minutes we ought to see them."

We climbed onto the larger boat by the ramp Canales had built along one side for hauling the porpoises aboard. I went to the stern, shielded my eyes with one hand, and looked down the channel. There was a slight wind now, and once or twice I mistook the glint of sunlight on the shallow swells for the fin of a porpoise. But the error was momentary. It had been a long time since I had last seen porpoises in this channel, but I remembered how unmistakable their appearance always was, the great bland shapes sliding out of the gray water, as startling and unwarranted as if they had burst forth from the earth itself.

Mr. Granger kept to his station at the steering wheel, joining in the reconnaissance with the binoculars. Canales was lecturing the teenagers on the bow.

"Now these animals have a blowhole right on top of their heads. That's like their nose, that's how they breathe. You have to keep that thing out of the water, otherwise they'll drown just the same as us. Okay?

"All right. We're going to net them in shallow water so all we'll have to do is stand there and hold them up till we're ready to load them on the big boat. Me and Jeff'll be in the skiffs—we'll get to them first, but as soon as you see us spread that net, you have Dude open it up all the way and haul ass to help us. I don't want any of these animals to drown."

All three kids nodded solemnly.

"Now when you get hold of them they'll thrash around a little bit—hell, you would too—but you just hang on. Don't believe it when somebody tells you they won't bite." Canales held his right hand out for their inspection. He had shown it to me earlier—half a dozen round, evenly spaced scars, a wound that looked like it had been put there by a factory punch. "But you just keep your hands out of their mouths and you won't have to worry."

"Goddamn," one of the kids said. "First you tell us they're practically tame. Now I find out they can bite my hand off."

"They won't." Canales grinned. "I promise."

"Shit."

"What if they jump over the net?" another asked.

"They won't think to do that. They're smart as hell but some things just don't occur to them."

"I don't know," the first kid said, "this seems like a pretty half-assed operation."

"That's why we hired assholes like you to help us."

"Ha ha," the kid said flatly. I turned back to my surveillance of the washed-out horizon. Near the cut on the island side of the channel I saw a half-dozen fins break water. They rose in silence and authority out of the flat, lambent surface. They were glossy and full-bodied, from this distance a deep, deep gray. When they submerged another group surfaced among them, as if in rotation.

I could sense how profoundly alien they were, yet at the same time I felt my body give a small involuntary lurch forward, wanting to join them. I remembered then that first occasion on which I had seen them. I could not have been more than three years old, crossing with my mother on the Port Aransas ferry. She pointed toward the jetties, toward the shapes rising and spouting from the water, and said reverently, "Look, honey, those are the fish that saved your father."

It did not occur to me now to mention my sighting to Canales. It was a private vision. He saw them soon enough anyway.

"Over there," he said in a near whisper, as if the porpoises were some kind of fleet-footed terrestrial animals that would startle and run at the sound of his voice. "Okay, Jeff, let's get in the boats."

We slipped over the side again into the skiffs, untied them from the piling, but held them in place for a while with our hands. We watched as the porpoises caught up, swimming even with us in the deeper water of the channel, breaching infrequently now but with a collective rhythm it seemed the whole herd assumed responsibility for maintaining. I saw the big male with the triangular fin, the harem keeper. He was broader than the others, and looked when he breached like the overturned hull of a shallow-keeled boat.

"We'll give them a lead before we take off," Canales said. "Then very gradually, very slowly we'll work our way around to the far side and try to herd them out of the channel. We don't want to tie together yet but let's stay real close." He turned and looked at me with a challenging stare.

"Okay?"

"Sure," I said.

"Remember not to fuck up."

In his boat Canales was kneeling on one knee, his head down like a quarterback whispering a Hail Mary before the game. His concentration was unnerving, because I understood for the first time that we were going to succeed. The image rose again in my mind, the man and the dead porpoise, each with a grim, fixed smile.

When the herd was a hundred yards up the channel we started our motors, infesting the morning air with the smell of gasoline and two blue clouds of exhaust. At Canales' signal we slipped into gear and set forth in tandem into the channel, the pontoon boat bulldozing its way through the water behind us. We swung west toward the mainland and closed in slowly upon the herd. I saw the porpoises, in reaction to our presence, drifting toward the other side of the channel. They did not seem disturbed.

Canales pointed to a little pod of three or four animals that had broken off from the main herd.

"We'll try them," he shouted above the noise of the boats. "Let's tie off now."

With the boats idling we found the ends of our nets and joined them together, so that now we were one craft.

For another quarter mile we followed the pod. They were

close to the lee side of Padre Island now, feeding, rocking up and down almost in place. The main herd had moved farther north and were about to enter the bay.

Canales looked over at me in a stern, quizzical way and put his hand up in the air, ready to give the signal for us to draw apart and encircle the pod. He waited until we were about twenty yards away—the porpoises still rocking up and down like buoys, a lighter shade of gray now that we were closer to them—and lifted his arm a little higher, tensing it, then brought it down in a furious swipe. We opened our throttles at the same moment and headed away from one another to form a circle with the net. Even then the porpoises did not seem particularly alarmed, and I had made a ninety-degree arc before they bolted off toward the open water. I thought we would have no trouble closing the net ahead of them, but when I looked back for Canales I saw his boat lying still in the water, the net tangled around the propeller shaft. I cut my motor back and watched the porpoises submerge and surface again fifty yards up the channel. They were entering the bay.

"My fault," he said. "Stupid mistake. I fed the net out on the wrong side of the motor. Totally my fault."

Canales kicked the side of his boat a few times, but he had calmed down by the time I pulled alongside.

He seemed to want me to acknowledge his magnanimous assumption of the blame, but I said nothing. Mr. Granger anchored the pontoon boat just off the channel.

"Looks like a real mess," he called.

Canales jumped in the water and began unraveling the net.

"You need some help?" I asked.

"No. Take a nap or something."

I boarded my section of the net and, when I saw how long Canales was going to take, tossed out my anchor. He worked for forty-five minutes. When the net was free he climbed back up into his boat and folded it into the stern as carefully as if he were folding a parachute.

Canales consulted the spiral notebook again and threw it

back into the tackle box with disgust. "They've probably gone out the ship channel by now," he said. "It's much too deep for us to set there. So much for the scientific method. Let's head up into Aransas Bay and see what we can scare up."

In the technical sense, Aransas Bay is not a bay at all, simply a place where the gap between the mainland and the offshore islands is wide enough to warrant a name. We threaded our way through a chain of spoil islands and picked the channel up again on the other side. It was midmorning now. One of the kids in the pontoon boat had taken off his shirt, revealing the broad pink baby-fat shoulders of a high-school lineman. I was definitely uncomfortable in my wetsuit, but I knew the water would be cold. If I took it off now I would just have to struggle into it again later.

As the morning wore on the color of the water changed from pale brown to a green that gave the illusion of clarity. But this was a surface change, a reflection of the sky. By midafternoon the water would be a vivid blue but would still not have lost its opacity. The color of the bay was a mirage—beneath the surface sheen it was always dense and murky.

We patrolled Aransas Bay for an hour without seeing anything. We were about to cross under the bridge and try Copano when two porpoises breached suddenly in our wake. They submerged and then surfaced again no farther than fifteen or twenty yards away, seeming deliberately to keep pace with us, even slowing down somewhat as we idled the boats and fastened the ends of the net together once again. They were already headed for shallow water, and we simply kept a respectful distance until the time came to spread the net. Canales gave his attack signal again. We tore away from each other at top speed, playing out the net into the circular wake. The water that had been still all morning seemed to rise up now against the intrusion: the hull of my boat smashed against each small swell it passed over, jarring my teeth.

We had already half-encircled the porpoises by the time they had grown suspicious. They rose backward out of the water with a great shivering lunge of their flukes and spiraled back in again, heading for the gap, the way out of the net that was being diminished each second. When Canales and I passed each other, closing the circle, I marveled at how neat it was: the high-speed maneuvering, the completion of the prescribed pattern provided me with an aesthetic rush. I cut the engine back and the noise it made disengaged itself and drifted like a cloud over the water. The circular wake had not yet lost its form.

Then I saw the porpoises plow in desperation into the net on opposite sides of the circle, hitting it at high speed, raising spouts of water and dragging a dozen floats down with them, and the raw edge of our handiwork began to assert itself. I sat there for a moment, hoping they would come up on their own. It seemed inconceivable that we could ever get them out.

"All right, hurry!" Canales yelled. He threw out his anchor, then stood up in the boat and signaled frantically to Mr. Granger, who was still plodding toward us in the big boat from several hundred yards away. Then Canales went over the side. His head reappeared as I was kicking off my huaraches.

"It's deeper than I thought," he said. "Fuck!"

I jumped far out from the boat into the water. My right foot landed on something broad and gristly, and in the next instant a terrific pain took root in my ankle. I felt the stingray slide off along the bottom of my foot, leaving its barb implanted. The pain did not subside in the slightest—it riled and inspired me. I took off for the other side of the net, to the place I had seen the porpoise strike. I felt the barb fall out as I kicked, dropping off like a scab but leaving its poison behind. Now I was having trouble breathing and my heart was beating recklessly—it seemed to be hurrying me along, wanting me to catch up with it, to fall within its wild rhythm. I did not want the porpoise to drown. Trapped in the buoyancy of my wetsuit, I felt myself moving toward the creature in the frustrating listless way one rushes toward the rescue of a loved one in a nightmare.

At last I reached the spot where the animal had disappeared. There was still a gap in the string of floats on the surface, and I could see the tension in the line that held them. I dove underwater and swam for the center of the gap, fighting against the wetsuit and feeling the sting of salt water in my open eyes, a complement to the great unwavering pain in my ankle. The visibility, of course, was very poor. I could see perhaps six inches and was not even sure anymore I was heading in the right direction. But I could feel the panic of the porpoise, its awful need for breath.

Then I saw the shape in the murky water. It was thrashing about in despair, enmeshing itself deeper into the diamond stitching of the net. I stood up and took a breath. The water came to my chest, and I worried that it would be too deep for me to support the porpoise. Nevertheless I submerged once more, planted my feet into the muddy bottom, took the animal's agitated bulk into my arms and shoved it upward. The porpoise resisted at first, almost throwing me off, but it grew calmer the closer it got to the surface. I took another breath, lifted with all my strength, and finally the broad, blunt expanse of the porpoise's head broke through the surface. The spiracle opened like a chasm, and the dank, hot air exploded in my face.

"You got yours?" Canales yelled from across the diameter of the net.

"Yeah," I shouted, looking back over my shoulder. Canales' porpoise was on the surface, lying very still, like an animal in shock beneath the jaws of a predator.

My own porpoise was quiet too, but I could feel its tension. Only its spiracle was moving now, producing an incessant distress call. *Thweet. Thweet.* With my arms cradling the underside of the porpoise, rocking it like a baby, I began to feel light-headed. I laid my head along the creature's back and saw daylight through a curious hole the size of a quarter in its dorsal fin.

"Ride 'em, cowboy," Canales yelled as his porpoise tried to buck him off and submerge. I looked away, back through the hole in the fin.

The pontoon boat came alongside and two of the kids

jumped into the water, startling the porpoise. I held on tight as it tried to lurch away, still hopelessly entangled in the net. When it was calm again I let the teenagers take over, though at their touch it lapsed again into panic and shook violently from side to side along the axis of its body.

Finally it was still. I gave myself to the wetsuit and floated on my back in the water. My heart was beating so rapidly from the toxin I felt I had to work to get a breath in between palpitations.

"You know you're bleeding?" one of the kids asked.

"I stepped on a stingray."

"No shit?"

"No shit. Remember to keep that blowhole out of the water."

"Son of a bitch won't let us. Wants to commit suicide."

When I was sure the porpoise was safe I swam over to the big boat, climbed up the ramp and onto the deck. Mr. Granger looked down at my ankle with a grave, fretful expression.

"Stingray," I explained.

"Oh, lord," he said. "I've heard of people dying from that."

"I'm all right."

"No, you're not, Jeff. You just lie back there. I'll get you to a doctor."

But my heart was beating so rapidly I couldn't lie still, and Canales was calling for us to get the boat into position.

"You just hold on, mister," Mr. Granger shouted back. "We've got a hurt man here."

"Go ahead," I said, "I'm fine. I promise." I looked over at the two kids who were holding my porpoise on the surface. They had thrown their heads back and were imitating the animal's distress calls and laughing.

Reluctantly Mr. Granger got behind the steering platform and brought the boat alongside Canales' porpoise. The four of us hauled it up the ramp like deckhands loading an unwieldy piece of cargo. Twice on the ramp it tried to hurl its bulk back into the water, but once it was on the deck it was very still.

My porpoise was easier to board. It was not as large as the other one and allowed itself to be worked up the ramp without a struggle. But when it was on the deck next to the other porpoise it began a wild series of distress calls and slung its body back and forth with such abandon that I had to lie nearly full length across it to keep it still. My face was close to the porpoise's face, which even in terror wore an immutable expression of serenity. Only its eyes, I thought, gave the creature away: the whites were prominent, crowding the calm brown iris, and somehow that engorged, colorless tissue conveyed an unnervingly clear picture of shock and hurt.

When it was quiet again I got up and stood over the beached form of the porpoise, saw it whole, realizing that perhaps this was something I should not be seeing at all. I remembered those sleek, mysterious shapes my mother had pointed out to me a long time ago. When their dorsal fins had rolled across the surface of the bay the forms that remained beneath the water had been unimaginable to me. Now it seemed somehow inappropriate for me to glimpse those bodies in their entirety. They looked naked and bland, like the bodies of turtles that had in some way been extracted from their shells.

I sat down beside the porpoise. My ankle was genuinely better now. The pain had centered into each of the separate barb wounds, so that what I felt was a prickly sort of discomfort. My heartbeat was settling, and I was breathing easier.

Canales squirted water from a spray can over the porpoises to keep their skin from drying out. They were still calling out to one another.

"Two pretty good specimens," he said. "The one with the hole in her fin is a little beat up. That looks like a propeller scar right behind her dorsal." I hadn't noticed it: a seam like the stitching on a baseball. "The other one's perfect. Really a nice-looking animal. Both of them are young. That's good. A male and a female. That's good too."

He clapped Mr. Granger on the back. "Good work, boss. We got us a show."

"They seem pretty shaken up," Mr. Granger said.

"They'll get over it. A porpoise is a very smart animal, very shrewd. They'll catch onto what a good deal they've got. Free fish. Applause."

He turned to me. "We'll have to give you a Purple Heart. Those stingarees are nasty little animals."

"I'm taking him to a doctor," Mr. Granger said firmly.

"I'm all right now." I was trying to shut out the porpoises' distress calls, which were more intense now that the boat was moving.

"There's a lot of poison in there yet," Canales went on.

"I'm okay."

"You're the expert."

We headed back toward Corpus Christi Bay with the two living creatures suddenly quiet now on the deck. I felt for a moment as if I was going to faint, but the spell passed and I was restored to reality. The high-school boys followed in the skiffs, gamboling with their machines in the wake of the boat. In an hour we were turning into the pass that led to Port Aransas and on out past the jetties to the wild blue water of the Gulf.

Chapter 2

The story that my father had been "saved" by porpoises was something I had come to regard in recent years as a piece of family apocrypha. Perhaps this was because, with my parents dead, there was no one left to tell it to me. As a child I had of course believed it wholly. Long before the public infatuation with porpoises began, the creatures were in my mind, as benevolent and watchful as guardian angels.

My father never told the story directly, and his forbearance seemed to add to its credibility. He sat by indulgently as my mother, who was prone to romanticism and misinformation, repeated it nearly every night for years after that first sighting on the ferry. I think she was consciously trying to provide me with a personal myth and that my father understood this and decided not to interfere. As the facts grew more tenuous and evocative each time my mother presented them, he must have seen the patterns of a legacy, a family trust. He let it ride.

The event itself was probably commonplace. My father was a fighter pilot in New Guinea during the war, flying an odd plane with a double fuselage that looked like two insects mating in air. Once during an aerial skirmish he was forced to bail out over the open ocean, and it was three days and nights before he was found. He had a small inflatable raft and a few days' worth of emergency rations, and was probably not in any great physical danger so long as the seas remained calm, which they did. But something got to him, almost immediately. His mind froze with terror and loneliness. As a working seaman—he had been a shrimper before the war and would be after—he could no more have afforded to contemplate the infinite purposeless ocean than to stare unprotected at the sun. But parachuting down to it, in shock from the battle and the loss of his plane, he had mislaid his defenses and now faced it whole. Within hours he was seeing mirages: there on the horizon was the Nueces Hotel, where the nurse he had just met—my mother—had booked them a room that looked out on the tame water of Corpus Christi Bay. The water came right up to the lobby—he had only to paddle a hundred yards, step out of the raft, and sign the register. But of course the hotel receded, and the bay itself followed, detaching itself from the ocean the way the moon had once torn away from the earth. He was alone again.

On the second day they came to him. They must have been a different species—Pacific bottlenoses, or spinners—and they came no doubt out of simple curiosity and stayed because of social instinct. He did not get out and ride on their backs—if he had entered the water with them at all they would probably have left. But they stayed with him for a day and a night, occasionally nuzzling the raft, buoying it up with their backs in the manner in which they support the injured and distressed of their own species. They were warm and living, and they stayed with him, turning his void benevolent.

By the time I was born, the incident—I think probably even the war itself—was a dream to him. But it was rooted quiescently in his consciousness, and my mother was always ready to draw it to the surface. She had been a Kansas debutante from a small musty town. I remember visiting there, seeing a great-grandmother who impressed me as hardly anything more than a composite of ancient odors and knickknacks. Everything in her world had the same forlorn value: footstools, slipcovers, brittle sheet music, the prairie itself under a winter sky.

My parents married just after the war, and my mother came to live in Port Aransas. I used to think of her looking out at that gray water for the first time, at the slimy twitching things her husband pulled forth from it to make a living for them. She never liked the ocean—it was like a nightmare version of Kansas, a prairie that would not bear one's weight. I think she clung to my father's simple adventure because she wanted to believe that something existed beneath the surface of that water that was capable of treating her with kindness.

My father, as I said, never talked about it. He was a taciturn, reverent man who believed in a hybrid Catholicism of his own invention that he never inflicted upon his family. He sat in his glossy armchair, diligently reading *As a Man Thinketh* or a biography of the Curé d'Ars, but I remember understanding, at a very early age, that his true religion was elsewhere. It was a sort of totemism, and came into evidence every time he saw a porpoise, whereupon he became rapt and silent, as if what he saw rising out of the water was the gracious shape of his own happiness.

When I was old enough he would take me out on his shrimp boat for brief one- or two-day runs. I saw the open ocean, which was vast, blank, and horrifying. That my father could detect life there at all amazed me; I believed him to have a form of genius. He would haul up, on still, warm nights when the deck was lit by an arc lamp against the suffocating darkness, mounds of throbbing sea creatures: crabs, sea slugs, ribbonfish, flounder, an occasional shark snapping witlessly at the air; all of this studded into a pile of shrimp that seemed sometimes as tall as I was. My father and the rig man would pull on heavy gloves, sit on the deck, and decapitate handfuls of shrimp with the idle finesse of crocheting women.

Later I would lie in my tiny bunk and listen to them speak in Spanish in the wheelhouse, gossiping with other shrimpers on the radio. After a while my father would come in and wake me, handing me a Dramamine and a glass of water, and then lie down in the bunk below me and snore in pitch with the heaving of the boat until he woke again a few hours later and rose like a sleepwalker to check the try nets.

In the morning there would be porpoises, ocean-going porpoises with sprigs of seaweed festooning their dorsal fins. I remember dimly an unfamiliar species—small, mahogany-colored, speckled like fawns. We scraped the trash fish overboard through a hole in the gunwale, and I saw the porpoises' faces through the clear water, the tentative courtly way in which they took the fish into their jaws.

My father died when I was seven. The porpoises had not saved him for long. He had a heart attack and lay for almost two weeks in an enduring coma. Mr. Granger took me to see him early on, before he began to waste away. It was nearly Easter, and my mother was sitting by the bed holding a bundle of fresh palm fronds as if they were a bouquet that my father, rousing himself from his coma, had just handed her. He lay on his back, his eyes closed, his body rocking back and forth so evenly, with such a regular cadence, that I thought for a moment he was not sick at all, had in fact recovered and was performing calisthenics to regain his strength. Then he grunted, and his body lurched out of its rhythm for a moment, and I knew he was lost to us. I imagined the coma as a separate physical environment, like the idyllic woodland scene I saw when I peered through the peephole of a hollow Easter egg. I hoped my father was happy there. Both my mother and Mr. Granger wanted me to try to speak to him, but I refused, seeing that he did not want to be disturbed.

I think my mother would have packed me up and taken me back to Kansas after the funeral had it not been for Mr. Granger. I remember him in those years—he was middle-aged, in his prime, and the eccentricity and sentimentality that must always have seemed outlandish and suspect before had found its place. At least it seemed so to me. He was wholly appropriate and credible. Somehow he possessed the hard-won, white-tuxedo authority of a George Sanders, but there was not a worldly or cynical trace in it. He fascinated me. I enjoyed watching people—friends of my parents—meeting him for the first time. They were hardly able at first to keep from giggling at his high voice, his strange clothes, his undisguised fretfulness about everything, but then something in his manner would snare them, draw them in, so that by the end of the evening they were flattered by his smallest attention.

My father's death broke his heart, and afterward he remained solicitous of my mother, maintaining an odd asexual deportment that over the years I came to recognize was not suspect in any sense. He found a crew for the *Rapture* and put his personal accountant in charge of our affairs, so that by the time of my mother's death the boat was clear and the house nearly so, and from their sale I had more than enough money to finance the dissolute years of my college education. He was the benevolent proof my mother had once looked for in that empty seascape, and though I sensed his vulnerability was greater even than mine, that a seven-year-old's grief was healing faster than his, I counted on him and clung skittishly to his presence.

I've never been clear about how he came into our lives in the first place. He was at least twenty years older than my parents, and must have seen them less as friends than as godchildren. Apparently he had no family of his own, and for much of his early manhood had wandered in Argentina—he called it "The Argentine"—roughnecking for oil companies, riding muleback for weeks along primitive trails. When he returned to America he settled in Corpus Christi, because it was a pretty city and, besides, it was where his ship docked. This was long before the seawall was built, when the shorefront was nothing but an abrupt mud beach set out before the business district. He lived there for a while in a bayfront hotel, and then one day crossed over to Port Aransas. There were no roads across the bay then, just railroad tracks suspended on pilings above the water over which a kind of bus traveled. The hurricane that had passed through six months before had left almost nothing of Port Aransas—most of the houses were gone and the few people living on the island, including my father's family, had pitched tents next to their boats. With his roughneck money Mr. Granger opened a bait house, had a sign painted that said "Tarpon Capitol of the World," and gradually nursed the town back into existence. With more prescience than acumen he began buying into oil leases as well, and by the time Roosevelt came down to Port Aransas to fish he was a rich man. He was rowed out to the presidential yacht for a drink.

He never married. Perhaps he was homosexual, but if he was I doubt that it was a trait he ever consciously revealed to himself. I believe he lived his whole life as chastely as a priest. Perhaps that was at the root of his devotion to my parents, the long habit of pure, worshipful love. His selection of them was not arbitrary, but I doubt if it was destined either. They were a pleasant young couple whom he saw often fishing together off the pier, two people so kind and unremarkable his half-century of reclusiveness had broken down before them.

My father's death pulled Mr. Granger and me closer to my mother, but over time not that much closer to one another. We became two planets circling the same sun in different orbits, and when she died, unexpectedly and very quickly, of complications arising from a hysterectomy, we both spun off into space. This was when Mr. Granger began to prepare for the boom. He saw the tourist industry spiraling wildly, like a hurricane, along the great curve of the entire Gulf Coast, and he believed that it was only a matter of time before it centered along the sloshy bays and lagoons of Texas. To some extent his vision worked, and to accommodate it he altered the face of Port Aransas like a boy tinkering with a model railroad layout, building a yacht club and a bank and a little shopping mall with a billowy concrete awning that an architect had told him "stood for" the flight of sea gulls. And people came, but it was not a boom. It was not Florida—you could be certain of that by simply looking out over the muddy water, at the tar-stained beaches where the surfers rode the paltry breakers but more often sat on the beach dreaming of real waves, waxing their boards and sprinkling meat tenderizer on their man-of-war wounds. Still Mr. Granger counted on the boom and prepared for it without avarice or guile, like a host preparing his house for special guests.

A few months after my mother's death, when I had graduated from high school, I left the coast, I thought, for good. I left with a strange bitter fascination over my orphanhood, feeling like an astronaut who had just dropped the booster stage of his rocket and was silently heading toward a deep and alluring space. I relegated my sorrow to a backwater of the imagination, a place I knew I would never want to visit again in physical fact. I bought a brand-new Chevy II and a backseat clothes rack and a dozen paisley shirts which had been recommended to me by a clerk as "what the kids are wearing." I spent a summer in Austin, virtually alone, living in an expensive off-campus apartment and spending my days at Barton Springs reading whatever books the Kids Were Reading. It was a long, critical season. When it was over I went to the university, began my gradual dishevelment from paisley to army surplus, paid my roommates' rent, financed a band called Crude Dude and the Scissor Kickers, was suckered into a brown rice diet for two weeks, and in a few years received a notice from the university in the mail. I had apparently graduated with a degree in anthropology and could have a diploma if I paid a forty-dollar library fine.

Then came the era's prescribed postgraduate year of homesteading in Arkansas. There were six of us, living on twelve acres secured by the last of my fortune, and we nursed our communal fervor with great care, always speaking to one another in low, soothing voices, moving about dreamily and simpering with feigned contentment. We built a two-story shack, in whose kitchen we began to cook fewer and fewer lentils and more Kraft Dinners. During the days we sat on the crude porch, eating Ritz crackers and watching our twelve acres accumulate with old car parts. We grew so paranoid of our neighbors we pulled up our subsistence crop of marijuana, and we all sank into despair if our subscription copy of *Time* was a day late. One of the women became pregnant, and the baby was of course born in the house, with the aid of a midhusband, who wore an instrument on his head that gave him a sort of gnostic demeanor. He was paid in mescaline. The baby gave us something to watch. The father would sit with her in the loft, letting her play with his skimpy beard, singing "When you're lost in the rain in Juarez . . ." while the rest of us gazed upward, charmed and disturbed. Later someone's parents sent an old TV on the bus. We hooked it up to a generator and started out watching just the news and an occasional episode of *Dragnet*, but when we began to sit around watching daytime TV, taking turns holding the antenna for better reception, I admitted to myself finally it was not working at all.

"I'm leaving," I told the girl I had drawn in the communal lottery, as we sat along the bank of the creek accumulating ticks and watching a water moccasin sidle into a den on the other side.

"I suppose," she said condescendingly, "you have to do what's right for you."

So I accepted a long-standing invitation to visit friends in Santa Fe. I wanted away from the gloomy Ozarks as I had wanted away from the gloomy Texas coast. I found a job in a little bookstore off the plaza and rented my own little adobe house and every morning ate blue corn tortillas for breakfast. In winter we would load ourselves into a van and drive to the Jemez mountains, where we would sit down naked in hot springs beneath aspens whose pale bark seemed moonlit even in daytime.

Living alone, I grew fastidious and thrifty, and during the course of several years became a solid citizen of the Santa Fe subculture. The place suited me, and in all my time there I only left it once, when a friend who had forsaken skiing convinced me to go along with him on a package diving tour to Belize. I had not thought about salt water in years, but as soon as the suggestion was made I was helplessly caught up in it. In high school I had done some diving along the Port Aransas jetties on those rare days when the clear water came close into shore and hovered like a cloud over the pass, but it had still been muggy coastal diving, and since I lived now high above sea level, in sharp air and light, I wanted to experience water with a concomitant purity. We boarded a plane in Albuquerque with a group of earnest young sportsmen and flew over Texas, across that painful stretch of coast into the clarity of the Caribbean. The water was as pure as the air of the Sangre de

Christos, and had a strange desert warmth. I passed a simple vacation there, in another element, and went back to Santa Fe unchanged.

A year or so after Mr. Granger's visit I quit my job in the bookstore. I had fallen in with film people by then and could count on periodic work in whatever training films or commercials were in production. Usually I was the grip or assistant production manager, but once I landed the role of the villainous trucker who causes a four-car smashup in the highway safety film *Defensive Driving or Death—The Choice Is Yours!*

Then a big cocaine dealer moved into town and said he wanted to get into the exploitation market. He had a script, which he had written himself in a Oaxaca motel room, called *Bigfoot Stalks!* and seventy-five thousand dollars to spend on its production. I was offered the role of Bigfoot because in the past I had demonstrated such versatility and because I was reasonably tall. They paid me six hundred dollars up front and promised another six hundred when the film was finished, plus one-half of a percent of profits, which I was assured I would never see if the film was a success because of all the "Hollywood rip-off types" who would litigate the money into their own pockets. But I would see my name in the credits—"And introducing Jeff Dowling as Bigfoot"—and I was told there would surely be a sequel, which would be more of a character study of Bigfoot than the original, and thus would give me a chance at stardom.

So every day for two months I climbed into a dank costume that shed all over the marginal actresses I was called upon to dismember. Since I was frequently required to pounce from boulders onto innocent young couples' picnic lunches I outfitted the Bigfeet themselves with size thirteen Dr. Scholl's foot pads.

I began to fall in love with the seamstress who constantly attended me. "Hold still," she would say with a mouthful of pins while I stood before her in my costume, shy and hulking. At other times she would speak to me soothingly, as to a captive bear, and I would respond with the rapture of an animal in love.

Out of costume I did not seem to mean quite as much to her, but she moved in with me just the same. It was pleasant. We would sit in the bathtub and look out a small window across a stretch of undeveloped desert at the blue-tinctured mountain skyline, with Sandia Peak looming there like a beached whale. Between us at such moments there was some tentative and disinterested talk of marriage, an event that would be timed with the simultaneous premiere of *Bigfoot Stalks!* at every drive-in theater in the country.

One night Mr. Granger called, after a particularly arduous day in which we had spent eleven hours shooting my death on the "miraculous" spiral stairway that, according to legend, an uncommunicative carpenter who looked suspiciously like St. Joseph had built without charge and in defiance of the laws of gravity for the destitute nuns of a local church. (We used a replica—the nuns wouldn't let a man in a gorilla suit desecrate the real thing. The set designer said it wasn't miraculous anyway.)

"It's your grandmother or somebody," the Seamstress said, handing me the receiver. I said hello and heard Mr. Granger babbling about porpoises.

"Here's the thing, Jeff. They've got one of these places up in Galveston. A big one. But there's not another trained porpoise on the whole coast. People in Corpus don't want to go two hundred miles to see something like this, but they'll sure as hell drive across the bay!

"Now, I've got a man here to run it, used to work at Sea Park out there in California. He needs an assistant, and I talked him into giving you a try. Jeff, it would be perfect. You could come home."

I could come home. For a moment I half believed it, as if the only thing that had kept me away for all these years was the lack of an opportunity to train porpoises.

"I don't see how I could leave everything here," I said.

"Oh, sure you can! You think it over. You do that for me and then call me collect tomorrow night. You have the number?"

"Yes." I had memorized it as a little boy. My parents had

told me, *Call Mr. Granger if you need something and you can't find us.*

"Jeff," he said before hanging up, "I know what these animals meant to your father."

But I could not get a fix on what these animals meant to me. I could not, for a moment, bring them clearly into my mind. I was used to that other beast, the mythical terrestrial one in whose skin I had lived for two months. It was the porpoises that seemed mythical now.

"You're not seriously considering this?" the Seamstress asked.

"I don't know."

"Jesus, you really are. I'm going to the kitchen and meditate. Let me know if you decide to do something ridiculous."

Fifteen minutes later I broke her off in mid-mantra. She scowled, unlotused her legs, and climbed down from the kitchen table.

"So you're going down there? To Walla Walla, or whatever?"

"Corpus Christi."

"Whatever."

I looked at her handsome, indifferent face.

"You don't mind that much," I said.

"I don't understand, that's all."

"I just want to go home. It might not be for long."

"You never seemed particularly homesick before."

"I know," I admitted. But some new element had been introduced. I was a little mystified, and sad because I knew that the cordial relationship between the Seamstress and me could not bear the weight of this new longing.

I wanted to go home. It was not the porpoise training—that was just a job offer, an excuse to resettle. No, I thought it might be the porpoises themselves. The idea of those creatures was suddenly vibrant in my mind. There had been spells of nostalgia before, but I had ridden them out. This was different, graver. A channel had opened up through which I could see into that part of myself that never came to light anymore, the part that was not isolated and imperturbable but deeply in need of some half-forgotten form of human contact. It was the porpoises. They were mediums, restoring to me the voices of my parents, the texture of that forsaken past. If I was skeptical about the old family saga of my father's rescue, I was helpless against its power. It was mine, an heirloom I had to go home to claim.

"Okay," the Seamstress said. "You have my blessing, for what it's worth."

By leaving before the filming was completed I forfeited my percentage of the profits, but I didn't have that much faith in the film anyway. The director said there was no problem with my leaving. Only incidental footage was left to be shot—extreme close-ups and long shots—for which anyone could wear the Bigfoot suit.

"Hey," he said, "remember, it'll be playing soon at a theater near you."

I sold my books, gave away my eight place settings of plastic dishware, a few albums, a few sweaters I never wore. All the rest of my belongings fit into the trunk of my car.

"I'll come down to see you," the Seamstress said. The house was now hers and a friend's, a weaver, who moped about the living room looking for a place to put her loom as we said good-by.

"I know you will," I answered, and muttered, not entirely for form's sake, or for nostalgia, but because I wanted to believe it, "I love you." For once she had the tact to say it back. I kissed her face, and it was clear she would not come down to see me on the humid coast of Texas. She could not make the passage—she would implode as soon as she hit the flatland.

By the time we reached Port Aransas the wound in my ankle was merely a nuisance, a throbbing discomfort that underlay the rest of my perceptions. Despite Mr. Granger's frantic insistence when we docked I refused to see a doctor—the pain seemed to have a very clear and reasonable course to run that I did not want to interfere with.

The porpoise pool was formed by a sort of dock that extended from shore and enclosed about a quarter-acre of water just off the ship channel. It was ten feet deep—having been dredged and shored up against the beach side—and water flowed freely through a chain-link fence that formed the underwater borders of the pool. On the mud floor Canales had installed a false bottom, a submerged grate attached by ropes to pulleys by which we could haul the porpoises out of the water if the need arose.

Above the waterline the facility was still under construction, a jumble of raw unweathered lumber which two carpenters at the moment were transforming into bleachers. They had already finished the high fence that bordered the pool on three sides, and I noticed they had constructed a huge wooden arc to go over the main gate, an arc that read, so far only in penciled outline, DUDE GRANGER'S PORPOISE CIRCUS.

We tied off at the far end of the dock, and it was no great effort to roll the porpoises into slings, transport them across a few feet of planking, and lower them gently into the pool.

They swam rapidly around the perimeter, the female traveling close to the larger male, her beak resting beneath his pectoral fin. Gradually they quit circling and came to the center of the pool. They expelled their breath in a way that seemed to me as plain as a human sigh and sank beneath the surface. They rose again, of course, over and over, but did not stray anymore from the center of the pool.

We stood there and watched them, and the carpenters came down from their unfinished bleachers and watched them too.

The bodies of the porpoises seemed to have changed in shade. They were no longer the glistening deep gray color they had been from a distance. Now they were as muted and cloudy as the water in which they swam. Bringing them in on the boat I had noticed the pinkish cast of their stomachs, the veins standing out there through a layer of blubber that had seemed oddly translucent. And across the upper parts of their bodies I had noticed faint streams of a very pale gray where the lifelong flow of water across their bodies had marked them.

I sat down on the first row of bleachers, aware of the poison remaining in my system. It seemed to have gone to work now in beneficial ways, providing me with a keen visceral happiness rooted in a sense of dislocation, the calm security of shock.

Mr. Granger paid off the high-school kids—a hundred dollars each—and shook hands ceremoniously with each of them. They wandered off, out the front gate of the compound, without looking back at the creatures they had hauled out of the bay.

One of the carpenters stood at the side of the pool, retying his ponytail as he watched the porpoises.

"They as smart as people say?" he asked Canales.

"Sure," Canales said.

"Now I know they're not fish. I read that. What are they, reptiles?"

A look of professional disgust came over Canales' face. He unzipped his wetsuit and began to squirm out of it.

"Mammals," he said.

The carpenter snapped his fingers, chiding himself for not remembering. Canales pulled off his wetsuit and let it fall onto the dock. Underneath he wore a pair of surfer's trunks, with the wax pocket in front. There was a pale line between his toes where the strap of his rubber thongs had screened out the sun. He reminded me of boys I had known who worked on the big fishing boats out in the bay and whose job it was to remove hardheads from the lines of squeamish tourists and smack the fishes' skulls against the railing—boys who seemed to have no home or family, who probably passed their shore time as mascots in the rough bars on North Beach, and whose arrogance toward everything that surrounded them had always inspired me.

I took off my own wetsuit and pulled on my Bigfoot promotional T-shirt in its place. The carpenters went back to work. The noise they made did not seem to disturb the porpoises, but Mr. Granger sent them home anyway, telling them to come back in several days when the animals were better adjusted. When they were gone Mr. Granger and Canales and I sat around the dock for a long time without speaking, looking down at the creatures in the water. They surfaced continually in the center of the pool, exhaling with a sharpness that bordered on distress, the way a poor swimmer will pull up from a crawl and gasp for air before moving on again.

"What we should do now," Canales said, without lifting his eyes from the porpoises, "is go get us some lunch. I'll come back and check on them tonight—I've got some errands to run in Corpus—but for now the best thing is to keep out of their way, give them a chance to adjust."

But he didn't move. He kept staring at them.

"I think we could have done better than that female. She's pretty dinged up. I don't mind that myself, but people see scars on them and they think you're torturing them or something. The male's good, though. Christ, he's perfect."

We left the compound and walked down the oyster-shell road to the Marlin Spike, the restaurant Mr. Granger owned near the ferry landing. It was a classy coastal restaurant, meaning it served mostly frozen cod from the North Atlantic at inflated prices. A hostess came drifting across the plush red carpet. She was wearing a sailor's hat. She said, "Ahoy."

"Ahoy," Mr. Granger answered. The restaurant was almost empty. The only other diners were a middle-aged couple—the man wearing a blue blazer, boat shoes, and a gold-braided skipper's hat he held under the table in his lap and seemed ashamed of. The woman was very thin and pale, and wore a chic boating outfit that looked like a pair of pajamas. So much for the boom.

The hostess seated us at a picture window that looked out at the ship channel. The two ferryboats passed one another like awkward beasts in an inconclusive mating ritual. Canales put his finger casually on the glass, pointing at a spot in the channel where a small pod of porpoises were swimming back and forth.

"That's not feeding or mating behavior. They're trying to figure out what the deal is with their buddies over in the pool."

I looked over at Mr. Granger. There was no emotion apparent on his face, but I thought I saw something anyway—a film of sadness, like the faint passage of water across flowstone.

"Ahoy," the waitress said.

"Ahoy, honey," Mr. Granger said back to her. We all ordered Bloody Marys and fried shrimp. A dapper little man in a leisure suit sat down at a piano beneath a mounted tarpon and began a medley of movie themes.

"You boys like this restaurant?" Mr. Granger asked Canales and me. We both nodded obediently.

"There are more people here at night. A lot of young folks, too, you'd be surprised. This town has needed a nice place to eat for a long time."

"Wait'll we get these animals working," Canales said. "This whole place is going to take off at once."

Mr. Granger smiled, somewhat indulgently I thought. When his shrimp came he ate each one absently and arranged the tails in a semicircular pattern on his plate.

"How's your ankle now?" Canales asked me.

"Fine," I said, bending down to scratch it.

"I've never been stung by anything myself. Just bitten. I knew a guy, he was collecting shells or coral or something on the Great Barrier Reef, picked up a stonefish"—Canales snapped his fingers—"dead in thirty minutes. Phenomenal."

He threw his last shrimp tail onto the plate and leaned back in the booth. "Well, I'm satisfied. We did a good morning's work and had us a good lunch. I think we've got two pretty decent animals, all in all. They don't seem to be real tense. A lot of porpoises, those little Mediterranean jobs, they'll just pine away right before your eyes. But old Tursiops, they're built to last.

"Like I say, we'll just let them alone the rest of the day. I'll be back from Corpus late tonight and I'll check on them then." He looked at me. "If you want to drop in on them before dark and make a few reassuring noises I'm sure they'd appreciate it. Just don't spook them, and remember to keep the gate locked."

I nodded, and then the three of us filed out, Mr. Granger

stopping to shake hands with the piano player and to talk for a moment with the cashier. He bought us each a chocolate-covered mint.

Outside Canales went on ahead, and as Mr. Granger and I walked back toward town he passed us in his pickup on his way to the ferry.

"Do you like him?" Mr. Granger asked me.

"In a way."

"Well, Jeff, he knows his business. He's damn smart. He had a friend out in California he wanted me to hire, but I kept on about you. I knew you'd catch on right away, and you're a kind person, I know that about you. And that's the sort of person you need to work with porpoises."

I looked down at the ground, at Mr. Granger's white shoes as they emerged in cadence from beneath his long suit coat. I did not feel entirely like a kind person. I was troubled by the violence and confusion I had brought into the porpoises' lives.

"I've got to see a man in Tivoli about a lease this afternoon," he said. "What are you going to do?"

"I'll hang around here. Drop in on the porpoises later, like Canales said."

"Where are you staying?"

"In Corpus."

"You go over to the Salt Sea and tell Lois I said to give you a room. No sense in you having to drive back and forth thirty miles every day."

I promised to do that. I had stayed in Corpus deliberately, these first few nights, to make my homecoming as gradual as possible. But now when Mr. Granger left for Tivoli I walked all over town in a nostalgic stupor, breathing in the salt air, which was so sharp I felt a mild sting high in my nasal cavities.

I strolled out to the end of the jetties, a half mile out into the Gulf. A wind came up, and I stood there exposed and shivering, almost engulfed by the spindrift created by the granite boulders. A long time ago I had gone diving at this spot, at the mouth of the jetties, and seen a school of manta rays above my head. They had blocked the sunlight, which spilled over the edges of their wings, making them look beveled and radiant. It seemed to me, as they coasted leisurely above me, that they were imprinted with some great purpose, that they were on their way somewhere, drawn along by a dim and hypnotic longing.

The water was not so clear now as it had been that day, but a hundred yards farther off I could see it growing bluer, shaking off the mud and dusky effluents of the inland water. Out in that clarity the great sandbar lay submerged, like some quiescent sea monster, guarding the only natural pass through the barrier islands for a hundred miles.

A Spanish explorer named Pineda, charting the great curve of the Gulf coast for the first time, discovered the pass in 1519. He had been plying along the coast for months, dispensing names to inlets and rivers according to the liturgical calendar, and his discovery of the big sluggish bay that lay beyond the pass fell on the feast day of Corpus Christi.

He had a few skirmishes with the Indians here, the Karankawas, a starving, capricious, unappeasable people who took an occasional porpoise for food from their dugout canoes but who seem to have subsisted mainly on insects and prickly pears and yaupon tea. Over the next three centuries they massacred, not without cause, Spanish, French, and Anglo colonists. They were no good at alliances. They believed that what they dreamed must immediately be put into action, and in the end their imagination and inflexibility finished them. At Boy Scout campfires we used to hear about how Stephen F. Austin's colonists had killed all but a dozen of the whole Karankawa nation, and how these survivors—stark naked, very tall, their lips and nipples pierced with reeds and their bodies smeared with alligator grease—plowed through the surf on Padre Island in a few canoes and headed out to sea, where they disappeared forever.

Pineda, in discovering Corpus Christi Bay, had kept his ship well off the bar that guarded the pass, but in the future others were less prudent. Scores of ships foundered there over the next few centuries, until finally some enterprising settler—an ancestor of mine—hired himself out as a bar pilot, guiding the ships around the barrier in his lighter and helping to salvage those few ships that did not make use of his services. There were several bar pilots in my family and a few schooner captains as well, who sailed across the primeval bay loaded with timber, lime, fruit, or railroad iron to be transported to the mule trains on the mainland.

I stood at the end of the jetty, feeling that slight heritage, and watched the open Gulf as it was subsumed into the calm water of the bay. I felt in balance, a creature of the littoral.

Leaving the jetties, I went to see our old house. It was still there, high up on its stilts, having withstood two severe hurricanes since my departure. I went blank looking at it—it was strangely unevocative. My memories of the house seemed distant and formal. The dunes that once surrounded it had been blown back by the hurricanes and resettled several hundred yards inland, so that my old home looked exposed and weakened.

Someone else had it now. The new owners had enclosed the porch in some sort of corrugated green plastic, their bright blue Volkswagen Rabbit an alien presence in the garage below the house where I used to clean shells, soaking them in Borax until the hermit crabs crawled out to die.

The house once had an unimpeded view of the ocean; my parents and I used to watch TV and see beyond it through the big picture window to the surf, pale as an afterimage in the moonlight. That view was spoiled now by dozens of houses that had seized upon the homely necessities of island architecture and turned it into a style. There were ranch houses and chalets raised up on stilts, and rambling mansions with elevators.

That was part of the boom. Then there were the condominiums, the McDonald's going up in the center of town for which Mr. Granger owned the franchise. It was all his doing, but he was as innocent a despoiler as the hurricane that could one day level all he had built.

I spent the rest of the afternoon in my car driving down the beach all the way to the national seashore, swerving the wheel so that my tires would pop the man-of-war sacs littering the shoreline. By the time I got back to the porpoise circus it was almost dusk. Before I unlocked the gate I stood outside for a moment, smelling the fragrance of unpainted lumber and listening to the creatures inside, the gentle wash of sound they made in the pool, followed by their hard, explosive breaths.

I opened the trunk of my car and rummaged around my still unpacked belongings until I found my face mask. Then I went inside. The animals lifted their heads out of the water just enough for their eyes to rise above the surface and see me. I sat down on an unfinished bleacher seat and wondered what they saw: a human being, a land creature watching them with a vague air of sorrow and apology they would not be able to read.

For a moment longer they stayed close together at the surface in the center of the pool, then each lifted a tail into the air and let it slowly and evenly follow them down into the water.

I took off my T-shirt and entered the pool with them. The water was as cold as a mountain stream, and for a moment, as my feet sank through the grate into the bottom of mud and pulverized oyster shell, I could not catch my breath. I surfaced and swam in a breast stroke to the place I had seen them go under, but they surfaced again on the far side of the pool, raised their flukes in tandem, and submerged again into the murky water where they were lost to me.

Then with a discreet lapping sound they rose from the water about fifteen yards away, close enough for me to smell the stale air they expelled from their spiracles.

I swam back to the dock and picked up my face mask. It was a prescription mask. The two wide circles of glass set into the lens gave the whole thing the appearance of the face of an owl. Putting it on, I always felt transformed, as if the owl's face brought with it something of an owl's perception. With my vision restored, the twilight was invested with clarity. The sky had the look of a stained-glass window barely illuminated by evening light. All the way up the ship channel, all the way past the jetties and out into the open Gulf, the water was motionless and taut. An offshore rig on the horizon turned on its lights in the same soundless, delicate way the first evening stars began to appear.

With the mask in place I took a breath, dropped beneath the surface, and swam toward the porpoises on the other side of the pool. The visibility extended maybe eighteen inches—looking back toward my feet I could see no farther than the empty belt loops of my cutoffs. My hands seemed encased in an amber gel. But in this close space I did not feel threatened or predatory. I had the feeling that the trapped air in my lungs would last forever if I used it wisely enough. I did not want to surface, to break the spell for something as trivial as air. I was at home here, in this drab water that would not hold light. Every molecule I passed through seemed a separate, visible thing waiting to be charged, to be filled with information.

At some point I came into their territory. I felt myself moving through a latticework of signals, being tracked and assessed. For the porpoises I existed now as an impulse, a sonar signal.

I rose and took a breath, looking for them on the surface, but they were still submerged. I went down again and swam toward the center of the pool. Then in the dark water the knowledge came to me that they were very close. With a kind of instinct I extended my hand and felt a pectoral fin graze across my open palm, and after that the firm gritty passage of a tail fluke, then finally a cool submarine wake that broke apart over my fingers.

I saw the eye of a porpoise keeling along no more than eight inches in front of my mask. I could make out the tiny hole in the dorsal fin and the long unbroken genital seam when the porpoise performed an abrupt log roll.

My breath was gone now, but I held myself down a little longer, hoping for something like a second wind. The stingray wound, aggravated by the salt water, was hurting again, but the pain was like a voice from far away, a voice nagging at me about something insignificant. As I was about to spring up to the surface I felt another pectoral brush me across the shoulder, a strange, light, deliberate touch, behind which I could sense some effort at trust, reassurance. Suddenly I was on the surface, flooding my lungs with air.

When I climbed back onto the dock the porpoises took up

their old station in the center of the pool. I stood for a while, shivering, drying myself with my T-shirt, and watched the moon begin to rise over St. Joseph Island across the channel. I could hear the soft explosion of each breath the porpoises took, and I could hear as well the surf on the beach, the radios of the season's last campers in the state park, and gusts of music and dialogue from the Crow's Nest, the open-air theater that Mr. Granger owned down the street.

I got some dry jeans and another shirt from the trunk of my car, brought them back to the pool, and put them on. The moon by this time was high enough to cast a wake on the water, and I could see that as it rose the wake would trip across the jetties.

Though I had a motel room in Corpus, there did not seem to be any place for me to go, so I sat down on the bleachers once again and watched the steady surfacing and sinking of the porpoises, the mist they expelled that was still visible in the dark. They revealed nothing but their backs now, with the dorsal fins that sometimes flagged spiritlessly over to one side. That morning I had set out with Canales not believing that this could be possible, that a creature so shapeless, so large, so unrevealing, could be captured. But now, suddenly, here they were. The porpoises were not furtive, but the water that enveloped and sustained them seemed to do so at least partially from their consent. It was a living cloak that they drew over themselves, that kept them from our sight, that was never meant to be removed.

I did not hear Mr. Granger come in and walk onto the dock in his white crepe-soled shoes, in fact I was not aware of him until he was standing very near me, with his hands deep in his suit pockets, watching the porpoises. He said nothing for a long time, then he squeezed my forearm and said, very softly, without taking his eyes off the porpoises, "By golly."

We left together soon after that, locking the gate behind us.

"Well," he said, "how about going to the movie? Remember when I used to take you over to the Crow's Nest when you were a boy?"

I nodded. "What's on tonight?"

"Oh, *Captain Nemo*—something. *Captain Nemo and the Underwater City.*"

It sounded sufficiently lightweight. I walked with him down to the theater.

"It's an awful print," he said on the way. "By the time we get them they're held together by Scotch tape. Right now I'm working on getting those two Flipper movies, so when we open up the porpoise circus in the spring we can have a double feature over here at the same time."

I had not been to the Crow's Nest in eleven years. Though it had been repainted, it had not changed in the slightest. Lois was still behind the popcorn machine. She looked at me with a puzzled expression for a moment, then gave a strange, dry little whoop and came out to hug me. She had not aged so much as mummified, but there was a gnarled strength to her yet. Her husband had died in the 1919 hurricane. She had told me once how she had watched from the house as he hung onto the fence with his fingers, his body flung out like a windsock until finally he tore loose and fluttered away forever.

"I want Jeff to stay at the motel," Mr. Granger told Lois. "You got a room for him, don't you?"

She patted my head. "Why sure, honey. I'll fix you up after the show."

"I'll come over tomorrow," I said. "I've got a room in Corpus tonight."

"Whatever you want to do, honey. Y'all gonna see the show?"

"Thought we might," Mr. Granger said.

"It's a good one," Lois said.

The movie was half over when we went inside, and the theater was nearly deserted. Mr. Granger preceded me down the aisle, his popcorn in one hand, asking me at each row in a loud whisper, the way he had done when I was a child, "Is this all right? What do you think?"

I slipped into a row toward the back, sat down, and looked up at the stars. Nothing had changed. The same constellations were there, still framed by the same four walls that had framed them eleven years ago, and the exposed roof caused a breeze, a slightly chilly breeze, to circulate through the theater, imparting an astonishing freshness that I could not remember experiencing since childhood.

Two boys were riding their skateboards down the aisles, producing a ratchety sound that I found soothing. I took my eyes off the movie and watched them glide in the strange hybrid light that the screen and the unimpeded moonlight made.

There were few patrons. Several rows in front of us I noticed the heads of a woman about my age and a small boy who kept turning to her in frustration, demanding an explanation of the plot.

Mr. Granger set his popcorn on the arm of the chair between us, nudged my shoulder repeatedly, and pointed to the box. I grabbed a big handful and watched the movie. How many times had I seen Captain Nemo on this screen, always courtly, benevolent, gifted, but always wrong, fundamentally wrong? This time Nemo was played by Robert Ryan, near the end of his life. His underwater city rested beneath a clear dome that looked like the membrane of a jellyfish. There were the usual comings and goings, the attacks by sharks and moray eels. The people who were Nemo's prisoners (or "guests," as he insisted with impeccable courtesy) frolicked in the deep, clean, well-lit ocean until it was necessary to escape, whereupon Nemo blew himself and his city up once again.

Mr. Granger was asleep by the time the feature was over and the previews came on. I woke him up, knowing this was what he came to see when he went to the movies—coming attractions. He had Lois run every trailer available, regardless of whether the movie had been ordered. So we sat and watched scenes from *Rome Adventure*, *The Legend of Boggy Creek*, *Valley of the Gwangi*, and *Flipper*. A porpoise—a dolphin, they called it—lifted his head out of the water and shook his neckless body so that the animal seemed to be nodding. "Eh—eh—eh—eh," Flipper said, then swam beneath the surface where an underwater camera followed him, recording the one fixed expression on his face, that of self-knowledge, contentment.

By the time the previews were over Mr. Granger was asleep again and beginning to snore in a low, rasping way, an old man's snore. When I woke him he looked up at the blank screen with a puzzled expression, unable to understand why there was nothing there.

"Do you want to stay for the beginning?" I asked him.

"No, Jeff. You go ahead. I think I'll go on home."

I followed him out. In the lobby the woman and her son were standing at the concession counter.

"I want a Coke," the boy was telling his mother.

"No," she said, "you can't have a Coke." She held up a thermos. "I brought you some orange juice."

"I want some popcorn."

"All right, you can have some popcorn."

Mr. Granger spoke over the woman's shoulder to Lois.

"Good night, Lois."

"Night, Dude. You come see me tomorrow, Jeff." She handed the little boy his popcorn.

We walked in silence up the road, past the hotel where Mr. Granger lived, toward my car. I watched his shoes glaring in the moonlight. When we came to the pool we both stopped outside the gate and listened, but we could hear nothing—no lapping water, no clicks or whistles.

"They must be asleep," he whispered. "I wonder how they keep from drowning when they fall asleep."

I shrugged my shoulders.

"You went swimming with them tonight, didn't you?"

"For a little while."

He laughed. "I think you have a talent for this business, Jeff."

"Maybe," I said. "I don't know."

"You take care of that ankle. If it starts hurting again, you call Dr. Rush. I'm serious."

"I know," I said. "Good night."

I drove onto the ferry. In the perfect moonlight the water of the ship channel was a lithograph gray, and as we crossed over it I could see deep into Corpus Christi Bay, almost as far as the city itself. I could certainly see the aura its lights cast on the southern horizon—the sky was pale there, and the stars, shedding their own light, were lost in the confluence.

In the broad, jagged wake the ferry left behind I noticed a pod of porpoises moving up to ride the bow. I rushed forward and stationed myself where I could watch them when they arrived, but they changed course abruptly. A few moments later I saw them breaching high into the night air, heading out to the Gulf.

When the ferry docked I took the old familiar road that led around the northern hemisphere of the bay, following it until it became a highway, and following the highway until it became a boulevard lined with palm trees. All familiar. The boulevard led through a recently refurbished suburb down onto a sea-level spit of land that gave way in the distance to the lights of the harbor bridge, curving upward from the earth like the spine of some great supine animal.

At the crest of the bridge I could see all the earth and sea I had come home to. Several spoilbanks emerged from the milky darkness of the bay, and one or two sailboats with running lights, but otherwise the bay was featureless, and the lights that fringed it seemed tentative and imperiled. But it was home. I took my foot off the accelerator and glided into the city.

Chapter 3

In my motel room on the bay I wrote a letter that night to the Seamstress, telling her I missed her, which I did. "It's no myth about the porpoise's intelligence," I wrote, then wondered if she was even aware of the myth. She was not unintelligent, she simply had a habit of ignoring information. During the height of my infatuation with the Seamstress I had of course seen this trait in a positive light, thinking of her withdrawal from the world of knowledge as saintly and charming.

But now I wanted someone to talk to, and after eleven years' absence no one came to mind. My high-school friends were grown up now, like me. They were teaching at the local junior college, or running their fathers' businesses—indeed, when I turned on the tube I saw one of them standing woodenly in a leisure suit before a roomful of sofas. Perhaps a few of them had conformed to the archetype of their generation—gone to the war and died, or been paralyzed, or come home whole; or ducked out from it all, bought land in British Columbia, formed a band, lingered for ten years in graduate school. I would have been surprised if they were not all back now, their blood having cried out in the end for the sultry air of the coast that had bred them like mosquitoes.

There was no torpor anywhere like it. My sojourn in New

Mexico, in that clean air, had been a long, depraved hit of some illicit gas. Now I was back on the coast, moving with effort through the heavy, sluggish, barely breathable atmosphere. It had claimed me too. I was coming down from my high.

I looked out the window of the little stucco tourist cottage, at the black void of the bay, and considered walking down the bluff to the shore. But I remembered the muddy beach, the fount of stagnant air that would be there, the tiny waves, the shore littered with milk cartons and bleach bottles and dead cabbageheads.

But it could be a pretty basin of water. On a clear day the sky would reflect itself there and the water, if impenetrable, would be a dazzling blue, and the city itself—its skyline and seawall—would seem a model of tranquillity, reduced and placid, like a diorama in which tiny plastic people bustle about with earnestness and security.

I finished the letter to the Seamstress on that note, on that image of blue sky. It was not late—only ten o'clock—so I got into my car and drove down Ocean Drive past the T-heads, the docks where the excursion boats and yachts were moored. I saw a sign for a bank, with a grinning porpoise as its logo. There was another porpoise on the sign of a seafood restaurant, and there was a Blue Dolphin motel now that featured the animal standing upright on its flukes, wearing a butler's costume and smiling.

I ended up at a place called the Lonesome Coyote, which I had heard mentioned as a tolerable establishment with live music. I had my hand stamped with the word "Friday" and went inside. A cosmic cowboy band in high pointed straw hats and snuff tins in their breast pockets were whining a song called "Cocaine Cowgirl." In the middle of a steel solo the lead guitarist took his hand off the frets of his instrument and guzzled half a quart of beer.

"Heeeeeeeeeee yowwwwwwwwwww!!" the crowd called back in admiration. They were mostly young pimply kids wearing the same sorts of rodeo hats the band wore, or else ten-gallon felt numbers with hatbands made of pop tops. They held their girl friends by the back of the neck, as if they were handling rattlesnakes, and the girls stood patiently beneath this grip, their clean simple smiles and glazed eyes shining in the dim light.

The cowboy tradition was a recent innovation, a cultural graft from the Texas heartland, and it seemed out of place on the coast. But I was in a mood to be indulgent toward it and decided to stay as long as I had a beer in my hand.

I wandered outside to the yellow light of the patio. Here the patrons seemed a little older—my contemporaries. I even recognized an old classmate. We looked at each other briefly, severely, he said "How you doin'?" and I said "Fine."

I was not very surprised to find Canales here. He was sitting by himself at a spool table, trying to roll his coaster around its circumference.

"Hello," I said.

He slid the coaster under his beer. "Hey, sit down, man! Don't worry, you won't be cutting in on any action. Can you *believe* this town? There's not a chick here over statutory age. I was getting so antsy earlier I almost decided to drive all the way to Austin. But I figured I better stay close because of the porpoises."

"They're fine. I checked on them."

"Good," he said, and sipped his beer. "How's your sting-aree wound?"

"Better."

"That was fun today, wasn't it? Catching those porpoises?"

I shrugged. I pointed with my longneck beer at the shark's tooth hanging at Canales' throat.

"You catch that yourself?"

"Damn right," he said. "At Bob Hall pier. A nine-foot tiger. Caught it on this big Penn reel I have about the size of your head."

"I never did any shark fishing myself," I said. "A friend of mine used to swim bait out."

"Hey, I swim my *own* bait out. Rump roast. USDA *choice*."

Canales shifted his weight in his chair, smiling to himself, and laid his coaster over the hole in the middle of the spool table. There was something likable about him, some irony or savvy that was discernible only in his relations with himself. I had known others like him in high school, Mexican-Americans who had bailed out of their heritage before it became fashionable, who had become smooth and anglicized, ending up perhaps as anchormen on Midwestern TV stations where their names were mispronounced, styling their hair, winning disco contests, while their *hermanos* down south walked about humorlessly in brown berets and sunglasses, staffing community action centers where kids were shown slide shows about the dangers of sniffing paint.

He turned to signal a waitress and I saw the stern classic Indian profile, a simple characteristic that gave him a stronger alliance to this country than I could claim.

"No," he was saying, "this town is really dead. Did you grow up here too?"

"In Port Aransas."

"I imagine that's even worse. You know what we used to do for kicks? We'd steal bowling balls from Buccaneer Bowl and go up to the Harbor Bridge about two in the morning when there wasn't much traffic and just let them loose. They'd roll all the way to Portland."

I smiled and nodded. A tall, snaky woman in antique clothes came over, and Canales ordered a pitcher from her. She brought it a few minutes later. She had an odd, weary attractiveness, and I was not surprised when Canales tried to get her to sit down.

"I'm *working*," she insisted, though she kept her smile and her spacy, flirtatious manner.

"You're talking to a man who's had his head inside the mouth of a killer whale," Canales told her.

"Sure."

"Jeff will back me up on this, won't you?"

"I might as well," I said.

"We're porpoise trainers," Canales told her.

"I'm really thrilled," she said. She was holding her empty serving tray against her hip, swaying back and forth good-naturedly.

"Sit down then," Canales repeated.

"Maybe later." She drifted away.

"What is the *deal* with this town?" he said.

I shrugged. Dancers were spilling out onto the patio floor. The music had softened to hard-core country lullabies:

> *Don't know whyyyyyyy*
> *Ah feel so lonesome*

> *Don't know whyyyyyyy*
> *Ah feel so blue*

A breeze swept across the patio, a cool salt breeze, the barest sign of autumn.

Canales filled our glasses from the pitcher and leaned back in his chair and looked up at the moon.

"Well," he said, "what do you think?"

"About her?"

"Anything."

"You haven't taught me about training the porpoises yet."

"You'll pick it up."

"How long will it be before they're trained?"

"Depends on the animals. Some porpoises are dumber than others. In six months, if they're not absolute cretins, we'll have them doing coordinated high bows, tail walks, all that shit."

"Mr. Granger says you have a lot of experience."

"Yeah," he said frankly, "I do. I was head trainer for a while at Sea Park before I started free-lancing. That was when Bill Mason was curator. You ever see his show?"

I nodded. I remembered a scene from *Adventures with Animals* in which Bill Mason was dragged across the Brazilian pampas holding the tail of a giant armadillo.

"What do you mean, free-lancing?" I asked.

"I went on the road with this porpoise I had. Barney. Took him around to shopping centers all over the country for about two years. It was an unbelievable hassle. I had this collapsible Plexiglas tank that I'd haul around with me in the bus. I'd keep Barney right behind the driver's seat when we were traveling. He had a little pool about the size of a coffin with an automatic sprinkler system to keep his skin from drying out. I'd be driving that bus, popping uppers and stopping every four hours to give ol' Barn some vitamins or medicine or whatever. Then I'd pull into town and of course nothing would be ready. The shopping center director was supposed to have eight guys there to set up the pool, that was part of the contract, but they were never there. So Barney had to sit in his little pool for another day, and then I'd have to neutralize and salinate the water before we could let him in. That made him happy, getting into that big pool again.

"I'll tell you, that was so weird. The whole thing. I was never away from him for two years, not for a minute. It was like being married to him. Some nights I'd be driving along about four in the morning, trying to make Saginaw or Eugene or wherever, with maybe a blizzard outside, and I'd pull over to check on Barney. And I'd just get weirded out, looking down at that creature. He could have been from outer space, you know? It was like I was dreaming the whole thing. Then I'd see him watching me through the Plexiglas and start wondering what was going on in *his* mind. I know everything there is to know about porpoises—I could take the fuckers apart and put them back together piece by piece—but sometime I would just like to know what's going on in their heads."

The waitress slunk by again, giving Canales a friendly smile as she passed.

"Anyway," he went on, "he died. Of course. One day the tank gave out. I wasn't paying enough attention, and the assholes who were helping me set it up left out a couple of bolts on one of the panels. Barney was whipping around the edge of the pool, building up speed for his high bow, then the whole thing falls apart, he flies out of the tank like a torpedo and goes right through the J. C. Penney window.

"The thing was, he wasn't even hurt physically. But he couldn't handle the trauma. He just checked out. That night the SPCA and the TV stations and kids with tears in their eyes were all outside the bus yelling abuse at me while I sat in there trying to convince Barney to stay alive. You ever seen a porpoise die of a heart attack?"

"No."

"Their tail just sort of lurches up and they go 'Uhhh!' and their blowhole stays open. It's very quiet, very fast. I've seen it happen a lot—hell, at Sea Park we'd lose five or six a year at least. You don't hear about that."

"You didn't tell me about the mortality rate before," I said.

"Don't worry," he said, "we've got primo conditions. We've got open water so we don't have to screw around with chemicals and salt. Plus, like I told you, I'm no vet, but I'm a good porpoise mechanic. I'm not going to blow this one. The Marine Mammal Commission is breathing down my neck after the scene with Barney. They wouldn't even give me a capture permit. I had to have Mason step in and sponsor me."

Canales finished his beer and poured another one from the pitcher. Talking about Barney had made him gloomy. The waitress came over again, her purse slung over her shoulder, and sat down.

"My name's Sara," she said.

Canales introduced us. "I figured you'd be drawn irresistibly to us," he said.

"I want to hear about the killer whale. That's like a big shark, isn't it?"

"Worse," Canales said.

"So what was your head doing in its mouth?"

"Waiting to get bitten off."

He told her about Karluk the Killer Whale and Finny the Sea Lion, who had to be threatened with a baseball bat to perform, and about the emperor penguins he had once trained that would simply shut down and die if somebody looked at them cross-eyed.

"Well," she said in a deadpan voice, rolling her empty

beer glass between her palms, "it sounds like a pretty interest-ing life all right."

"You could say that." Canales grinned. He was very effec-tive with her, and I thought perhaps that animal training had given him an edge that way. He had a sure perception of ges-ture—he knew by the way a creature regarded him what it was trying to get away with, what it was dying to offer.

"I better go," I said, noticing their shoulders were touch-ing. "I want to get there early in the morning."

"Don't leave yet," Canales said.

"Yeah," Sara murmured without interest.

"No, really."

"Well, I'll see you in Port A. Tomorrow we'll try to get them to eat something."

I wondered if I should tell him about swimming with them. I decided not to. He extended his hand, fingers up, of-fering a power handshake. I could see a small tattoo distorted by the cordage of his forearm, a porpoise jumping through a heart. Out of equanimity I offered my hand to Sara, in the old courtly way.

I walked back through the bar. There was a different band now, with a female fiddle player who stomped her boot on the floor in a becoming manner. I watched her for a while, until the set was over and she came to the bar. She was my age and had a harsh, pretty face. She looked at me very frankly, and I made a sort of half-nod in her direction before I left. I was a man with responsibilities.

The next morning I was awakened by the sunrise over the bay. I watched it for a while from the picture window of the motel, then checked out and ate breakfast at a little café on Ocean Drive my father had sometimes taken me to. A half hour later I was driving off the ferry into Port Aransas. No one was at the pool. I unlocked the gate and went inside. The por-poises were swimming in opposite directions, exhaling in loud resonant gusts that made their bodies sound perfectly hollow. When I came closer they moved away from the perimeter of the pool and stayed in the center, lifting only their backs when they breached.

It was not difficult to tell them apart. The female was smaller, and there was the hole in her dorsal fin and the scar tissue behind where someone's propeller had struck her. The male, though, was in perfect condition—he seemed wary but not alarmed. Neither of them showed any interest in reviving whatever it was that had taken place among the three of us the evening before. The female dropped out of sight now for long periods—two or three minutes—before surfacing again in the precise center of the pool.

Canales showed up a little later, driving a pickup load of fish, frozen blocks of smelt and herring which we carried into a big meat locker in the little shed that had been built beneath the bleachers.

"I think the female's a little morose," I told him when we had finished with the fish.

"Yeah, look at her. She's going straight for the bottom. That's a bad sign."

"Why?"

"She's a sulker. Or she's dumb, or high-strung. The other one might bring her along. God, he's a prize. Look at the way he's swimming—clockwise. That's excellent. Most porpoises'll swim counterclockwise."

"Why does that make a difference?"

"You train a porpoise by using its natural behavior. If you like the way it moves—zap!—you reinforce that. What we have here is an animal that has already essentially trained himself to swim opposite his partner. It'll be no problem at all to teach them to jump over a bar from opposite directions. It's all very natural."

So we sat and watched the porpoises a little longer. Canales was looking for usable motion, something that could be incorporated into what he termed not a "trick" but a "behavior." I was looking for something else. I watched them to convince myself that they were real, but I had no success. I could not believe in them, but there they were anyway—odd, plaintive almost shapeless. Wild things, wild animals dredged up from the sea.

"Now we'll see if they'll eat," Canales said. He went over

to the meat locker and took out two frozen herring, which he thawed somewhat beneath the water faucet.

"Of course they *won't* eat. I know that already. But you've got to let them know it's available."

He threw a fish out into the center of the pool. The female sank immediately to the bottom. The male shied away as well, but he was not frightened.

"Come on, you guys," Canales said. He turned to me. "You have to keep talking to them. That's one of the ways they get to know you."

I nodded. He went to the shed and came back with one of those long-handled nets used to skim fallen leaves from swimming pools.

"One more chance," he said to the porpoises. "Thirty more seconds."

They did not take the fish.

"Okay, you blew it. Too bad."

Canales skimmed the fish out of the pool with the net. "You've got to let them know it's not going to be there forever," he said. "They're on our schedule now, and they'll just have to realize it."

"How long will that take?"

"The male, I'd say three days. The female won't have enough sense ever to take it by herself. She'll just watch him and finally she'll catch on. They have a big adjustment to make, you can't really blame them. Porpoises in the wild won't eat dead fish—it's like you or me eating carrion. They have to be pretty hungry before they'll accept it. Once they do, though, they're under control."

Sara showed up at the gate a little later. Canales had invited her, and I could see from the offhand way he greeted her that they were already lurching toward intimacy.

"You really weren't kidding," she said, leaning down to the pool. "Oh, they're so cute. Poor things."

The male lifted an eye just above the waterline and looked at her for a moment.

"What are you going to call them?" Sara asked. She dangled her polished nails in the water and spoke under her breath, "C'mere, boy! Here, boy!"

"I don't know," Canales answered. "Squeaky, Porky, Flippy, Flappy, whatever. You have any ideas, Jeff?"

I looked down at the porpoises, unable to think of anything to call them.

"We could call the little one Peewee and the big male Smiley," Canales suggested.

"How original," Sara said.

"All right then," Canales said, "we could call the male Charlie. No, that's that tuna's name."

"I have an Aunt Wanda," Sara said. "I've always liked that name."

Canales considered for a moment, and then nodded decisively. "Okay. Wanda for the female. Does your aunt have a husband?"

"Lloyd."

"That's no good. You can't name a porpoise Lloyd. What about Sam? Or Sammy, that's better. Jeff?"

I shrugged.

"Wanda and Sammy," Sara said quietly, watching them.

She left soon after the christening, after a very broad display of eye contact with Canales that left no doubt as to her disposition for the evening.

Canales and I did little for the rest of the day except observe the porpoises, watching for reinforceable behavior. He lectured me about the philosophy of animal training, how it was a process of shaping, containing, a sculptural process, the pairing away of great blocks of irrelevant natural behavior and shaping the material that was left.

"You'll see when we start with them," he said.

In midafternoon he tried to feed them again and elicited no response, though it was somehow evident that the male—Sammy—was interested. Perhaps it was the still, wary manner in which he let his body hover on the surface near the fish. I could sense the alarm and desire that the half-frozen herring excited deep in his imagination. Wanda, however, stayed submerged, and on her rare trips to the surface came up at Sammy's side.

Before we left for the day we performed an experiment.

"Get down below the bleachers where they can't see us," Canales said. "When I tell you, we'll raise our heads and take a look."

We stayed hidden for half a minute, and then when Canales indicated peered over the bleachers. The porpoises' heads were raised high out of the water, up to their ventral fins. They were spinning slowly along the axis of their bodies, as if levitating. They were looking for us.

"The fuckers are fascinated by us," Canales said.

I went to the Salt Sea to claim my room. Lois wasn't there—she was already at the theater, popping popcorn and threading the film—but her nephew, a bloated middle-aged man named Buster, was minding the office. He gave me a key and told me to make myself at home. The room was clean and bare, with a little kitchenette and an old black and white TV. Above the bed there was a painting of the surf, the kind that brings good prices in shopping-mall art galleries because of the illusion of the sun penetrating the swells. For a moment I wished I had brought a picture of the Seamstress to hang on the wall beside it, a picture of her in her oversize backpack, smiling on some mountain trail.

I unpacked my few possessions: two pairs of corduroy jeans, a few shirts, my huaraches and tennis shoes, underwear, socks, diving equipment. I shoved the backpack that had contained all of this under the bed. Now I was settled. I walked to the store and bought provisions. At a postcard rack by the checkout counter I found a picture of a porpoise leaping clear from the water with a lighthouse in the background. The porpoise looked heavy, pregnant.

"The antics of the porpoise," the back of the card read, "are an endless source of amusement for residents and visitors alike in colorful Port Aransas, Texas."

I threw the postcard into my shopping cart. On the way home I stopped at the library just as it was closing and checked out the only book they had about whales and dolphins. Back in my room I heated a can of soup, tacked the postcard against the far wall where I could see it from the bed, and then leafed through the book. There were pictures of flensed carcasses on whaling ships, of hundreds of pilot whales butchered in an inlet. Dozens of species of dolphins and porpoises were represented, some looking, with their blunt snouts, like primordial fish, others with long thin birds' beaks rooting blindly in the mud of the Ganges River.

Finally I came across *Tursiops truncatus,* the Atlantic bottle-nosed dolphin, soaring through a fiery hoop.

"In general," the book said, "toothed cetaceans with beaks are known as dolphins, those without as porpoises. The Atlantic bottle-nosed dolphin, familiar to patrons of oceanaria all over the world, is properly a dolphin, but is also widely known as a porpoise."

I stared at the pictures for a long time, at the pretty girls in bikinis swimming with the porpoises—or dolphins—and the strange bliss on the animals' faces, as if all that mattered to them was to be loved by human beings. I read through a chapter on echo location and understood that, conceivably, they could see *into* one another, that despite all the experiments humans had made to understand their language, the porpoises themselves communicated almost unconsciously, knowing one another's condition, intentions, fears, all in one persistent wave of awareness.

When it grew dark I took a walk, past the surfing shops, the bars, the Catholic church, the bait stands, the rows of charter boats, and the frames on the docks on which people hoisted their sailfish and tarpon and—once, and the image was persistent and troubling—a porpoise.

I walked out onto the big fishing pier, all the way to the transverse that stood above the farthest breakers. The pier was littered with trash fish, hardheads and gafftops, their razor-sharp dorsals erect and vengeful. Old women in bonnets and tennis shoes were casting out into the darkness, and at the transverse the shark fishermen tended their great reels in silence beneath the arc lamps. At their feet lay the milky body of a five-foot hammerhead shark, a fringe of dark, frothy blood around its mouth where the jaws had been cut out. The shark was still synaptically alive, and it moved the strange beam of its head from side to side irryhthmically. I watched it without emotion: it was just one more unimaginable shape the black ocean had given up to the land.

The Crow's Nest was showing *The Green Slime*, with Robert Horton and Richard Jaeckel. I thought perhaps Mr. Granger might be inside watching it—he went to the movies often, indiscriminately—but when I walked by the Tarpon Inn I saw him out in front, swaying on a porch swing directly beneath a bare yellow light bulb. He was looking out toward the ship channel and did not notice me until I spoke to him, whereupon he stood up and gave me a funny little bow. He was holding a strange drink in his hand, a foamy lime concoction that made me think of the movie at the Crow's Nest.

"Come on up and I'll fix you one of these," he said.

"What is it?"

"I'm not real sure what you'd call it. Some kind of daiquiri, I think. I invented it years ago, before you were born."

He led me up the broad outside stairway to the second floor, then opened the door to his room and stood aside as I passed through.

"You haven't been here for a long time."

"Not since I was eight or nine."

"It hasn't changed much. A few years ago I had it painted. Then I had this little icebox brought up, so now I'm pretty self-sufficient. Of course I never did cook here anyway. I'll go out for a sandwich if I get hungry, over to the Marlin Spike or the Dairy Queen. Sometimes I'll drive over to Corpus and have a shrimp cocktail at the Petroleum Club."

Mr. Granger took a can of limeade out of the little refrigerator and poured it into a blender near the sink. I sat down in his rocking chair, remembering the room, the smell of old linoleum and after-shave, its aura of desperate, heartbreaking tidiness. It was as anonymous as the room I had been given at the Salt Sea. When I had first come up here, as a boy, it had astounded me because I had known that Mr. Granger was rich, and had assumed that wealth was something that sought its own level, that people as a rule lived and behaved in ways that were bounded by what they could and could not afford. Seeing the place where he lived had drastically altered my perception of Mr. Granger—he seemed for the first time a powerful being, a force in my parents' lives. The room exuded sadness, loss, but there was no hint of dereliction in it, no trace of someone out of control. I felt now, as I had when I was a boy, privileged to be here.

A great musty pile of prewar *National Geographic*s sat at the foot of Mr. Granger's bed, which was neatly made and covered with an ancient bedspread, patterned with llamas and parrots, that he had brought back from South America as a young man. On one wall there was a fishing map of the inland waters of our part of the coast, and next to it a photograph of my parents in the wheelhouse of the *Rapture*, holding me up to the camera.

Mr. Granger handed me my drink. "You want to wait till it settles down a little bit before you drink it. You've got vodka in there, and limeade, and just a touch of root beer concentrate."

We both sat there, silently watching the drink deflate.

"It's not bad," I said when I took a sip.

"I used to make it for your folks."

I creaked away in the rocking chair. I felt very comfortable.

"Did you know we named the porpoises today?" I asked.

"That's what Mando told me."

"We named them Wanda and Sammy."

"Those seem like good names. He says you're working out fine."

"I was reading a book tonight. It seems that they're really not porpoises. Strictly speaking, they're dolphins."

"Do you think that's what we should call them?" He looked concerned.

"I don't care," I said.

"We want to be correct."

"I think it's probably simpler to call them by the name everyone already knows."

"That's a good point, Jeff." He set his drink on the nightstand and studied it for a moment. Then he took off his glasses, his old wire frames, with the motion of someone unwinding a bandage from his head. When they were off and he was wiping them with a paper he'd taken out of his wallet, the exposed flesh around his eyes looked like the dead white skin that might have been hidden under a bandage. It seemed painful for him to have the glasses off, as if the sallow light of the room stung his eyes like salt water. He squinted against it, but there was still no focus to his face.

When he put his glasses back on he looked over at me and pretended to be shocked.

"When's the last time you cleaned your glasses?"

I laughed. "Years ago."

"They look like the windshield of a car that's been out on a dry caliche road. Hand them over here."

When I took them off and passed them across to him, the room lapsed into a familiar, comfortable blur. I watched Mr. Granger's fuzzy hands, nearly indistinguishable from the white lens paper they held, busily working over my glasses.

"This paper is made specially for eyeglasses," he lectured. "I buy it by the case, carry it around with me every place I go. Now," he said, handing the glasses back, "try that."

I put them on and the room snapped back into a clean, precise order. The quality of light had changed.

"Now I'm going to give you some of these," he said. He opened a drawer and pulled out a dozen of the little packets and poured them into my hand. I knew it would do no good to protest, so I stuffed them as well as I could into the pockets of my jeans.

Mr. Granger sat back on the bed and crossed his knees.

"You use those," he said. "Don't just throw them away."

I nodded indulgently. He leaned forward and rested his elbows on his knees.

"Are you glad you came down?" he asked.

"I think so. I'm glad to see you again, and I still think of this as home."

"It's in your blood, Jeff. Or in your genes, like they say nowadays."

"I'm still uneasy, though, about the porpoises. I thought they'd be happy and cuddly and as intelligent as everybody says. But there's something else there too, something about them that bothers me. I guess I always thought that they'd know who I am and what I wanted from them. But they don't know anything about me."

"You know," Mr. Granger said, going over to the sink to make us another drink, "I'm not as sentimental a man as people think I am. I've hunted all sorts of animals—doves, javelinas, deer—on just about every hunting lease in South Texas. I have to, it's part of the business I'm in. Some clients you play golf with, others you hunt with. We'll sit up there in those blinds, and right across from us there'll be an automatic feeder with an electric eye that throws out corn at a certain time of the day so that we'll know when to start looking for the deer. Then when one of them comes up we'll unload on him. Usually this man will keep the head if it's got any kind of rack at all and give the meat to his Mexicans if he happens to think about it. I'll tell myself that it's a shame, and that's all I'll think about it." He was silent while the blender was on. "But these porpoises, they're different. You can't think of them as animals, can you? Or fish either, of course. I guess I feel a little sorry about what we did to them."

He brought me my drink. "What I'm saying to you, Jeff, is that if you want to, we'll let them go tomorrow. I'll pay off Canales, and that will be that."

I thought for a long moment, or at least convinced myself that I was thinking, because my answer had been there all along. I did not want to let them go. I wanted them to understand me.

"No," I said. "Let's give it a try. At least for a while."

Mr. Granger brightened. This was what he badly needed

to hear. "They'll be happy, Jeff. They'll see that we don't mean them any harm. We just want them to be happy."

By the time I finished my drink Mr. Granger's room seemed very warm, with an almost visible shimmer of comfort. I settled back in the chair—it seemed impossible to leave. But in a moment I pulled myself up and said good night.

"Don't leave so soon."

"I better, or I won't be able to move."

I remembered the night I'd spent here so long ago, on the last night of my father's illness. I had not understood why I could not sleep in my own house, especially since the next morning was Easter, and I was afraid when Mr. Granger picked me up and brought me back to his room and put me into his bed while he sat in his rocking chair in his pajamas. Most of the night I only pretended to be asleep. When the phone rang I watched Mr. Granger rise from his chair and answer it. He mumbled and sat back down. I drifted in and out of sleep. Once when I woke he was crying, and another time he was shuffling around at the foot of my bed.

In the morning I looked down at the Easter basket he had placed there and I knew that my father was dead. I was very hungry. I asked him if I could eat the foot-high chocolate rabbit in the center of the basket. He said to go ahead. My mother came at midmorning and took me walking on the beach and told me. "I know," I said, and broke down.

She held me and said, "We'll have some breakfast, okay?" The thought of breakfast restored me, filled me with hope and happiness. I had never been so hungry in my life.

Now Mr. Granger held open the door, and looking at him, I knew that grief would never be that simple again.

"Sleep well," he said, "and don't be such a worrywart."

I walked home along the main road. A dune buggy sped by me, screeched to a halt, and backed up. A kid pulled himself up on the roll bar and asked—in the Tex-Mex catch phrase, "Kitty combate?"—if I wanted to fight. In the glow from a nearby streetlight I could see the surfing cartoon on his T-shirt, his adolescent scowl. I stood there for a moment and actually deliberated. I had heard of the therapeutic value of a good fight.

"No," I said finally, "I don't think so."

"You pussy!" The kid threw a half-filled beer bottle at me, but his aim was so wild I didn't even bother to dodge it. It landed on the oyster shell without breaking and the dune buggy peeled out.

At home I stared at the postcard I had bought, the porpoise leaping high in Lydia Ann Channel, seemingly about to give birth. I thought I would dream about it, hung there in the sky, delivering its calf into the open air. But I had another, more disturbing dream instead—my parents in the wheelhouse of the *Rapture*, their faces glassed over. They were saying something I didn't understand and pointing to the landscape, to the flat seacoast that trembled and rose up against them, capsizing the boat and drawing it down into its substance.

Chapter 4

Canales was right: for three days the porpoises would not take the dead fish. Each time it was offered, though, there was a barely detectable change in Sammy's attitude. By the second day he nudged the fish slightly with his beak, and when another was thrown in several hours later he actually took it into his mouth and spit it out.

"Tomorrow he'll go all the way," Canales said, skimming the fish out. And the next day Sammy took a herring in his mouth, thrashed his head back and forth very slowly, and let the fish fall back into his gullet. Canales blew his whistle to reinforce the act.

"Good boy!"

He threw another fish out. The porpoise regarded it tentatively, then ate it as well. While this was going on Wanda remained, as usual, on the bottom of the pool. Once or twice, though, she rose near Sammy and regarded him curiously before going back down.

"How long will it take with her?" I asked Canales.

"I doubt if she'll hold out for more than a couple of days. You can tell she's already interested."

"What if she doesn't eat at all?"

"We'll force-feed her. But I don't think we have to worry.

She's dumb. She doesn't have any ideas of her own, so whatever Sammy's doing is what she's going to pick up on."

She came up the next day and nuzzled Sammy as he was taking his fish. I detected a coyness in this act, but I knew she was hungry, repulsed, afraid, a dozen things that the deportment of her body could not show us. It was as if she were demanding something from Sammy, some explanation as to why he was eating the dead fish. She did not seem to equate it with sustenance. Finally, though, she understood, and took a piece of smelt into her mouth and dove to the bottom with it.

Over the next week the porpoises grew more active, though they still stayed in the middle of the pool and though Wanda remained for the most part on the bottom, rising only to breathe or to feed. She made me think of the dolphin in the book I had checked out of the library—the one with the narrow beak that rooted in the mud of the Ganges. I would stand on the dock, placing myself deliberately in her line of vision when she surfaced. I wanted her to see me, to acknowledge me the way she had the night I had gone into the pool with them. But I was only another object on the dock, another fixture above the waterline, like a buoy or a lighthouse.

"The next step," Canales said, "is to get them to eat out of our hands. We'll keep dropping the fish a little closer to the edge of the pool, closer to us. Soon they'll get the idea that they can swim over and pick it up and there's nothing to be afraid of. Then we've got them. Then they trust us."

So we taught them to trust us. Over time they swam up to our hands, which held the fish, and lifted their eyes above the surface, so that when they took the food they were watching us. We blew our whistles, then, to let them know they had done the right thing, and they slipped below the surface and were instantly swallowed up by the muddy water.

For three weeks we worked on these preliminaries, coaxing them into understanding our position, conditioning them to the objects—our open palms, the bright red target ball, our human forms themselves—that it was necessary for them to recognize if they were to evolve into the perfect state we had imagined for them.

This was a good time. I would wake each morning from a dream that was tamer and more rational than the reality I knew existed at the pool. Very quickly they came to love us, and at the first sight of us each morning they would leap in high, precise arcs from the water, an astonishing, improbable welcome that left me dizzy.

The adjustments I made to their company were very subtle. For the first week I could tell the porpoises apart only by the obvious external markings—Wanda's dorsal hole, her propeller scar and smaller size, Sammy's unspoiled surface and heft. It was an intellectual process, searching for the signs. But gradually I became less reliant on the field marks. It was a matter of conditioning myself to quit looking for human reactions to be displayed on cetacean faces. I became fluent in understanding a broad range of emotions that had no apparent outlet in the porpoises' bodies. I thought I understood them as they understood one another, through a kind of constant internal readout.

Sometimes, though, human and porpoise seemed to coincide in their expressions. I was convinced there were moments that the famous fixed smile really aspired to be just that. Besides the eyes, that smile was the great standard of the porpoise face, and it was surprisingly expressive. Its rigidity, I discovered, was as much an illusion as its constant attitude of mirth. If the smile did not actually change (and there were days when I thought it did), it nevertheless managed to convey moods that, through much trial and error, I was able to read. The mouth drew its expression from the eyes, the way the bay on any given day was influenced by the color of the sky. Yet it was not the eyes one looked at, it was the mouth. Sometimes its downward curve seemed less severe, extending almost playfully along the head to the pinprick that marked the ears. At other times the mouth was set in that quavering way in which humans smile just before they are about to break into tears.

Fear was the simplest emotion to spot. It arose in the porpoises less frequently now, occurring only for a moment when we introduced something—a prop, a ball, the red target on a longer pole—into the pool. At those moments I would see, directly in their eyes, a glimpse of that terror that had been there on the day of their capture. The whites would engorge, overwhelming the soft brown irises.

They remained skittish about outright physical contact with us, even after they had learned to take fish from our hands. As they approached us to touch their beaks to our palms (for our palms were their true target, for which the red ball was merely a substitute), they went through a whole physical repertoire of longing, hesitation, anxiety, afraid of what we would do to them if they came too near.

It became plain very early that Sammy was exceptional at anything we wanted him to do. There was a clarity of purpose in his every move, as if every one of our requests were something he had already conceived in his own mind.

In all professional respects, Wanda was a problem. She was shy and slow, and continued to hug the bottom of the pool as if it were the only thing in her new universe she could believe in. She would, Canales predicted, be barely adequate as a foil for Sammy during a performance. Even Sammy seemed exasperated by her timidity. She got in his way and dogged his progress with us. In time his confidence seduced her away from the bottom and from the safety zone of the center of the pool, but any progress she made was simply an effort to keep up with him. He was growing away from her, and she was afraid.

I did not think of her as stupid. The first time she pressed her beak against my palm I felt that the act was an end in itself, the sign of a covenant, whereas for Sammy it had simply been another base to touch. When she swam up to me and hesitated, I thought of the human quality of reserve. She withheld a part of herself from every activity, and I found that admirable at the same time the professional side of me found it exasperating.

It is an odd experience, to fall truly in love with an animal.

It is off the scales. There is no way to assess what is happening, no way to take your own emotions seriously, no release short of perversion. It was not the sort of love that required release, but I won't pretend it wasn't, in its way, sensual. One cannot love the gray, bulbous, taut-slick form of a porpoise and not enter some trackless territory of physical longing.

As a boy I had dogs. I worried for their safety and enjoyed their company, but I did not stay awake at night thinking of them. I would not simply put down my fork at a meal and daydream until my food became cold, as I did frequently now.

This infatuation came as a surprise to me, and I was not sure I welcomed it. At the end of the day I could still see and feel and hear them, my hands would still be stinging from contact with the cold salt sheen of their bodies. When I closed my eyes I would see their open mouths, each small perfect tooth, the strange tongue that seemed to be rooted at the front of the jaw, the hard bony beak pocked with tiny dents that were like the pattern in a carpet.

It was all much more a part of me than I was prepared to admit. I told myself it wasn't "love," that it was nothing more than what anyone feels after a day of work, the shoe salesman who cannot close his eyes without having to watch an automatic recapitulation of each shoe he placed on each foot. But a shoe salesman doesn't hunger for that kind of vision, he doesn't lie in his bed at night waiting for it to begin. I did. A part of my world fell away during those weeks. I swooned.

We did not enter the water with them again for a long time. What we did now was all work and drill and maintenance. At some point our teaching them to trust us became teaching them to perform. My hand was, in truth, a target now, what they must watch and live for; my voice was a police whistle that they heard when they made some gesture that pleased me. Canales drew graphs and had them Xeroxed, and bought two clipboards. We worked on basic behaviors—high bows, tail walks, "singing"—and after each of our three daily sessions we would note on the charts the rate of progress, the amount of fish consumed, overall disposition.

Wanda wanted desperately to please us, Sammy to please himself, and I to be made explicable to them both. I was not comfortable being an object of confusion to another creature, I wanted my motivations and intentions to be plain to them. I felt increasingly as if I did not belong to an authentic species but to some alien race that had been put onto the earth without cause, and cursed with the desire to explain its presence.

It was an anthropocentric conceit I could not help trying to overcome in an anthropocentric way. This was a trap Canales did not fall into. We were the "bosses," the porpoises had to do what we told them. It was a simple and not entirely graceless attitude, and in practice I could not help but adopt it. During the training sessions I worked close to the bone, learned to be explicit about basic things. If when Wanda went over the bar, she grazed her belly across it, if she did not raise her body far enough out of the water for her tail walks, I had to correct these things by withholding her reward, leaving her in confusion about what she had done wrong until she tried it again and happened to get it right.

"What we need is a theme," Canales told me one day. "Something to hold all the behaviors together. Pirates, Porpoise University, shit like that. When I was on the road with Barney we had this Laurel and Hardy type thing. I'd be the straight man. I'd say something dorky and Barney would jump up out of the tank and splash me. It worked pretty well. We need to come up with something like that.

"We also need a sexy chick. She'd fall in the pool and pretend to be drowning and Sammy would rescue her, and then Wanda could pretend to be jealous. Or she could get in and dance with him. Ever seen a girl dance with a porpoise?"

"No."

"It's kind of cute. Ballroom dancing. I'll talk to Dude about getting a girl on the payroll."

The carpenters came and built, to Canales' specifications, a kind of pulpit on the far end of the dock. We climbed up onto this structure and onto a metal ladder that rose high over the pool. Leaning forward at the top of the ladder we were able to hold our props—the bar, or hoop, or the red target ball on the end of a pole—twelve feet above the surface of the water. The porpoises were nowhere near that height yet. Looking down at the impenetrable sheet of water, I felt it unrealistic to expect that the animals would ever make it up there.

But the training was so incremental the improbable was accomplished almost unnoticeably. We brought them up inch by inch through the hoop or across the bar. With the target we led them higher out of the water each day and shaped their high leaps and acrobatics by blowing the whistle at every new apogee they reached.

Usually they would consume their daily ration of fish as rewards, though when they did badly much of it would be withheld and given to them at the end of the day in one dose.

"That's to show there's no hard feelings," Canales explained. "That tomorrow we start over. A lot of trainers use starvation techniques, but not me. I have respect for these animals."

When we left at night Sammy and Wanda would swim with us to the edge of the pool and follow us with their eyes as we left the compound. As we locked the gate we could hear their whistles, their worried splashing, as if they feared they could not survive for even a night without some form of human guidance. Canales and I fell into the habit of going out for a beer a few nights a week and then afterward making a final check on the porpoises to make sure they were calm. On these occasions he would lecture me on some fine point of training, and I would nod my head soberly and patiently.

I knew that I was a good trainer, that I was a better trainer in fact than Canales was. I was less temperamental, my hand signals were clearer, it did not upset me when the porpoises did something wrong.

Canales at times reminded me of my high-school football coach—"No, no, *no*, son! Do it again!" Porpoise training was merely a craft for him in which the medium happened to be living creatures.

But his knowledge of porpoises was sound. He had read all

the books I had recently been plowing through, read them more carefully than I would have guessed, and his assessment of the literature, what was worthwhile and what merely trendy, I found to be generally accurate.

"Don't talk to me about that asshole Cousteau," he would say over his beer. "All that sanctimonious crap. Read his early books, the ones where he goes out and *harpoons* porpoises. And those Sierra Club creeps. 'The cetacean brain is ten times larger than the human brain.' They'll believe anything that makes humans out to be second rate. They don't care about porpoises, they're just using them to put down the human race. Sure, porpoises are smart. But if they're smarter than us how come they're not teaching *us* tricks?"

Some evenings I would stop by Mr. Granger's room at the Tarpon Inn and watch television with him until it was time to go to sleep. He sat there in an almost reverential silence, accepting everything that appeared on the tube. The bionics, the "relevant" sitcoms in which families gave and suffered abuse, the endless procession of archetypes—psychotic detectives, dopey women, sidekicks, prescient sheepdogs living among families of insipid moppets—all this evidence of the nation's diseased vision he took at face value, in innocence. He would sometimes laugh softly along with the off-key, computer-enhanced laughtracks, and turn to me as if for confirmation that what he saw there on the TV was really funny. I would smile reassuringly.

More often I went straight home and read about cetaceans from a big coffee-table book I had bought in Corpus with the proceeds from Mr. Granger's extravagant paychecks. I read *Moby Dick* again, this time watching out for the interests of the prey, those cousins of Wanda and Sammy that were so unutterably monstrous and strange I could barely stand to think about them.

I worried that I was becoming too withdrawn, had inherited that vague, attenuated manner by which my father had maintained his distance from the world and which I had always admired. It was a condition that for most of my life I had cultivated a little, so that I was secretly pleased when teachers would take me aside and say, "Don't be so shy!"; "Pay more attention to what is going on around you!" But now the state had seized me, there was no artifice in it, and there were times when I wanted away from it. My father could walk around nearly in a trance and one still felt attuned to him, drawn to him; he was not self-absorbed in his isolation, as I felt I was becoming.

So I decided to rally, to make an effort, to turn my thoughts away on occasion from warm-blooded sea creatures to members of my own species. One night I called the Seamstress.

"Oh," she said calmly. "Hi."

I told her about the porpoises. I could hear her inhaling a joint over the phone.

"What about the movie?" I asked.

"They've finished editing. I think it's going to be released sometime next fall. We all had a big party the other night and Richard—that's the guy that replaced you—shook hands with the mayor. Wearing the suit, you know."

I let a pause sag into the wires between us.

"Well, listen," she said, "I don't want to run this up on you."

"No."

"Keep up the good work with the fish."

"They're mammals, like you."

"Oh, I may be going to the Coast. The West Coast, not whatever coast you're on. This guy Richard's moving there. He's got a job in the Baba Ram Dass cassette library. I might ride along in his U-Haul. Just for the ride."

"I bet."

"Nothing like that."

"I bet."

"Was there something you expected of me?" the Seamstress asked.

I had to admit there wasn't.

"Well, I better go. It was sweet of you to call. I sort of miss you. That's as honestly as I can put it. I think about you some-times. I'd like to keep in touch, I really would."

"I'll be here," I said. "You have the address. I'll be getting a listing. Give me a call."

"For sure," she said.

In the grocery store the next day I ran into someone who claimed he had been to high school with me. His name was Mark, he was rather short and fastidious-looking, and when I tried to remember him in school I could not dispel an image of the full-grown man before me sitting attentively in a wooden desk.

Mark invited me to dinner at the condominium he and his wife managed near the beach. I didn't know what to do but ac-cept, so the next night I was sitting with them in their living room, looking out a picture window at the offshore rigs and eating snack crackers from a tray. Mark and I didn't talk much, having discovered that we did not belong to the same circles in school or, indeed, to the same grade. We simply went over the list of homeroom teachers, refreshing our memories about their neuroses and eccentricities, and then talked about our re-spective businesses.

"Well, Jeff, let's hear about those porpoises," he said, just after finishing an account of the Byzantine negotiations that led up to the closing of a motel he had recently purchased.

His wife was a busy woman who was always sweeping up crumbs with her hands and refilling drinks and trying to perk up the conversation from her station in the kitchen. She had decorated the living room with Hummel figurines and pastel wallpaper and throw pillows and sprayed it with some delicate and insubstantial scent that made the air seem bad.

They had no children, just a high-strung dog of some exot-ic breed that seemed to drain their energy and keep them barely within the range of civility to one another. She had bought the dog as part of her decorating scheme, had envi-sioned it sleeping in the little wicker basket in the corner, bun-dled up with its squeak toys. But the dog merely ran over the furniture, snorting and drooling and humping the legs of the guests. She said she wanted to get rid of it, to find it a place in the country where it would be happy, but Mark had developed an affection for it and would not let her. He stroked the short knotted hide behind its ears while it waved its hind leg and dribbled urine on the carpet. There was something pathetic and honorable in his alliance with the animal.

"I mean we have an obligation to the goddamn dog," he said.

"Maybe if we have to keep him," his wife said to me, "you could help us to train him."

I did my best, but it was impossible to hold the dog's attention. I hoped that my failure would somehow dampen our relationship, but Mark called me regularly, inviting me to dinner, and I accepted whenever there was no way out of it. Once he asked if I would mind if there was "a fourth," and I said of course not before I realized what he meant. They had gotten a recent divorcée for me, a big-boned woman who kept lighting cigarettes with kitchen matches and smothering the room in sulfur fumes as we watched TV. I had to volunteer to take her home, and when I declined to come into her house she touched my forearm and whispered, "I understand."

They didn't call me after that, but in a few days I ran into another classmate, one that I remembered. His name was Overturf—he had never gone by his first name—and he had changed little since high school. He was still lean and sly, seasoned by a decade of drug abuse. I remembered him as slightly brilliant, an impression he still managed to give off though much of his intensity was gone and he seemed irretrievably mellowed.

Overturf owned land in Port Aransas and lived there most of the week, but his business was in Corpus. He mowed lawns there, or rather was at the head of a lawn-mowing empire; he himself mowed only one day a week. He said he made $50,000 a year and invited me over on his day on to see how. I was vaguely interested and took him up on the invitation the next time I felt like taking a day off from my own work.

Overturf had a big pickup with a double cab in which he drove around town picking up his six-man crew. Those that couldn't fit in the cab sat in the bed, which was loaded with dirt and brush and greasy lawn mowers and edgers. They drove around from lawn to lawn and put in a fourteen-hour day. I watched them for a few hours, stupefied. Their average time for a lawn was four minutes, and Overturf had contracted for blocks and blocks of flat residential yards. They mowed sixty yards a day.

"There's no secret to it," he told me as we watched his minions swarming over the grass, actually running behind their mowers. "Used to be a yardman was somebody who'd poke around on his hands and knees all day and get maybe three or four dollars for it. If he was lucky the maid would bring him out a sandwich at noon. I've just upgraded the profession a little bit. Streamlined it. I tell all my customers 'No flower beds, no leaf bags, no trimming around the flagstones.' We're professionals."

When the yardmen were through with a block they passed around hip flasks, slapped each other on the back, and called each other "Hoss," then whooped and loaded their machines onto the bed of the truck. One of them was a woman, and she seemed amused to be a part of these male bonding rituals and took obvious pride in keeping up with the work. She seemed bright and self-assured and unattached. I liked to watch her leg muscles working as she pushed her mower, the concentrated set of her features under her straw hat.

Her name was Irene. I invited her on a whim to the Yardmen's Ball, the annual black-tie rite Overturf had told me about that celebrated the end of the season. The affair was held at a private club and there must have been nearly a hundred yardmen there in tuxedos, representing various lawnmowing factions throughout the city. Overturf gave a speech, and there was a kind of parody of the Academy Awards, in which miniature gilded lawn mowers were awarded, and after that a formal dance that soon degenerated into a drunken brawl.

Irene and I left early, but when we were alone she turned vague; she seemed uncertain about how to deal with a man beyond the mores of camaraderie, genuinely puzzled as to what I could possibly want from her. I kissed her, knowing it was hopeless. She looked at me as if I were very strange.

It took me a few days to get over that, as if I had indeed committed some grave blunder, had been mistaken all along about the way the world worked. I returned to my work, morose, confused. It took the porpoises to draw me out of this mood; I gave them my full attention, no longer distracted by attempts at human intercourse, and began to feel secure again, and concentrated, and not alone.

The first norther did not come until early November. The wind fanned the languid water of the channel and blew down the few remaining tents in the state park. The last of the tourists went away, and the summer people taped their sliding glass doors and picture windows, applied their security decals there, and went back to the Midwest or to West Texas. The surfers appeared now in wetsuit tops. They stood on the beach most of the day examining the waves and walking up and down like shorebirds. Mr. Granger closed down the Crow's Nest for the winter.

I came to work early in the mornings and stood on the pulpit in the cold wind, watching the gray shapes below me following my hands. Three or four times a week a small skiff cruised by the dock, guided by a woman in a bright-blue waterproof parka, the same woman I had seen that first night at the Crow's Nest with her little boy. Sometimes, when I was out of her sight and she thought I could not see her either, she let the motor idle about twenty-five yards out and looked at the pool through binoculars.

When the norther had blown itself out the mild weather it left behind had an edge to it, a vague wintry drift. I read in the paper that the first whooping cranes of the year had arrived at the wildlife refuge, fifty-one of them.

"Take a good look at those birds," my father had told me when I was a boy and we had taken the excursion boat out to see them. "There won't be any of those left when you grow up."

The cranes picked their way through the marsh that day, oblivious to the boat. Their white plumage seared itself into my memory, as something lost and unredeemable. But here they were again, still wintering in the same place, still breeding and replenishing themselves.

The training began to accelerate. There would come a point in the tedious step-by-step process at which Sammy would see the object we had in mind and work toward it directly. By the middle of November he could walk across the pool on his tail and perform a nearly complete frontal flip.

Wanda, of course, came along more slowly, but once she understood what it was Sammy was doing she seemed eager to imitate it. She was not well coordinated, and it seemed to me she was less than single-minded about the whole enterprise, unable to think in terms of simple leaps and twirls that must be attained. There was something more she wanted to understand.

I thought of them like this, as conscious beings grappling earnestly all day long with the problems we presented them. Surely it could not have been easy making sense of us, and I found pleasure in my work at that point where man and porpoise both stopped trying, and achieved something together. It might be a simple wave of a pectoral fin, the most uncomplicated of all our behaviors, that drew us together and held us for a long moment in some special sanctum before everything grew distorted again and unnatural.

Of all the behaviors the one that was most pivotal was beaching. A very gradual ramp had been constructed at one corner of the pool, and very slowly, using the target, we began to coax the porpoises out of the water. It was a classical progression, but it took even Sammy a long time to come all the way out and lie there helpless on the ramp with the weight of his body bearing down on him.

"It's definitely a weird thing for them," Canales said. "A porpoise does not beach himself unless there's something really haywire somewhere. It's the one position where they're totally vulnerable."

Once Sammy had been drawn out of the water onto the ramp he invented his own variation, swimming around the pool for speed and then lunging out of the water and sliding on his belly along the ramp so that he almost collided with us as he took his fish. Wanda hauled herself up in the old painstaking way we had taught her, rising out of the water by a surge of her flukes and dropping onto the ramp, staying exposed just long enough for me to toss the fish into the open trough of her mouth. If I was not immediately forthcoming with the fish she would leave anyway, and all my efforts to get her to stay longer were fruitless.

"We'd better write that in as a joke," Canales decided. "Think of some funny reason why she jumps right back in the water."

"How about terror?"

"Yeah, that's really funny. I can tell you've got a bright future in this business. Seriously, though," Canales said, "we *do* need a girl in the show. Somebody we could teach the ropes to. She could be an assistant. Then one of us could have an occasional day off."

"Fine with me," I said.

"Do you care who it is? I mean, she obviously can't be a pig, right? Just some reasonably pretty, fairly bright girl."

"You've got somebody in mind. Sara, right?"

"She doesn't really get off on waitressing that much. She's been sort of asking me to help her scout out her career opportunities."

So Sara quit her job at the Lonesome Coyote and came to work soon after. For the first few days she wandered around the perimeter of the dock, looking bored while Canales and I worked the animals. They grew used to her and would let her rub them behind the pectorals, but her presence did not excite them in the slightest. We taught her the hand signals—the counterclockwise spiral that meant a front flip, the outspread arms that signaled the coordinated tail walk. I took her up to the pulpit and showed her how to draw the porpoises in with her hands until they were stationed directly beneath each open palm, their heads out of the water watching for the signal that would tell them what to do.

She had a rather glum interest in it all, an overall mood that seemed totally dependent on how Canales treated her off duty. They were living together in a little ground-level house behind the dunes, a pleasant place whose plastic wood-grain paneling Canales had covered with his mementoes. There were pictures of Karluk the Killer Whale and assorted porpoises, of a pilot whale and a sea lion. A large part of the living room was taken up by Sara's stereo system, with which she rendered down an impressive collection of progressive country albums.

She had recently, at age thirty, developed an ambition to become a singer in that genre. She had a wan, not unpleasant voice, which she attributed to good living. She ate no meat and made chocolate chip cookies out of carob and whole wheat and honey, which Canales and I nibbled on politely.

Sara had had three abortions, and spoke of them so frequently I began to understand they had had some sort of therapeutic value for her. But she loved children, she said, it had just never been the right time for her. She needed the right man to have children with. Besides, she might have to go on the road someday soon. And then there was the basic ethical question involved in raising a child in a world that was nothing less than a carcinogenic hothouse.

One day we all brought our wetsuits (Sara had one from her surfing days) and entered the pool with the porpoises. They avoided us at first, Wanda taking up her old position at the bottom of the pool. But then very quickly they grew delirious with excitement and began to swim with us, allowing us to be towed on their dorsal fins and gently raking us up and down the legs with their teeth.

"You better watch out for that," Canales told Sara. "That's foreplay."

"It's more than I get from you," she said.

Every day after that there was a free period during which we went in with them. Canales wanted the porpoises to get used to us being in the water. He especially wanted them to feel at ease with Sara, because she was needed for what he called the Roman Chariot Ride, a behavior in which she was to stand with one foot on each porpoise and ride around the pool.

The trick took a long time to set up. Sara practiced her balance while Canales and I accustomed the porpoises to the double bridle they would have to wear to support her. Then began a delicate round of negotiations so that the porpoises would tolerate her standing on their backs. It was not easy convincing them; each step of the behavior had to be laid down with extreme care, as if we were building a house of cards.

Finally Sara and the porpoises were able to manage a trip around two sides of the pool, an event comparable in our minds to the first flight of the Wright Brothers. Mr. Granger was there, and it was when Sara tried to acknowledge his applause with a wave that she fell off. But while it lasted it was a riveting vision, a classical one: the girl borne across the water on the backs of two creatures that had risen from the gloomy depths to her aid. I remembered the day we had captured them, how improbable it had seemed then that they would ever rouse themselves in the slightest from their fear and shock. I was proud of them, and proud and ashamed of myself, aware of a nagging reserve that had, over the months, become less and less insistent. All I knew was that when Sara fell off, and Canales and I blew our whistles in congratulation so that the porpoises knew they had done it right at last, they did not swim over to Canales though he held out the fish that was their reward. They came to me.

By the end of that day the behavior was perfected. Sara and Canales left early. I stayed behind to give the porpoises the balance of the day's fish (plus a little extra) and to put some salve on a fungus Wanda was developing behind her right pec. The two of them leaned their heads against the dock and opened their mouths and made the creaking sound from their spiracles that I had learned long ago was a sound of contentment, expectation. I placed the small stiff fish, a handful at a time, into the open mouths and watched them disappear down the porpoises' narrow throats.

They were still excited from the day's success when it was time for me to go, and they did everything they could, from their element, to keep me there. They splashed me on the way out, and Wanda did her uncoordinated front flip and swam on her back waving good-by as if she knew the gesture, out of context, would charm me into staying. When I was outside the gate I waited a long moment until their splashing and squeaking had finally wound down, and then I went home.

I heated a can of chili on the stove and spent most of the evening reading about famous dolphins and porpoises—Pelorus Jack, Opo, a dozen dolphins who voluntarily came in from the sea to swim with children on the beach. All the stories ended in the deaths of the animals. All true animal stories do.

On the *Tonight Show* a man wearing a bush jacket was holding a leash to which a lemur was attached. The lemur was climbing around on Johnny Carson's shoulders with a strange, otherworldly delicacy that suggested the creature was weightless. Carson looked at the camera and gritted his teeth as the thing paced behind his neck. The man in the bush jacket, whom I recognized as Bill Mason, the famous wildlife entrepreneur and Canales' former boss, was chuckling and saying, "Now, Johnny, just be calm." Then the lemur's face stared at the camera also, and those great bug eyes were the only thing on the screen with integrity.

"I saw your friend on Johnny Carson," I told Canales when he came over near midnight to get a beer.

"Mason? Yeah, he's on there all the time. He's such a hot shit I can't stand it."

We went to a shrimpers' bar near the bait stand and sat at a booth by a window that overlooked the channel. A few commercial craft moved in silence across the dark water. Canales put a quarter into the table jukebox and punched a Willie Nelson song. He waited until it came on to collapse against the vinyl.

"That was damn good today," he said. "Sara and those porpoises. Tomorrow I think you and me ought to try it in case she gets sick or quits or something. That way one of us can still do the behavior. Course it won't be the same with a guy, but it's still an interesting trick."

I nodded, and we listened to the song.

"You think Sara's working out okay?" Canales asked.

"Sure."

"She's talking about going up to Austin. There's some band there she thinks might need a girl singer. You ever heard her sing?"

"Just a little. At work."

"She's awful. She's sort of a sad case, you know? Delusions of grandeur."

"You think she'll leave?"

"Probably not. There's this guy she's in love with."

"Not you?"

"No, I'm the guy she lives with. She's in love with this steel guitar player who's so stoned all the time he can't even remember his name. She's a masochist."

Canales finished his longneck and ordered another. It was hot in the bar, and he took off his coat and rolled up his sleeves very carefully. He held up his hand.

"See what she gave me?"

It was a ring shaped like a porpoise. He took it off and twirled it around in front of his face.

"That's one thing about being a porpoise trainer," he said. "You accumulate a lot of crap like this. Every Christmas that's all I get, porpoise paperweights and porpoise salt and pepper shakers."

Canales talked for another hour, edging closer to bathos with each beer he ordered.

"I should have married Barney. He was the only thing that ever loved me. If queers can get married I don't see why a guy and porpoise can't.

"Tell me when I start sounding pathetic," he said.

"I can take it."

"No, let's get out of here. Let's take a walk."

We paid our bill and took our customary walk up the road to the porpoise circus. Canales did not talk anymore. I think he sensed what I did: that any fondness we might develop for one another would somehow be shy of real friendship.

We were several hundred yards away from the compound

when I heard something—a series of hollow splashes and the faint sound of angry male voices.

"Somebody's over there," I said.

"Where?"

"At the pool."

We stopped to listen. I heard the splashes again, louder this time, and from far away a sound that rooted me to the road with panic, the distress call: *thweet—thweet.*

"*Run!*" Canales yelled. Then I was drifting along the dark road as in a dream, my heart beating wildly, Canales' labored breathing just over my shoulder. And a peculiar sensation, an intense body vision of what I would find when I reached the compound.

In the darkness I saw a big car, a Lincoln, parked by the gate. There was a ladder on the outside of the wall, and without thought I scrambled up it and dropped down onto the top row of bleachers. I heard a splash and then another, this one landing on solid flesh.

"Hey!" Canales screamed, climbing over the wall.

Everything was silent now down at the pool except for the distress calls of the porpoises. It was too dark to see who was there or how many there were.

I started down. I heard footsteps climbing the bleachers.

"Hey," a voice said. "It's okay. No harm done."

The voice was out of range, but I lunged for it anyway and grabbed someone's pants leg. I pulled myself up to his waist and fell back down the bleachers with him. It seemed to take a long time for us to reach the bottom, alternately falling on top of one another or catching a limb in the troughs between the rows of seats. When we reached the bottom row I lost him.

"Jeff!" Canales yelled, but I didn't know what he was warning me about until I felt something crack against my forehead. I told myself as I was falling that it must have been a baseball bat, because it sounded like a home run. I was losing consciousness, but I resolved to pitch forward in doing so, and had the good fortune to latch onto my opponent's belt. This contact revived me, it was a purchase on my own awareness. I held on, feeling my strength recharge. The bat struck me on the back and on the legs, but the guy obviously had no angle to work from. Other footsteps were scrambling up the bleachers toward the ladder.

"Let me loose," he said, and then added, as if to appeal to my sense of sportsmanship, "Come on."

I could see him then, a little: a young face, the ubiquitous scowling face of the high-school terrorist. He hit me again and pulled me up with him to the next row of bleachers. I heard the car starting outside the compound. I was losing focus again.

"Let me go, you creep. We didn't hurt your fucking sharks."

Rallying, I aimed the bottom side of my fist at the place the words had come from and felt the septum crack and the nose splay beneath it. I struck again, missing this time and scraping the flesh of my palm along a row of teeth. He got loose then, and I grabbed blindly and got an ear in each hand and pulled down hard, expecting them to rip like torn sleeves. He yelled as if they had, but they remained attached. And I got a mean kick in my chest that sent me rolling down the bleachers again. I was out before I hit the bottom.

Perhaps five minutes later I looked up. Canales had found the lights, and the compound was lit up like a football field.

"Christ," he said. "Are you okay?" He was bleeding from the nose.

I nodded. It hurt.

"I heard them smack you from the other side of the pool. They had baseball bats and two-by-fours, it looked like. There were three of them."

"What about the porpoises?"

"I think they're all right. They're making a big racket. I'm going to call an ambulance, then I'm going to call the pigs."

"Never mind the ambulance," I said. "It's not that bad. I can go anywhere I need to in a car."

"You haven't seen yourself. You might have a fractured skull."

"I doubt it," I said, though my head was beginning to throb.

"Okay, I'll just call the police. But do me a favor and don't move."

I lay very still and listened to the distress calls of the porpoises beside me in the pool. I could hear the wild porpoises in the channel answering them, but Wanda and Sammy stayed near me, on my side of the pool. They were calling to me.

Turning my head a little, I was able to see them. They both had their faces out of the water, nodding their heads the way they did when they had performed a behavior well and were expecting fish, but I could see the panic in their eyes. Wanda was bleeding near the spiracle, the blood tinting her breath when she exhaled.

"It's all right," I said to them. "It's all right."

I let my body slide into the pool. The water was shockingly cold, and the salt water that entered the wound on my forehead seemed to flow straight into some central nerve center, the pain was so shrill and cauterizing. Treading water with my feet, I took Wanda into my arms and held her close, in the human way. She lay still, and her breathing became less and less erratic. Underwater Sammy swam against my legs.

"You crazy fucker," Canales said when he came back from the phone. He had to pull me out; I couldn't climb onto the dock on my own.

"I think they're okay," I said.

"Now you've probably got pneumonia besides."

"I don't remember anything," I said. "What happened?"

"Just some classic punks. They thought Sammy and Wanda were sharks. They were beating on them from the dock. Stupid porpoises must have swum right up to them at first. They probably got a couple of good licks in then, but I doubt if they could have done much but scare them after that. One of them was on you. I got the fish knife and chased the other two around a little. They all got away in that goddamm Lincoln. I think you clobbered one of them, though."

"I broke his nose," I said. "I felt it."

"You're lucky if he didn't break your head. You've got a lump there about the size of a baseball."

The sheriff came and walked around the perimeter of the

pool awhile, looking at the porpoises, who cowered in fear at the far end of the pool.

"Probably just some kids," he said. "You didn't get their license number?"

"No," Canales said. "It was a Lincoln."

"Probably just some rich kids from Corpus out for a little meanness," he said philosophically. "I'll have my deputy cruise by for the rest of the night. You might think about getting you a security guard if these fish are that valuable."

He turned to me. "You want me to call an ambulance for you?"

I shook my head. I was sitting up by this time, holding it, cupping the lump with my hand.

Mr. Granger came through the gate, shook hands on the run with the sheriff, and studied my head with a worried disapproving look.

"I'm taking you to the hospital right now," he said. "And that's that."

"Don't worry about the animals," Canales told me. "I'll stay with them awhile and check them over. I think they're fine, physically at least. Don't worry."

Mr. Granger supported me as I walked to his car. It seemed to take forever, and I was greatly relieved to collapse onto the leather seat of his Seville. He took me home first, and I changed painfully from my wet clothes.

"You need some new clothes," he told me, tying my shoe for me.

We took the southern route into Corpus, along Padre Island. The big car glided with precision down the road. Mr. Granger was in shirt sleeves, and his hair, which was usually slicked back on his head, stood out a little around his ears.

"Those kids must have been on drugs," he said. "That's the only explanation I can think of. You shouldn't have tried to stop them, you should have just called the police."

"Sammy and Wanda could have been dead by then," I said.

"Well, you came within a hair's breadth of being dead yourself, young man."

I held my ice pack tighter against the swelling.

"I'm going to forget the whole thing, Jeff. I'm going to let them go and forget the whole thing. It's just not worth it."

I looked out at the peaceful, vacant highway and the dark coastal plain indistinguishable from the night sky, and knew I wanted to live here for the rest of my life. I loved the name of this place, some Spanish word sufficiently bastardized to mean nothing now except the land and water that so many different creatures held in common as home: Aransas.

"Is it?" Mr. Granger asked.

"What?"

"Worth it?"

"Let's talk about it when my head is clearer," I said.

At the emergency room we found out I did not have a fracture. They cleaned out the wound and gave me some pills for the pain.

"You look pretty ugly with that bump," the young doctor said, "but you're perfectly all right."

On the way out I saw myself in the unlighted window of the coffee shop and looked away, it was so grotesque. The strange mound attached to my forehead reminded me of the bulge found on the heads of certain cetaceans, what my whale book called the "melon."

Mr. Granger drove me home and insisted on following me into my room and getting me into bed.

"You've had a big shock," he said. "I want you to stay in bed all day tomorrow. I'll check on you in the morning."

"Fine. Thank you."

When he was gone I sat up on the bed and remained motionless until the room stopped swirling around me. I looked at the clock: three thirty. I dug my sleeping bag out of the closet, took the pillow off the bed, and walked out to the car. When I sat down behind the wheel my brain seemed to spin inside its skull like a gyroscope, but it was a short drive on deserted roads to the porpoise circus, and I made it easily enough.

As I was unlatching the gate the sheriff's deputy drove by.

"Just checking," he said. "You okay?"

I nodded.

"You look a little dazed. That guy really lit into you, didn't he?"

"Sure did," I said.

"Well, you never can tell. Maybe we'll catch them. Won't make any difference if we do. You take care now."

When he had driven away I went inside and spread my sleeping bag out on the dock. The two porpoises, sensing I was going to stay with them, calmed down and swam back and forth in front of me. I went over to the freezer, left some fish out to thaw, and took one of the pills I'd been given. Then I climbed into the sleeping bag and fell asleep.

I was awake, though, when the norther blew in. The cold wind rattled the metal supports of the bleachers and whipped up the water of the pool. The stars disappeared behind a front of solid cloud. I snuggled deeper into the sleeping bag, fell asleep again, and was awakened this time not by the cold or the pain but from a sensation of being needed.

I turned my head to the pool and saw the two sleek heads there, like puppets, watching me. I stretched out my hand and touched their beaks, and they moved up and down in the water. For a moment I thought they were going to jump completely out of the water and onto the dock, but they were satisfied just to have me touch them, to reassure them I would not leave them alone.

"Go to sleep," I told them, "go to sleep now."

Chapter 5

When I woke up just after dawn my head ached violently and my teeth were rattling with cold. The porpoises were asleep, and for a long moment I did not move, simply lay there and watched them rising slowly and unconsciously to the surface for breath.

I stood up, bundling the sleeping bag around me, and took another pill. The porpoises woke immediately and began swimming on their backs with their pectorals out of the water. I had Wanda come over to me so I could check out the wound near her spiracle. There was a bruise there now, but I was confident the injury wasn't serious. I wasn't so sure about her psychological condition—she moved about the pool sluggishly and spent a lot of time on the bottom. Sammy was unmarked and more than anything else seemed relieved, grateful that we had saved him.

When I began to open the gate to leave, Wanda leaped high out of the water and began squeaking indignantly.

"It's all right," I said. "I'll be back."

I went to my car and looked at my forehead in the rear-view mirror. The swelling had not gone down, but I drove over to a restaurant anyway and had breakfast, keeping my head turned toward the window so it would not offend anyone.

A parade of shrimpers was cruising out from the jetties into the Gulf, and a big excursion boat was headed that way too, out to the snapper banks where its few patrons would fish with electric reels.

At home I put a fresh ice pack on my head and phoned Canales.

"I was just on my way over to see them," he said.

"I think they're doing pretty good. I stayed there last night."

"That was dumb."

"I don't care, I didn't think they should be alone."

"How's your head?"

"No fractures, no concussion. It just looks ridiculous."

"Jesus, I'd like to get those bastards. I'm so irritated I can't sit still."

"I'm going to sleep," I said. "I'll come over when I get up."

"Don't worry. We're not going to work them for a few days. I'm going to go over later this morning and rent us a security guard. You sure you're all right?"

"Fine."

"That was dumb, sleeping out in the cold like that. I have to hand it to you, though, you're dedicated."

"Don't tell Mr. Granger I did that. Lectures just make my head hurt worse."

But then Mr. Granger himself called as soon as I had hung up with Canales. I told him that I had slept soundly all night in my own bed, that I was much better, and that I was going back to sleep.

I fell into a mild, dizzy sleep, and when I woke in the late afternoon my head felt better and the swelling had gone down somewhat. I put on my coat and walked outside. It was warm now, though the sky was still gray. It seemed to me the cold weather of the night before had been something I had imagined.

At the pool I met Mr. Hillson, the security guard, an old man who giggled when he talked and whose dentures shook

when he giggled. His gun was made out of heavy plastic, mold-
ed in one piece with his holster. On the other side of his vinyl
utility belt he carried a plastic billy club. A shield-shaped patch
on his sleeve said "Island Security Agency."

"Gollee," he said, looking down into the pool, "I'd hate to
fall in there with them sharks."

"We've got a problem," Canales told me. "Wanda won't
eat."

I called her over to me. She came up to the dock and laid
her beak in my hands. Sammy tried to nudge her away and
take her place.

"Let me try," I said, and Canales handed me a few smelt. I
grazed one of them across her closed mouth but she broke off
from me and sank. Sammy opened his mouth. I tossed the fish
into his throat.

"We'll give her till day after tomorrow," Canales said.
"Then we'll have to force it down."

"We can't do that. She's had enough trauma as it is."

"Well, then she dies, Jeff."

"What if we let her go?"

"Come on. How long do you think she'd last in the wild?
Talk about trauma. Besides, we've got a lot invested in her."

So two days later, when she still had not eaten, we had to
force-feed her. We were able to coax her into doing her
beaching behavior, and before she had a chance to fall back
into the water I sat on her back, just behind the dorsal. She
tried to throw me off, but then she calmed down. Sammy
swam warily in the water behind me and once beached himself next to her so that I had to shove him back into the pool.

Sara was rubbing water onto Wanda's forehead, a useless
calming gesture. I watched as Canales took a fish in one hand
and pried open Wanda's jaws with the other, using his closed
fist to hold them open as he shoved the arm with the fish down
Wanda's throat up to its biceps. Straddling her, I could feel her
muscles reacting against the arm. When the fish caught in her
stomach Wanda gagged and thrashed, but the food stayed
down.

"Jesus!" Sara said.

I looked away, out to the Gulf.

"It's either this or she starves," Canales told me.

"I'm not saying anything."

He fed her three more fish that way. On the fourth something went wrong. The body beneath me spasmed, nearly throwing me off, and the fleshy lip of the spiracle snapped open and did not close.

"What happened?" I shouted at Canales.

His hand was deep inside her, feeling for the fish.

"She must have thrown it up. It must be lodged somewhere in her throat."

He kept probing with his hand. The lip of the spiracle tried to open and close, but was able to make only gasping sounds.

"I can't find it," he said. "Get off her! Hurry!"

As I rolled off, Canales rose up onto his knees, closed both hands into a double fist, and brought them down hard in front of the dorsal fin. There was a deep, hollow sound, and then the blowhole sucked in air again. Canales opened Wanda's mouth, took the fish out, and fell back on the ramp.

"We almost lost her," he said.

"Can we let her go back into the pool?" I asked.

"Yeah, I doubt if we did much for her appetite."

When she hit the water Wanda went straight for the bottom. Sammy went after her.

"Well," Canales said, "we can scratch the beaching behavior. She'll never do that again for us."

"I don't blame her," Sara said.

I walked over to the bleachers and sat down. My head and my heart were both pounding.

"Will we have to do that again?" I asked.

"If she won't eat," Canales said. "I don't look forward to it, either."

But the next day she did eat, and stayed near the surface almost the whole day. It was as if she had simply resolved to put her life into order again. She would not come near the ramp, though, and we were careful not to give any indication we expected her there ever again. We were just grateful to her for being alive.

We gave the porpoises a week off from training. At the end of that time my head was back to its normal shape, and Sammy was so bored we could not get him to stop after he had finished the first series of behaviors.

But there was an element missing in Wanda's performances. It was not simply her refusal to beach herself or to swim near the ramp. She had no enthusiasm for the rest of her behaviors, either, though she went through them willingly enough. She worked for fish now. Her affection toward us had not altered, but I could see she no longer associated us with everything that mattered to her. There was a part of herself she did not give to us anymore.

These are human interpretations. I don't know what Wanda felt, or if after the beating she had sufficient reserves of trust to feel anything. Her intellectual powers, as we perceived them, were still minimal. She still depended on Sammy's mastery of a behavior to pave her own acceptance of it; and her allegiance to Canales, who was short-tempered now himself and tended to shout at her and stamp his foot—"No! Bad girl!"—became increasingly tenuous. She began to rely on me even more than she relied on Sammy, who had evolved beyond her and was pleasing us more and more with every session.

Sammy had found the heart of the race. I believe he actually understood something of human wit, he worked so hard to make us happy; and the night of the beating he had learned something about human cruelty as well and had passed it effortlessly into his fund of knowledge. He was opening up to us; there was something about his strange form that began to seem explicable, familiar. The mystery was raveling away, and underneath it we saw a brilliant porpoise on the make.

It was Wanda I worried about. When I entered the water with her and she swam by so that I could grab her fin and swim with her around the pool, I knew there was some secret knowledge about herself she was trying to pass on to me. I could read it in the way she moved, see it in the immutable expression of her face, and hear it in the squeaking and clicking sounds she made for me. I would hook my finger through the hole in her dorsal and look up at the sky as she pulled me along, with Sammy indulgently following. At those times I could feel, even in the hard muscular thrust of Wanda's flukes beneath me, a delicacy that would not survive.

Sara by now was very proficient at the Roman Chariot Ride. She moved across the pool like a Cypress Gardens water skier.

"Smile more," Canales told her every day, and she would break into a cold grin as she undulated across the surface. She was regressing from a thirty-year-old waitress to a teenage surf bunny secure in the romance of her job.

"We've got to start putting this program together," she insisted. "I mean I've got to have some motivation when I'm riding across the pool. What's the point of all these behaviors?"

"We've got months to work on that," Canales told her.

"This is *show* business," she said. "You're supposed to *start* months ahead. I mean, the humans need rehearsals too!"

So over the weekend she and Canales developed a "concept."

"See," Canales told me, "we'll start out with the standard lecture about how porpoises aren't fish, et cetera. Then we'll talk about how they evolved from land animals. And that's where we'll put in the beaching, say something like Sammy's always had a hankering to try life on the dry land himself. Then we'll say, as long as he was at it, he figured he'd find out what it was like to fly, and that's where we'll put in all the leaps and shit. Okay, we've got all that out of the way. Then we'll talk about ancient legends, like that guy Arion? The one with the lute? That the porpoise saved, right? One of us'll do that. We'll fall in the water and Sammy'll come up under us and take us on his back and Wanda'll swim up and hand us a lute. And we'll ride around playing that for a while.

"Okay, then we have Sara's part." He put his hands out as if he were a movie director framing a scene. "There's this beautiful Karankawa maiden."

"Come on."

"Really. The legend of this beautiful Karankawa maiden. She's in love with this porpoise. She's pining away like crazy. We'll put Sara in the water with Sammy, dancing, and maybe we can work out a kissing behavior too. We'll talk over the p.a. about how this Karankawa maiden got saved when the rest of her people were all wiped out and how she was carried away to Porpoise City or someplace on their backs. That's where the Roman Chariot Ride comes in. That's the finale."

"There's no legend like that," I said.

"You think I don't know that? For Christ's sake, a legend is something you make up, isn't it?"

"It gives the show a narrative element," Sara said calmly.

"And she's going to write a song, too," Canales said.

"I was thinking maybe I could record it," Sara explained, "and sell little forty-fives of it after the show."

"It's fine with me," I said.

So Sara worked at night on the song and designed her costume, a sort of loincloth bikini. Her new enthusiasm, though, did not extend to the porpoises. She regarded them as props, or in her more sentimental moments as childlike helpmates. She had not, from the first, felt anything toward them, an attitude I could not understand. Canales, at least, had a sort of burnt-out reverence. He treated the porpoises the way he treated his truck, with regular maintenance and an appropriate, reserved affection for their existence.

But Sara was beyond even the illusion of emotion. She was one of those people for whom an animal is simply an adjunct to human life, not really worth noticing. She could never tell the porpoises apart with any proficiency, and her highest praise of them was that they were cute. Yet her indifference to animals made her no less vulnerable to human emotions. Despite the steel guitar player, she was clearly in love with Canales, and she clung to him most of the day like some bothersome plant whose tendrils he could never shake off.

When we were in the shed together, thawing fish under the water tap or cutting them up to stretch the day's ration, Sara confided in me as if she were bestowing a favor. Canales didn't talk when they went home, she said. He just sat there and watched TV. She felt like he was not serious in the slightest. He pointed out other women to her he thought were attractive. Sometimes he would ask her to stay home while he went into Corpus. He once threw a full ice cube tray at her.

After recounting this to me she would stand, brush the fish scales off her lap, and go out and kiss Canales and try to sneak her hand inside his pants. He would scowl and make her rehearse the chariot ride again. She was very competent at that by now. She could ride around the pool on the porpoises' backs and step onto the dock as if she were stepping off an escalator, walking off with such indifference that she had to be reminded to throw the animals a fish. Wanda and Sammy returned her indifference, and I thought if there was one sure thing about Canales and Sara's relationship, it was the fact that it was not blessed by the porpoises.

Most of the behaviors were down by Christmas. We were still increasing the heights of the poles and hoops, still working to coordinate their leaps with each other's, and we had a long way to go in perfecting the tail walk from either side of the pool, but there was no question we would be ready well in advance of the April opening.

On Christmas Eve Mr. Granger arranged to have a party at the pool. He wanted the porpoises to be in on it. It was, fortunately, a warm day, and he set up tables on the dock and brought eight times as many tamales as we could eat (made by the family in Refugio that made his clothes) and several gallons of eggnog. Mr. Granger wore a bow tie shaped like a holly leaf, with electric red and green lights that blinked in sequence. He set up a small tree on the pulpit and stood up there and toasted each one of us—Sara, Canales, me, Mr. Hillson (whose services we had not required for a month, but who was invited anyway). Mr. Granger was also careful to include Wanda and Sammy in his toasts. The porpoises lay in the water beneath him, making their clicking sounds and watching his hands. We were all embarrassed and pleased.

"To my family," Mr. Granger said, raising his eggnog glass.

"And I want you to know that includes all of you and especially my two friends down here. I never thought I'd have a porpoise for a relative, but it just goes to show."

We drank to that, that it went to show. Mr. Granger passed out elaborate gifts. "Mementoes," he said, "of our enterprise." Mine was a watch, engraved on the back with a porpoise leaping from the water and the words "To Jeff Dowling from Dude Granger, in deep appreciation for our friendship."

I knew better than to argue that it was too much. I had done that before when Mr. Granger had given me another expensive gift, and I had seen the disappointment and fear on his face. This time I said "Thank you" as simply as I could.

"Now," he said, "I have something for Sammy and Wanda." He unwrapped a volleyball and threw it into the pool. The porpoises swam away from it, as they always did from something strange, but gradually they came back beneath it, and in two or three minutes were playing catch with us.

Christmas Day itself was cold and overcast. I woke up early and walked down to the pool to check on the porpoises and play ball with them for a while, then I went back home and read. Mr. Granger had left the night before for one of those inconceivably vast ranches along the border, for a Christmas to which he had been pledged for two years. Canales called and invited me over to watch football. I told him there were friends in Corpus I had to see.

I went to the grocery store and bought a very small turkey and a paperback copy of *The Joy of Cooking*, then went home and read what to do. Stuffing looked too complicated, but the actual roasting of the turkey seemed simple enough.

The bird turned out all right, and I mashed a potato with a fork and heated up some green beans to go with it. I had only a pocket knife to carve the turkey, so I just tore the meat off with my hands and sat there with a paper plate on my knees watching football with the sound off. I noticed how the silence seemed to impel the players to their collisions, as if it were all rehearsed, each tackle and block an immutable, predestined thing.

I did my best not to think about Christmas with my parents, or even with friends in Santa Fe, where the season had always seemed more immediate than it did on the coast, with piñon logs in the fireplace and windows framed with real frost, an effect achieved from an aerosol can during my childhood in Port Aransas.

I did remarkably well in not thinking too much about these things. I looked up to the postcard tacked to the wall, curling upward under the influence of the gas heater, and wished—for the first time—that I was a porpoise, with no holidays to celebrate, living outside human understanding in the continuum of the ocean.

Chapter 6

Over the next several months we perfected all the behaviors. It was now simply a question of drill, of not allowing the porpoises to get away with fuzzy performances. Canales instituted a grading system. We could let the animals slide to A–, sometimes in extreme cases to B, but we were never to give them any more slack than that. The show had to be tight, perfect, when it counted.

I stood on the pulpit, my whistle around my neck, my hands at my sides in the neutral position. They waited for me to move those hands. I twirled my fingers, they spiraled, dancing. I pointed to the far corner of the pool with my right hand; Sammy disappeared for a few seconds and came up in the middle doing his spectacular back flip. I pointed to the other corner; Wanda did her less than spectacular front flip. Then I pointed in both directions at once, and they both torpedoed to opposite corners of the pool, shimmied up into the air and, propelled by their flukes, walked across the water and passed one another like two folk dancers. Perfect. A plus.

Sara and Canales practiced the script over the p.a. system. "What's that you say, Sammy?" Canales would read into the mike. "You don't *want* to do your high jump?" Sammy shook his head back and forth, making his *naaaa* sound. "Well, you'd better think again, young man. A lot of people paid good money to see you do it. What's that? You don't *care?* Let *Wanda* do it? Sam, I'm surprised at you."

And so it went, the porpoises responding to Canales' hand signals, completely innocent of any understanding of the insipid dialogue.

"You try it, Jeff."

"I can't say that shit."

"Hey, man, I put a lot of thought into this script. You might have some consideration."

"Seriously," I said, "isn't it enough that they can do all the behaviors? Why don't we just leave it at that? I mean, people are coming to see the porpoises, not how clever we are."

"You mean no narration at all?"

"Sort of. Yeah."

"Haven't you ever seen an animal act?" Canales said. "It's all showmanship. People don't give a shit about seeing the porpoises. They want to see what we can *do* with them. I mean, what did you think you were doing all this time? Did you think you were a scientist or something, studying their natural behavior? If you can come up with a better script, fine, but don't pretend you're not a huckster, okay?"

I saw he was right. None of it made any difference to the porpoises, and that was what counted. I fell in line. There was a different rhythm now with the human commentary in the background, and when we drilled the porpoises without the script their behaviors seemed curiously disembodied, like a ballet performed without music.

"Can't you enunciate a little more?" Canales would correct as I mumbled through the script. "Didn't you tell me you were in a movie once?"

Only by close attention to the porpoises could I get through it. I saw how they acted without embarrassment, and I learned my part of the performance as earnestly as they had learned theirs. The spiel went through my head day and night, and there came a point when it passed into nonmeaning, became a kind of mantra, so that we acted even more in concordance, the three of us leaving the tricks and the cheap jokes and performing some elaborate, cryptic dance together on another plane.

We taught Sammy how to pick us up for the Arion number, taught him to slide beneath our legs so that we were sitting just behind his dorsal fin. With practice we were able to stay astride just by locking our feet beneath him, so our hands were free to play the "lute," which turned out to be a plastic ukulele.

Sara finished her song and recorded it with a band so that she could lip-sync it during the show as it was played back over the p.a. The effect was dreadful, the lag between her mouthing and the amplified voice reminding me of a dubbed movie. And the song itself was a genuine oddity, backed by a steel guitar (played, I assumed, by her true love) and an attempt by the drummer at tom-toms. A lilting Indian dirge, sung by a pretty, strung-out woman in a loincloth bikini:

> *My heart belongs to someone*
> *Who lives beneath the sea*
> *My heart it will be broken*
> *If he does not set me free*
> *He may be just a porpoise*
> *But that's all right with me*
> *I'd rather love a porpoise*
> *Than live in mis-ur-ee*
>
> *Oh darling come to me across*
> *The waters of the bay*
> *Let me get upon your back*
> *And we will sail away.*
> *Far across the ocean*
> *To some distant shore*
> *Where me and my porpoise*
> *Will be happy evermore*

At the end of the song Canales or I would give the appropriate signal, Sammy and Wanda would position themselves for Sara to step on their backs, we would say "and so the princess, etc.," and off the whole entourage would sail into the sunset. Never mind that a real Karankawa maiden would have been naked, tattooed, malnourished, and glistening with alligator grease—the first time I saw it straight through I was, to my great surprise, touched.

A couple of days before the grand opening Canales took Sara to Mexico. She wanted a hammock and a pair of tire-tread sandals and a purse made out of an armadillo. Canales just wanted a break. While they were gone I ran the porpoises through their behaviors without the script, moving my hands like a bullfighter and feeling that animal mass and form rumble through the wake.

A man came through the gate, an old gray lanky man in a black shapeless suit and a fresh haircut that made his huge ears look like two birds that had just been flushed from a thicket. He shook hands distractedly. His name was Miles Randolph.

"The columnist from the Corpus paper," he said. "Civic events column? It's called 'Around the Coastal Bend.'"

I pretended I knew his column and that he was famous.

"These are the porpoises, huh?" he asked. Sammy was by the dock, his head still, looking the columnist in the eye. Randolph took out a pencil and began writing in a spiral pad that said on the cover PROFESSIONAL REPORTER'S NOTEBOOK.

"Your name again?" he said.

"Jeff Dowling." It made me uneasy to see him writing it down.

"How long have you been working these animals?"

"Six months or so."

"And you're opening this Saturday," he asked rhetorically.

"Uh-huh."

"Tell me about them. They as smart as you hear?"

"I don't know," I said.

He looked up from his notebook and looked at me sternly.

"Well, I'm sure you've got some idea. They as smart as a dog, a cat, what?"

"I really have no idea."

"Well, are they *stupid?*"

I threw each of the porpoises a fish.

"No," I said, "they're not stupid."

Randolph put up the pad and walked over to the edge of the pool. I could see Sammy opening his mouth, taking in water. It was evident that he was going to squirt him if he came closer. The columnist must have sensed this. He kept his distance and took out his pad again.

"What do they weigh?"

"Four or five hundred pounds."

"What do you feed them?"

"Fish."

"How much?"

"Fourteen pounds a day."

"Lot of fish."

"For us."

He walked around the pool a little more, inspecting the porpoises the way he might have inspected a used car.

"What kind of tricks can they do?"

"The usual porpoise tricks."

He laughed. "Maybe it's my imagination, but you don't seem real excited about these animals. You say you've been around them six months but you can't tell me if they're any smarter than a dog or a cat. Hell, son, all I'm trying to do is put your place here in the paper. Dude Granger's an old friend of mine. Now, I'll tell you what. I read somewhere that porpoises are smarter than people. You tell me if that's true or not."

"Well," I said, "they're just as smart as they need to be. I don't feel like I'm in any sort of competition with them, so I've never tried to measure my intelligence against theirs."

"But theirs might win?"

"It might."

He gave me a sober look. "Tell me something. If they're so smart, don't you feel sort of guilty keeping them locked up like this?"

"A little," I said.

"Hmmmm," he said. He picked up the volleyball. "They play with this?"

"Yeah," I said, "go ahead and throw it to them."

The ball landed in the middle of the pool. Neither Sammy nor Wanda went near it.

"They have their moods," I said.

He stayed around a little longer, trying to get me to open up. I was feeling not just unsociable but a little cruel. For no particular reason I wanted the man off the scent, I did not want to read about Wanda and Sammy in "Around the Coastal Bend." But I woke up early the next morning and bought a paper anyway at the restaurant where I had breakfast. The article was on the front page of the second section, under a picture of Miles Randolph so grainy that his ugliness was even more apparent than in real life. It was lame chamber of commerce stuff:

> Who would have thought that Flipper could be found in our own backyard, so to speak? Not many people know it, but the porpoises that citizens of the coastal bend frequently spot cavorting in the bays and ship channels are more properly known as Atlantic Bottle-nosed Dolphins, and are the same cute little fellows whose antics have delighted patrons of marine parks for years.
>
> Well, over in Port Aransas Dude Granger has decided that he might as well make use of one of that area's natural resources, so this Saturday marks the grand opening of Dude Granger's Porpoise Circus.
>
> The mammals were busily rehearsing when I dropped by yesterday and talked with Jeff Dowling, assistant porpoise trainer.
>
> "These animals weigh anywhere from four to five hundred pounds and eat fourteen pounds of fish daily," he said, as Sammy and Wanda, the two "stars" of the show, looked on. Dowling admitted he suspected the porpoises were "smart" but stopped short of saying they are as intelligent as human beings. Let's hope not!
>
> Still, Dowling says he feels a "little" guilty about keeping such delightful creatures in captivity, though Armando Canales, the head trainer, said over the phone, "I have to work for a living, you have to work for a living, why shouldn't they?"

Sara Wade, the pretty female member of the "porpoise team," said, "It's no different from anything else."

The first performance of the Porpoise Circus is scheduled for Saturday at 10 AM in Port Aransas. Admission is $2.50 for adults, $1.25 for children. . . .

I was early to work that day. Sammy and Wanda were so excited by this I could not calm them down. Sammy threw me the volleyball, I threw it back far across the pool, and he was underneath it when it hit the water. Wanda swam up next to him, wanting the ball, yet seemingly lacking in any knowledge of how to take possession of it. Something besides my early arrival excited them. I could sense their awareness that something was impending, that six months of senseless drill was coming to a climax.

Sammy was so worked up he even threw the ball to Sara when she and Canales arrived. She tossed it listlessly back, and the porpoise did not pursue the game any further.

"You see the paper today?" Canales said. "We got some free publicity."

"When did he talk to you?" I asked. "I thought you were gone."

"He called last night just when we got in. He said he thought you were a little weird."

"Yeah, I guess so," I said. "How was Laredo?"

"This guy tried to sell us a pig's head," Sara said. "That was sort of gross. The rest of it was okay."

Mr. Granger came at midmorning with an armload of newspapers.

"We're going to have to start a scrapbook," he said.

He stayed while we ran through a full dress rehearsal. Sara wore her loincloth, Canales and I our matching surfers' trunks.

The rehearsal went well. The tape of Sara's song did not start on time, so she was stranded for a moment in a field of static, but we could correct that easily enough.

"More feeling," Canales instructed as I was doing the opening rap, so I made it as broad as I could stand.

"I've got a big surprise," Mr. Granger said after the rehearsal. "Tomorrow is not just opening day for the Porpoise Circus, it's also the first day of the season for the Crow's Nest. Guess what I've got lined up?"

"The Flipper movies," I remembered.

"A double feature."

"Gee"—Canales almost sneered—"that's really great."

"I thought it'd be interesting to compare our porpoises to theirs," Mr. Granger said. "Maybe we can pick up some pointers."

"We'll be there," I told him.

In the next morning's paper there was a letter to the editor. A headline above the letter read "Statement of Porpoise," and the staff artist had supplied a cartoon as well—a group of porpoises rising up out of the water with angry looks on their faces and holding placards that read "Equal Rights" and "Freedom Now." The letter was rather long and was punctuated by a series of dots that suggested it had been substantially cut:

> I am deeply offended by your writer's smug assessment of dolphins as "cute little fellows" and by what amounts to a free advertisement for an institution whose sole reason for existence is the exploitation for human profit of creatures whose awareness and sensitivity are every bit the equal of our own. . . .
>
> I hope that those who go to see this "porpoise circus" will realize what a corrupt and demeaning institution it is. One is hardly surprised at Dude Granger's lack of any feeling for his fellow creatures. The man who has "developed" one of the loveliest spots on the Texas coast into an extended shopping mall is probably incapable of seeing dolphins as anything but another commodity. But I wonder how Jeff Dowling, the trainer who admits he feels "guilty" about what he is doing to the dolphins, can live with his conscience. . . .
>
> Dolphins—these are not porpoises—have emotions and modes of feeling we are only just beginning to appreciate. . . .

They should not be kidnapped and made to perform as
clowns in "circuses." That sort of thing is degrading to dolphins and humans alike.

Mary Katherine Severin
Port Aransas

I knew who she was. The woman in the boat who had
been spying on us all winter. All right, I thought, here it is.

Mr. Granger called. "Jeff, is what this woman is saying
about me true?"

"No," I said, "she's just looking for a villain. She doesn't
even know you."

"She says I have a lack of feeling for my fellow creatures.
You know that's not true. Anyway, they seem happy now,
don't they?"

"I think they really are."

"Maybe we should call them dolphins from now on."

"I doubt if it would make that much difference."

"I just want to be accurate is all." He paused. I could hear
his deep, therapeutic breathing over the phone. "Well," he
said, "I'm too old to worry about what people think of me. I'll
see you today at the first show. Are you nervous?"

"Not at all."

"I'm real proud of you, Jeff. I know everything'll work out
fine."

But I *was* nervous, more nervous than I had been when I
went before the cameras the first time as Bigfoot. I put on my
trunks, the T-shirt that said TRAINER, slipped my toes between
the rubber thongs of my sandals, and set out for the compound.

We had put the finishing touches on it just a week earlier.
The banner arced over the gate now, a leaping porpoise on either side. The wall of the compound was painted inside and
out a cerulean blue that contrasted sharply with the muddy
water of the pool and the drab vista across the channel to Harbor Island. Painted against this blue background were mer-
maids, starfish, seaweed, sand dollars, a waterbabies' seascape.

"All right," Canales told me, "I'll m.c. the first show. You do the Arion bit, okay? Then you'll take the second one." He was jumpy, he had a new haircut, and I could smell the hair spray that kept his hair from reacting to the breeze.

Sara sat inside the shed, holding her arms against her body as if she were chilled.

"I'm always like this before I go on," she explained. "They say if you're not scared your performance will be worthless."

I took some fish out of the freezer, held them under the faucet, sliced each one neatly into three bits, and threw them into the bucket as Sara sat on her folding chair, silently mouthing the words to her song.

"You're sure you know when to start the tape?" she asked me.

"Uh-huh."

"Right after Mando says 'Long ago in this part of the world. . . ' "

"I know."

People began arriving a half hour beforehand. I watched them from the door of the shed, the Port Aransas summer trade—a preview of it anyway. A lot of them were kids, wearing T-shirts with iron-on transfers of TV idols or current catch phrases. Before taking their seats in the bleachers the patrons stood on the dock and looked down at Sammy and Wanda. Sammy cruised up and down, parading before them. He even turned over on his back and waved hello with his pecs. The audience thought it charming.

Wanda stayed mostly at the bottom. "God, she's dumb," Canales said. "I just hope she doesn't blow it for us."

I saw a preadolescent boy raise an imaginary rifle to his shoulder, close one eye, and aim and fire at Wanda when she surfaced. His index finger moved, and he mimed a recoil.

The show went fairly well. Canales went out onto the pulpit and looped his microphone around his neck and began his recitation.

"Good morning, ladies and gentlemen, and welcome to the very first performance of Dude Granger's Porpoise Circus. Now, the animals you will see performing before you today *are*

Atlantic bottle-nosed dolphins, which we commonly call por- poises. One thing we would like to point out is that they *are* mammals—they *do* nurse their young and maintain a constant body temperature.

"Now I would like to introduce them to you individually. Sammy, would you please take a bow for our guests?"

Very few of them could have noticed the hand signal that sent Sammy on his high introductory leap. Canales tossed him his reward with so much sleight-of-hand that the illusion of Sammy's working only for fun was not disturbed. There were some pleased sighs from the audience, some applause, and I was unprepared for how well the dispassionate behaviors of the porpoises meshed with the audience reaction.

The applause excited Sammy, but he kept to the program. Wanda did her bow next, not so high or so smooth, but Canales and I looked at each other with relief when she left the water at all.

It all went so well that I found myself with the odd hope that something would happen to subvert it, that Wanda would stray out of line, refuse to cooperate, that Sammy would leap with all his might over the dock into the open water on the other side. There was my role, the patient, infinitely patient saboteur.

They introduced me as Arion. I feigned a fall into the pool and felt the sea beast between my legs, heard his grunts as if he were chiding me for not giving as much of myself to the show as he was. And there was Wanda, with a plastic ukulele in her beak, pressing it upon me. *Here, take this.* I took it from her mouth, and she sank in the murky water.

Sammy swam slowly and rhythmically, as he had been taught, and I merged with the rhythm and stayed astride. I played my two ukulele chords as we paraded in front of the bleachers, which were filled with a hundred pairs of hands fan- ning back and forth, creating a sound I recognized as applause. There were smiles behind the hands, children and old men and women, smiling their goodwill, their envy. I noticed the woman I had seen so often spying on us from her boat in the channel. She was sitting on the bottom row of the bleachers, holding a little boy in her lap. When I passed by she regarded me very soberly and looked away when I met her eyes.

I watched her from the door of the shed for the rest of the performance. She kept a hard grip on her son's shoulders, as if to keep him from enjoying himself, but when the porpoises took Sara upon their backs I could see that beneath her disgust she was entranced. She looked down, self-consciously shook her head, and made a half-hearted attempt to keep the boy from applauding.

There was so much cooing and applause when it was over Sammy and Wanda were filled with an unfocused energy, which they released by an indiscriminate replay of their behaviors. Half the audience came down to the pool before leaving, and Sammy and Wanda eyed the people with new interest, impressed by their potential for appreciation.

A dozen children assaulted me with questions about the porpoises' diet and their relationships with sharks, and I had to patrol the edge of the pool to keep kids from putting their hands into the water.

The woman and the boy had not yet left. They were standing on the other side of the pool, staring at the porpoises. I started over to them, stealthily, pretending to inspect the water. A kid was following me, pleading.

"I'll work for nothing. I'll cut up the fish. I'll do anything!"

"I'm sorry," I said, "We don't need any help. And we can't have anybody else around."

"Why not?"

"Because of the insurance."

"But I don't *need* insurance!"

"That's not it, it's real complicated. I'm sorry."

"Can't I just touch them?"

"No." I was watching the woman. She was starting to leave.

"How come?"

"Because," I said, realizing that this was one of the things I had vowed as an adult never to say to a child, "because if I let you I'll have to let everybody."

The boy said, almost under his breath, "No you won't."

"Look," I said, "I'd really like to let you. I just can't. I really can't."

He muttered "Okay" and went away sulking.

They were standing at the gate now, hesitating. I don't think she realized how intensely she was looking at me, because when I walked up to her she recoiled slightly and regarded me with a wry, puzzled expression. I just stood there, bewildered and embarrassed.

"I had the impression you wanted to talk to me," I said.

"No," she said firmly. She looked slightly amused; her green eyes contrasted in an odd, provocative way with the deep tan of her face. "Why did you think that?"

"You wrote the letter to the editor."

She nodded.

"So I thought you wanted to talk."

"Not really. I was just here to see which of my dolphins had ended up in your clutches. That one there—Wanda, is that what you call her?—I'd been observing her for almost a year before she"—she said the word coldly—"disappeared. She was always easy to pick out by that hole in her dorsal. She had a calf that died last April."

She gave me a reproachful look, as if I were responsible. I looked down at Wanda, who was swimming near me, away from the crowd of kids who were trying to touch her, and thought how little I knew about her and how much I resented this new information.

The woman watched her too. "How did you know it was me who wrote the letter?"

"I've seen you out in the channel all winter, watching us. You seemed very interested in porpoises. And—I don't know—the name seemed to fit. Mary Katherine, isn't it?"

"Yes."

I told her my name.

"I know. I guessed your identity too."

"What sort of work are you doing?"

"I wish you wouldn't talk to me like we were colleagues or

something. I'm working on a master's thesis, trying to get some sort of fix on the dolphin population around here."

The boy was sitting against her shins. She grabbed his hands and hefted him up to a standing position, from which he obstinately collapsed.

"Come on, Nat," she said, hauling him up again. "We've got to go."

"I'm not sorry about that letter," she told me. "I don't mean to sound rude."

"Maybe we could talk sometime."

"Because we have so much in common?"

"I don't know. I'd just like to talk."

"I'll give it some thought," she said. She led the boy out the gate, guiding him by a light brush of his hair.

In the shed Sara and Canales were smoking a joint and Mr. Granger was holding a frozen smelt in his hand, turning it over and over, trying not to notice them.

"You were all brilliant," he said when I came in. "I'm so proud of you."

Sara handed me the joint, but I waved it off. She took another hit and passed it back to Canales.

"It went smooth," he said with his lungs full. "I can't deny that. Pretty good crowd too, for the very first show."

Mr. Granger smiled and set the fish down carefully on the edge of the freezer. "Well," he said, "I've got some business now, but I'll see you all tonight at the Crow's Nest."

"The Crow's Nest?" Canales asked.

"The Flipper movies," I said.

"Oh sure. You bet."

I walked Mr. Granger out to the gate. He stood for a moment and looked up at the string of triangular plastic flags snapping in the breeze.

"I don't know about you, Jeff, but I have a real feeling of accomplishment. I don't know anymore whether it was right or wrong to catch those porpoises in the first place, but by God we haven't let them go to waste, have we? We've done something with them!"

For the next show Canales and I switched roles. It was my turn to provide the spiel, and I spun it out fairly well, without a hint of revulsion. By the four o'clock show the porpoises were full and were performing rather sluggishly, though this was not a fault the audience would have noticed. But I could sense the slight lag between a hand signal and the animals' response to it. It was merely cause and effect now, an intellectual exercise.

It was apparent that the porpoises could sense the wider arena in which their actions took place. The applause, that great sensory mass that hung over the surface of the water like a cloud, obviously stirred them, provided them with a pleasurable and very alien form of reinforcement.

I fed them the remaining day's fish after the third show. They swam up to the dock and rested their heads there side by side as I tossed the smelt and herring into their open jaws. I put my hand into their mouths and scratched their tongues, then ran my palm along the ratchety edge of their teeth. They were subdued, content, maybe a little sleepy.

"Let's all go get drunk," Sara said. "I'm so uptight I can't stand it. I think I heard somebody laughing at me during the second show."

"You were amazing," Canales said. "All of us were real pros. Especially the porpoises."

"Then let's all go get drunk," Sara repeated.

"Mr. Granger sort of expects us at the Crow's Nest," I said.

"Christ almighty," Canales said. "The man is just too *weird!*"

"I need a night out," Sara said, looking severely at Canales. "A *real* night out."

"I'll put in an appearance for all of us," I volunteered.

Mr. Granger was standing in the lobby of the Crow's Nest, passing out coupons good for a half-price admission to the porpoise show. I told him that Sara and Canales had stopped off for a beer and would probably be along later, then helped him pass out the coupons until the feature started.

The theater was packed. It always was, I remembered, on the first night of the season. When we had taken our seats I saw Mary Katherine Severin walking down the aisle with her boy. The boy's hand was held by a tall thin guy, older than me, with a blond ponytail that reached almost to the small of his back. The three of them found seats near the front. Her escort put his arms back to retie his ponytail, and I could make out his stringy biceps in silhouette against the screen, which was illuminated by now with a faded cartoon in which a little gnome jumped about a landscape of popcorn, candy, and soft drinks, intoning repeatedly in a deep, raspy voice, "Snack bar!"

The film broke twice during the credits, but held up well enough after that. There they were—Luke Halpin, Chuck Connors, Flipper bounding up out of the water and making noises like Porky Pig. He was a perfect bathtub toy—the fixed smile masked every cetacean emotion, every behavior not rooted in an obsessive desire for human approval.

The creature was fundamentally different from Wanda and Sammy, though all three belonged to the same species and shared much the same fate. But there was something about the conditions of the water in which they lived that stamped them, as surely as the environment of an Eskimo distinguishes him from a Watusi. The clarity of the water Flipper thrust himself through took the edge off his appearance. Within ten minutes I was adjusted to the animal's physical presence, and bored. It was not the story or the acting—I had not expected either to rise above the *Lassie* level in the first place—it was the way everything about Flipper was revealed, how easily he could be accepted. In the months I had been with Wanda and Sammy there had never been a moment that I could truly *believe* in them as real beings, as a part of my life. They were an indissoluble clot in my imagination. Most of the audience tonight, I imagined, would go home thinking of a cute fish living in the blue-tinted vistas of the sea, wanting above all else to help a boy in trouble. But I had seen too much, I could not believe the folklore.

Every appearance my porpoises made, each time they came up out of the murky water to take a breath, constituted a revelation. The density of the water assured them of something Flipper did not have, that he could never know about.

I remembered how facile I had been in the New Mexico air, how loose and engaging, how the Seamstress and I were pleased to be with one another, and how that pleasantness was the result, more than anything else, of knowing we were not crucial to one another. I had moved through that air so easily, like Flipper through his brilliant ocean. But here on the coast my passage through the dense air left a nearly tangible wake.

Most of the audience left after the first movie. Mary Katherine took her boy out to the lobby, leaving the guy with the ponytail alone while they bought popcorn. I could see her boy's sleepy but insistent face as they walked back to their seats. It was plain he was the reason they were staying for the second feature.

Flipper's New Adventure was even worse. The principals were changed—grade D television actors—and the production values even worse than I expected to see in *Bigfoot Stalks!* Mr. Granger fell asleep and began to snore, very loudly. I looked away when Mary Katherine turned around to see who it was. His head dropped a few degrees with each snore, so that it looked as if it would fall onto my shoulder. Just before it hit Mr. Granger jerked awake.

"Have I been asleep?" he asked out loud.

"A little," I whispered.

He was out again in thirty seconds, and during the rest of the movie I had to punch him awake periodically to keep him from snoring, until finally his head fell onto my shoulder and the sounds were muffled. I watched the rest of the movie feeling his breath and the light stubble of his face, tripping on the fumes of his after-shave. When it was over, Mary Katherine gathered her sleeping son into her arms and walked up the aisle with her date holding her by the back of the neck.

She saw me there, with Mr. Granger's head on my shoulder, and gave me a very frank nod that thrilled me. The guy with her glowered at me rather weakly and followed her up the aisle.

I shook Mr. Granger awake. He looked around and made an odd sputtering sound.

"Well, are you about ready to go?" he asked.

Lois was in the lobby cleaning out the little grease trap on the popcorn machine.

"We had us a good crowd," she said.

Mr. Granger yawned. "I think the boom is starting," he said.

I was too agitated to go home. It was not just the tension of opening day that made me so restless; it had something to do as well with the nod Mary Katherine had given me in the theater. The longing that resulted from that gesture was not strictly sexual—it was a broad front, it had the range of an adolescent's physical yearning, a vague irritating desire whose components cannot be isolated. I just wanted her.

Instead of going back to the Salt Sea, I went to the pool and pulled my sleeping bag out from behind the shed, where I had left it the night of the beating. It smelled of pine needles and encrusted salt. The porpoises were excited to see me, but I lay down in the dark without playing with them, feeling their eyes on me.

"Calm down," I told them. "You've got to learn to calm down." I closed my eyes. There was a splash and a heavy slithering sound. I turned over and saw that Wanda had pulled herself out of the water and onto the ramp beside me. Her tail was in the air, her mouth open.

I went over and got a fish and laid it gently on her tongue, but she closed her jaws and held the fish between them without swallowing it. I rubbed my hand over her body, over the rough scar tissue of the propeller wound and the smooth, firm skin of her forehead. She laid her head on my knee, with the fish still between her jaws.

"Go back in the water now," I said in my language, then made the open palm gesture that we could both understand.

Chapter 7

She came alone to the Porpoise Circus several days later, after the final show while I was feeding Sammy and Wanda the remainder of their fish.

I was not surprised to see her, and she made no excuse for being there. She simply said hello and stood out of the way as I went about my business. The porpoises rolled their heads slightly to the side to get a look at her, making their contented clicking sounds while they fed.

"We're almost through," I told her, feeling strangely unhurried. "We've got to finish cleaning out the bleachers and then lock up."

She nodded casually. "Don't rush."

Canales came out of the shed and began gathering up the props. I introduced him to her, and she forthrightly offered her hand.

"You're the girl who hates us, right?"

She only shrugged, not knowing how to answer.

"Well anyway," Canales said, "it's nice to meet you."

When he left she bent down by the pool and put her hand tentatively out to Sammy. He nuzzled her palm with his beak.

"He wants you to shove him down into the water," I said.

"He gets a big charge out of that for some reason. Just take your hand and grab his beak and push him in."

She shoved him into the water. He came up again like a buoy, his eyes closed and a look of bliss on his face.

"You going to lock up, Jeff?" Canales asked me. He looked at Mary Katherine suspiciously.

"Yeah, I'll see you tomorrow."

"We've got to rein Wanda in on that front flip. She's starting to slacken up again."

"I'll work on it in the morning."

Canales left. Mary Katherine played with the porpoises a few minutes more before I suggested we leave too. She stood behind me while I locked the gate, and then without discussing it we began to walk toward the jetties. She said nothing for a while and I kept silent too, thinking that she wanted the initiative.

Finally she spoke. "I guess I want to apologize. Because I was so sarcastic the other day. I was mad, and I still am, but I felt bad about stereotyping you like that. You seemed a little more sensitive than I wanted to admit, so I apologize. Of course the fact that you *are* sensitive sort of compounds the crime."

"Maybe I'm not as sensitive as you think."

"Maybe not. Probably not. God, I can't keep from insulting you. So," she said, broadly changing the subject, "how did you like the movies the other night?"

I smirked. She smirked too.

"That man you were with, the one who kept snoring. Was that Dude Granger?"

I nodded.

"I thought so. He seemed reasonably harmless."

"He's as harmless as anybody," I said. "You had him wrong in your letter. It hurt his feelings."

"I was angry," she explained.

"I know."

"Don't act so indulgent toward me. I'm not retracting anything."

"Do you really think it's necessary," I asked her, "for us to keep up this adversary relationship?"

"No," she said, "as long as we realize that we *are* adversaries, I guess it doesn't make much difference how we treat one another."

"Common courtesy," I suggested.

She smiled.

"Tell me about that guy you were with."

"Why?"

I didn't answer. She knew why.

"He's my ex-husband. He lives here, he's a roofing contractor. Sometimes he takes Nat and me out."

We reached the jetties and climbed up the skirt of granite boulders to the walkway.

"Would you like to walk out to the end?" I asked.

She nodded and we walked until the pathway ran out and we had to pick our way across the boulders. The jetty extended perhaps a quarter mile into the Gulf. On the other side of the Aransas Pass, behind the opposite jetty, we could see the white sand beach of St. Joseph Island, inaccessible and undeveloped.

When we had reached the end we sat down on the boulders just out of range of the spindrift. Mary Katherine stretched out her legs. She was wearing brown corduroy jeans neatly ironed and stained with salt.

"Do you really think your dolphins are happy?" she asked me. It was not a challenge. It was simply something she wanted to know.

"Yes. I'm not saying it makes everything all right, but I think they're happy now. They had some rough times at first."

"It's just a matter of time before they die," she said. "You know that, don't you? Last year at Sea Park they lost twenty-two dolphins and three pilot whales in two weeks."

"We've got better conditions here. We've got natural seawater."

"That doesn't matter. They're very vulnerable in captivity. They can catch viruses from *people*."

"It seems to me they have problems in the wild too," I

said. "Sharks, for instance. Or those mass strandings, or tuna fishermen or killer whales. None of that sounds particularly idyllic."

"No."

"What happened to Wanda's calf?"

"I don't know. It was probably premature. I did an autopsy once on a little calf I found washed up on the beach. It was no more than a few days old. You could still see its fetal folds. It died of malnutrition."

I turned and looked out to the Gulf. There were whitecaps breaking over the bar. A part of me knew that I was making excuses, that I was justifying myself now just so I could hold onto Sammy and Wanda.

"Why did you come to see me today?" I asked her.

She lay back on one of the boulders, watching the seawater surge beneath it. She seemed very relaxed.

"I suppose I wanted to see what kind of a person you were."

"I won't pressure you for any conclusions."

"You're pretty confused, aren't you? About things in general?"

"I'm learning."

"There aren't that many tortured souls like you in the dolphin business. Mostly it's just the basic macho types. Surf bunnies. People who are after a good tan."

"It's time for dinner. Would you like to eat with me?"

"Thank you. I'm eating at home with Nat."

"So this is the extent of our association."

"I don't know."

"I can't tell if you're being coy or what."

"It's just that I have a certain hostility toward you."

"I know that. What else?"

She stood up and started walking toward shore. We were halfway down the jetty before she spoke.

"I'm not saying you couldn't come over and have dinner with *us*."

I said okay.

"We can walk down to the pier," she said. "My house is back in the dunes a little way from there."

We walked close enough to each other along the beach for our arms to brush occasionally. The sand was studded with pieces of sand dollars, and I walked along in my habitual beachcomber's stoop, searching for a whole one.

"I shouldn't have lectured you," she said. "In a way I envy you, being so close to them."

Her house was weathered and stood upright on pilings. There were the standard marine ornaments—life preservers, seine floats, ski ropes—along the outside stairway.

"This is Molly," Mary Katherine said, introducing me to a girl in her early twenties who was sitting on a sofa in the living room reading to Nat and holding a sleeping baby against her hip with her free hand. Nat, in greeting his mother, woke the baby. It shrieked for a moment and then calmed down, hiccoughing, the pulse on the top of its head beating. Molly lifted her T-shirt and let the baby nurse. She had a very young, very pleasant face.

"Molly and I are each other's baby-sitters. We're both at school here. She's studying pinfish."

"Pinfish," Molly repeated, giving the word an ironic lilt.

"You can leave if you want, Molly," Mary Katherine said. "Do you want me to watch Joshua tomorrow?"

"Maybe. If Bob comes through with the Willie Nelson tickets. There's another one of those Dylan rumors, so they may be hard to get. The latest is he's buying a beach house here."

"Great," Mary Katherine said.

We stood around politely while Molly finished nursing her baby. Then she tucked her breast back under her shirt, kissed Nat on the forehead, and left with Joshua strapped to her back.

"Do you remember Jeff from the dolphin show?" Mary Katherine asked Nat. The boy nodded without speaking. He left the room and came back with a little plastic porpoise which he handed to me in silence.

"Wow," I said, turning the porpoise over in my hands, "that's really neat."

"Captain Nemo gave it to me," he said. "See, I was underwater and I was swimming around with Triangle Fin and then Captain Nemo, he said if I wanted—"

"Nat," Mary Katherine broke in, "Jeff can't listen to that right now."

"I don't mind."

"No, really. It's a very long story. As long as he wants to make it."

"Who's Triangle Fin?"

"One of my dolphins," she said. "A big bull. He has a low, triangular fin, like a grampus. I give them names like that. Wanda was Hole Fin, for example."

"What about Sammy?"

"He was too perfect. There was nothing special about him, so I probably never even noticed him in the wild."

Nat was standing by my chair, leaning against my shoulder and looking down at the plastic porpoise I still held in my hands. I gave it back and reflexively put a hand on his shoulders—it spanned almost the entire breadth of the boy's back.

"I have some fish," Mary Katherine said, "lots of it. David—my ex-husband—fishes a lot and he's always bringing over what he can't eat. I've got some fresh flounder and some snapper, I think. Any preferences?"

"I don't know. Flounder sounds good."

"Fine." She began to rummage in her refrigerator.

"I'll be right back!" Nat told me, and ran at full steam into another part of the house.

I went into the kitchen. There were little plastic magnets on the refrigerator shaped like fruits and vegetables.

"Can I help?" I asked.

"I can do everything. Make yourself at home."

Nat came running back in to show me the Adventure People, an extended family group with movable joints that he held in his open palms. The Adventure People were apparently on safari, judging from the gorillas and lions and cages that nestled with them in Nat's hands.

"I asked my parents not to give him war toys," Mary Katherine said, "so they give him this thing, with wild animals in cages."

Nat handed me the animals and the Adventure People a piece at a time, offering them for my appraisal.

"All right, honey," Mary Katherine told him. "Go play in your room now. Jeff and I want to talk."

Nat went to his room without complaint.

"I really didn't mind," I said.

"He knows how to play by himself," she said. She was slicing bell pepper to garnish the two flounder, which lay in a baking dish, their flesh neatly scored.

She looked down at them intently for a moment, at the ugly mouths and great gill slashes.

"Do you mind if I take the heads off?" she asked.

"Of course not."

"David says if you're going to eat meat you should know exactly what you're eating, you should always have it in mind. I suppose I agree with him."

"Take the heads off," I said.

There were gig marks on the flounder. I imagined this David character stalking through the marsh at night holding a lantern in one hand and a triton in the other, the mud sucking off his tennis shoes. It was a good place for him, I decided.

She put the fish into the oven and then began to make the salad. I watched her slice a cucumber and an onion, finding myself attracted by the simple ritual. It had been a while since I had seen that.

We ate on the porch, our view of the surf spoiled slightly by an uneven row of houses built perilously close to the beach.

"First good hurricane ought to clear those out," I said, "then you'll have a view."

"Maybe. My landlord tells me this place stood up through Carla and Celia both without a scratch."

It was cool on the balcony, an ocean breeze threading its way through the dense static air. I looked back inside through the sliding glass door and noticed a wall decorated with unframed eight-by-ten photographs of leaping porpoises.

"You take those yourself?"

"Most of them. There's a darkroom at the school where a friend did the printing."

There was another easy silence. I told her I liked her boy, who was still playing in his room, having eaten before we came home.

"Nat's a pretty good kid. He puts up with a lot."

"What's his father like?"

"David? He's just a standard hippie with a certain amount of charm. Less and less charm as the years roll by, actually. I'll tell you an embarrassing secret."

"What?"

"Guess what 'Nat' is short for?"

"Nathaniel?"

"Natural Bridge. I'm not kidding. David's pantheist phase. I think he was on acid and saw this huge billboard for Natural Bridge Caverns up in New Braunfels. He may have even gone on the tour, I don't know. The thing is, it really didn't seem so silly at the time. Of course I suppose you could say that about the last ten years in general.

"Anyway, poor Nat's stuck with it, and it's my fault as much as David's. I was smitten too, in my way."

She smiled in a strange conspiratorial way.

"Did you like your flounder?"

"Delicious."

"How about some ice cream? Or would you rather smoke some dope?"

"Let's do both."

I watched her roll the joint; she made it seem a simple down-home skill, like the preparation of the salad had been. The marijuana itself did not affect me—it was the ice cream afterward that made me high, high enough to look at her plainly, without embarrassment. I saw her broad shoulders, bared by a sleeveless T-shirt, deeply tanned and peeling; the hollow at the base of her neck, the unwavering set of her eyes.

She told me of her girlhood in Oklahoma City. In the zoo there had been an elephant, Judy, born on the same day in the same year as Mary Katherine. She used to place peanuts in each of the elephant's nostrils and watch them soar up to the mouth. She was very conscious of Judy's regard for her—it was courtly and restrained, and it broke her heart.

When she was twelve she saw a picture of a dolphin in *Life* magazine and began to cry. She wrote fan letters to John Lilly, begging to become his apprentice. When she saw her first dolphins, on a family vacation to Galveston, she had to turn away, she was touched in such a fundamental, debilitating way.

I told her the story of my father's "rescue," taking pains to let her know I only half-believed it. She listened very seriously. She had taken a long time to eat her ice cream, and it had melted now.

"That's marvelous," she said. "Do you believe it?"

"It seems more probable to me than those stories of porpoises saving drowning sailors, pushing them to shore, that sort of thing. I don't disbelieve it."

"I'd like to talk to your father."

"He's been dead for years."

"Oh."

Nat came in, pretending to need help with his pajamas, and his mother went back with him to the bedroom to put him to sleep. I looked around the living room and inspected her bookshelves. *Man and Dolphin, The Mind of the Dolphin, Dolphins, Mind in the Waters, The Porpoise Watcher, The Whale, Whales and Dolphins.* All hardback. There were other books as well—natural food cookbooks, college editions of the classics, various field guides and thick paperback potboilers so swollen with water damage I surmised she took them out with her on her boat.

She came back into the living room while I was still browsing and sat on the couch and watched me. She looked tired.

"Nat asleep?"

"On his way, anyway."

"Do you mind me rifling through your books?"

"No, of course not."

"I've read most of these," I said, indicating the books about cetaceans. "Not the real technical ones, though. I guess I'm still a layman."

"Most of the scientists miss the point anyway."

"You're a scientist," I reminded her.

"That's just my disguise. That's my way of being around dolphins."

"I'm in disguise too," I said.

"I know."

I stood there, holding a book, looking at her. We were both still high. I felt pleasantly awkward around her.

"I'm not completely acceptable to you yet, am I?" I asked.

"It might take a while. I don't understand you."

"I just feel some connection between us. I know it's premature to say that."

"It's a circumstantial connection. Us both working with dolphins. It's probably best not to get carried away."

"What about David?"

"That's not it. It's just me."

She leaned her head back on the couch and closed her eyes. I wanted to walk over and sit next to her but I felt detached and almost serene. There was no hurry.

"Thank you for dinner," I said.

"I enjoyed having you over," she answered, very properly.

"Do you ever let people come out with you in your boat?"

"Nobody's ever mentioned wanting to. Except Nat. I take him out sometimes."

"I'd like to."

"It can be boring."

"I'd like to see what you do."

"All right. Do you have a day off?"

"I can always switch with Canales for a couple of shows. How about Friday?"

"I usually get started around six."

"I'll buy you breakfast," I said. "We could meet at the restaurant."

"Okay." She got up and began to clear the table, scraping the flounder bones into a trash bag.

"I'll help you with that."

"Don't bother. I'll see you Friday. Let's make it five thirty."

"Good night," I told her.

"This is all against my better judgment," she said.

It was still dark when we met at the restaurant. We took a booth beneath a stuffed, glossy tarpon. She was wearing an old sweater and boat shoes, and she piled her equipment—a camera, tape recorder, clipboard—onto the table. She was very alert and seemed to be delighted by the fact that I was still half asleep.

The fact was I had not slept all night. I had been afraid, like an adolescent on the eve of his first date, that if I fell asleep I might not wake up on time. My interest in seeing her at work, at watching the wild porpoises in the bay through her knowledgeable eye, produced a pleasant subsidiary excitement, but mainly I just wanted to see her again.

She told me about her thesis. It was a kind of demographic survey of the porpoise population along a forty-mile stretch of inland waters. There were thirty-two individuals she could recognize simply by a glance at their dorsal fins and many more she could identify from photographs.

"There aren't as many dolphins around here as it sometimes appears," she told me, blowing on her coffee to cool it. "I think maybe a little over two hundred in all. Those are inland dolphins. How many there are in the Gulf I don't know. What's interesting is that they seem to be distinct groups of animals. You never see inland dolphins out very far in the Gulf, and Gulf dolphins seem to have very set inland limits."

We finished our breakfast and drove down to the university docks. We lined her boat out of a shed and into the canal. It was a Boston Whaler, the same kind of boat we had used to catch the porpoises last October. And the day was similar—the perfectly calm sheet of water, the early-morning air that seemed to rest like a heavy gas in my lungs, the overwhelming corrosive scent of dead fish and salt.

When we got into the boat Mary Katherine put her camera and tape recorder into a watertight plastic bucket. I sat in the bow while she started the motor and we moved toward the channel, leaving behind a blue cloud of gasoline fumes and a smooth clear wake.

"Sit wherever you want," she said. "There isn't much choice."

I remained where I was and looked back at her. The sun was up now. She squinted against it and smiled and took off her sweater. Underneath she was wearing a T-shirt, and I could see beneath that the outline of her bathing suit.

We came out just below the jetties. A cormorant flew beside us, keeping the pace.

"We're going to head up the channel almost to the end of the jetties," Mary Katherine shouted above the motor. "Then we'll go back down and around Harbor Island."

I nodded and looked ahead to the mouth of the jetties. Fishermen were already out, littering the space around them with cut bait, trash fish, coils of leader. The water was a pale gray-green, though far out past the jetties I could see its modulation into clear blue.

Mary Katherine said something into the microphone of the tape recorder and set it back into the bucket. A fisherman waved at us, and I waved back, remembering the serenity of early morning fishing with my father, the way each shrimp curled so poignantly to the shape of my hook.

Neither of us had sighted any porpoises by the time we reached the open Gulf. Mary Katherine spoke into the microphone again and turned the boat around. We ran inland for another hundred yards before she pointed off to the south.

"Over there," she shouted. "By the tide gauge."

Four fins broke the water. One of them was low, stunted, symmetrical. I had seen it before.

"Triangle Fin?" I asked.

She nodded. "And part of his herd." She spoke into the microphone again.

The porpoises were feeding. Mary Katherine kept her distance and took out the camera, but she could not get a decent shot. The porpoises picked up and moved west.

"They're headed up Lydia Ann," she said. "We might as well follow them."

She swung the skiff out of the main pass and into the narrow side channel between St. Joseph and Harbor Island. On its lee side St. Joseph was carpeted with a flock of white pelicans that our approach disturbed into flight. We passed the wreck of a World War II freighter and, further down the channel, the old Lydia Ann lighthouse that was in the background of the postcard on my wall.

The porpoises had disappeared. It was warmer now, and Mary Katherine took off her shirt. She looked lithe and fit in her bathing suit, the light blue material flaring out against her tan.

We rounded the northern curve of Harbor Island and skirted the intracoastal. It took us another forty minutes to reach the main channel again and begin closing our circle around the irregular hulk of the island. During that time we saw no more fins. We kept our silence, the little boat gliding smoothly across the placid surface.

We passed a series of rotted piers, the legacy of a failed resort development. Years ago someone had taken a few backwater acres and laced it with canals and every sort of marina trapping, but no one had ever built a house there. Now only the piers were left and the canals, which once had had a clean surgical precision but whose banks had softened and grown over with grass.

"There," Mary Katherine said, pointing to a large pod a hundred yards ahead of us. They were feeding, rocking up and down in the water without moving forward. As we approached them they did not swim away; they seemed instead to be moving toward the boat from both sides of the channel.

"You're going to get the special treatment."

"What's that?"

"Watch."

I thought for a moment that the boat had struck a reef. All

of a sudden the water looked very shallow and stippled, and it took me a moment to realize that it was filled with living things. Porpoises. Dolphins. There could have been several dozen swimming with the boat, escorting us, so close it seemed they were trying to lift the small Boston Whaler on their backs. I leaned over the bow and the tip of a dorsal grazed my chin.

"Here," Mary Katherine said. She took a face mask from the bucket and tossed it to me. "Put this on. I've got a little tow bar rigged up to the boat. We'll take turns pulling each other."

She cut the motor. The porpoises disappeared as smoothly as a subsiding wave.

"They're still here," she said. Her voice sounded stark and direct without the background noise of the motor. She threw a wooden bar over the stern. It was attached to the boat by two pieces of yellow ski rope.

"Go ahead and get in," she said. "Stay back from the propeller."

I slid off the stern and untangled the ropes and swam out with the bar to the end of their length. The mask was an old Voit, the kind they sell in drugstores, but it sealed well enough on my face, and looking into the water I could see that anything better would be useless in the murk. I felt the slightest tinge of panic, thinking of all the lower forms of saltwater life I did not wish to encounter.

When I was ready I signaled to Mary Katherine and she started the motor and slipped it into gear. The bar began to drag me forward. For a moment I could see nothing but the blue gasoline cloud above the surface and, when I put my head underwater, the white froth stirred up by the propeller.

Very soon, though, the turbulence grew orderly, forming into a wake that passed on either side of me.

Suddenly the channel was alive. To each side I could make out the great shapes that the dense water did not reveal so much as imply, as if the porpoises were nothing more than clusters of water molecules. One of the shapes made a parallel swerve toward me, regarded me briefly with its eyes, and then thrust itself upward and broke through the filmy ceiling above us.

After that the others drew in to look at me, close enough so that I could see the face of each, the slightest gradients of expression there. I rose with them for breath, and caught a glimpse of Mary Katherine at the stern. She was looking down at me, amused. I descended again. It seemed to me that I was in their charge, that they were racing somewhere, toward some goal, and were taking pains to see I was not left behind. I could feel the shudder of each stroke of their flukes, but somehow our passage through the water together was as effortless as it was urgent. I rose to breathe easily, without forethought, when I was ready.

"My turn!" Mary Katherine called. She helped me into the boat; there was something startling about the touch of her hands on my bare wet back. She dropped her cutoffs and put the mask on, her upper lip splayed by the hard rubber skirt, her eyes isolated and magnified behind the glass.

When she had gone over the side I saw how the porpoises dropped back from the bow of the boat and fell in with her, swimming very close, even touching her from time to time. All that I saw of her when her head was beneath the water was her bathing suit, a blue lolling presence with a consort of odd, gray, snorting beasts.

After a short time she signaled me to turn off the motor and swam to the side of the boat. I helped her over the sharp gunwale. She lay there for a moment with the mask perched on her forehead, the droplets of salt water drying up one by one in the hollow of her throat.

She smiled. "I told you you were going to get the special treatment."

The porpoises were gone, far up the channel now. I started the motor again and led us slowly toward the university docks. Mary Katherine dried herself in the sunlight of the bow. When we got back we unloaded her white bucket and checked the boat in on a clipboard hanging in the shed. I sat on a gasoline can, watching her put her clothes back on. There was a strange, forlorn intimacy between us.

"You look sort of upset," she said, briskly buttoning up the cutoffs.

"When we caught Wanda and Sammy we were using two Boston Whalers just like this one. I remember we were chasing them, and all of a sudden they turned around and swam back toward us. I couldn't figure out why. Now I realize they may have thought it was you."

"That could be." She was concerned. There was a hurt look in her eyes. I didn't understand at first that it was meant for me and not for the porpoises.

"Would you like some tea? I have some in my office."

The corridors of the marine science building were peopled with lanky graduate students with scraggly beards and buck teeth. They all seemed to know her. To reach her office we passed through a lab in which a man in a white coat was placing tiny fish at the crest of a wooden watercourse and charting their descent. He looked up from his clipboard and nodded at Mary Katherine.

She turned on a light switch in a room just off the lab. A fluorescent fixture overhead blinked tentatively and then flooded the small cubicle with light. On one wall there was a computer rendering of a porpoise. Her desk was six inches deep in monographs and manuscripts. She cleared a space and sat down.

"What do you do in here?" I asked.

She plugged in a hot plate. "Transcribe my data. Make little charts. All the clinical stuff I have to do. If I had it my way I'd just drop all that and go out everyday and *watch* them, but that's not the way it's done. What kind of tea do you want?"

She had scooped a handful of Celestial Seasonings teabags out of the desk drawer. I chose peppermint.

"I'll have to borrow an extra cup from the kitchen. If the water looks like it's going to boil over, you better unplug it."

While she was gone I stared dutifully at the beat-up saucepan she had filled with water. I heard the scientist in the lab say, under his breath and with no apparent irony, "Eureka!" I peeked around the corner and saw him holding a dead fish in front of his eyes by its tail fins.

Mary Katherine came back with my cup and fixed the tea.

She cleared more ground on her desk and drew her knees up.

"What are you going to do when you're finished here?" I asked.

"Try to get somebody to fund me so I can keep on doing the same thing. Maybe write a book for the university press. *The Vicissitudes of Tursiops Truncatus in the Texas Gulf Coast.* Something like that, I don't know. Something dull."

"That wasn't dull, what we did this morning."

"No." She played with the keys of her typewriter. "All in all I think I have a better job than you do."

"Meaning it leaves you with a clean conscience."

"I think you enjoy your bad conscience," she said. "It gives you some sort of edge."

I had to laugh a little. Beneath the fluorescent light her eyes were a strong green.

"You think I'm sentimental," she challenged.

"Who knows?"

"But it has nothing to do with sentimentality, with the fact that dolphins happen to be cute. It goes beyond that."

"Where does it go?" I asked, wanting to know, wanting to go there too.

"It depends on how mystical you want to get. I think primitive civilizations were onto it. There were bear people, toad people, crayfish people. We're dolphin people, you and I."

"Totems. Freud said totemism is a form of patricide."

"In what way?"

"I don't remember. I remember not believing him."

"You and I know what a simple thing it is. It's a simple emotion. Believing in the existence of other beings, that's all it is."

There had been a few people like her in New Mexico, devotees of one animal cult or another, people who bought records of coyote yelps and played them all night when the moon was full. Wanting to be Indians, to be one with Owl and Snake and Chuckwalla. But I could see she was already one, the choice had never been there for her to make.

She unplugged the hot plate. "I better get to work," she

said, but she did not get to work. She must have dropped off the desk with a volition toward me I did not notice at the time, because kissing her was a very smooth motion, an easy passage through the air that separated us.

"The inevitable," she said, her face now in my shoulder. I looked down at the top of her head.

"It wasn't so inevitable," I said.

"I didn't mean to sound fatalistic. I don't mind it happening, not at all."

She looked pensively off to the side, to the computer portrait, the dolphin rising from a sea spray formed from vagrant letters, like alphabet soup.

"Where will you be tonight?" I asked.

"Home. No, wait. I'm switching off baby-sitting with Molly. I'll be at her house. You could come over there, but it would be pretty hectic. Why don't we see each other tomorrow night? Molly could keep Nat. We could have dinner."

I agreed. I could wait that long.

"Jeff," she whispered, "I'll help you let them go."

It was not a dare, it was the promise of an alliance. I held her for a long moment, in silence, then kissed her good-by.

The crowd for the ten o'clock performance was filing out the gate when I arrived at the compound. It was a sparse crowd, with only a few hangers-on pestering Canales with the usual questions, which he answered grudgingly.

"You can have it," he told me when they were gone. "Wanda refuses to do her back flip, hits the bar every time on the high jump, gets in Sammy's way when he's building up speed for his big leap. Stupid fucking animal. She better watch her step or she's on her way to the glue factory."

Sara went into the shed, got an ice cream sandwich out of the freezer, and sat by the edge of the pool rubbing the porpoises with her feet.

"This tastes like fish," she said.

"Plus the Indian princess here forgot to rewind her tape

recorder so there she was mouthing the song and all you hear is static."

"Leave me alone."

"Maybe I better work the porpoises before the next show," I said.

"That won't do any good. Wanda'll just get full that way and she'll be even more half-assed than she is now. She didn't get much to eat the last show. Maybe if she's hungry she'll do all right this time, start thinking about holding up her end of the fucking deal."

"How much did you hold back?"

"Maybe three pounds. How was your boat ride?"

"Fine."

"What's that chick like? Bleeding heart, right?"

"She's okay."

"I'm going into Corpus for some R & R. You and Sara can have this chickenshit operation for the rest of the day."

When he left I went to the freezer and measured out three pounds of herring, thawed it under the tap, and shot it down Wanda's gullet, tossing Sammy a fish every now and then so he wouldn't get jealous.

"Are you supposed to do that?" Sara asked.

"I'm not going to work her if she's three pounds down. I want her to know the slate's clean."

"Look at her looking at you. She's in love with you. She hates Mando."

"That's because he hates her."

"She *is* really stupid."

"That's not the point."

"Sometimes I think he's cruel to her."

"How?"

"I don't mean like physically cruel. Sometimes he just seems to want to confuse her, you know? Of course he's that way with me, too, the way he decided just now to go into Corpus. Notice he didn't ask *me* if I wanted to go? I'm pretty pissed off, if you want to know."

"What does he do to her, Sara?"

"Like I said, nothing serious. He just sort of picks on her. When she makes a mistake he seems glad about it. He'll yell at her and stamp his foot and not give her any fish until she gets so worked up she wouldn't be able to do it right anyway. He just seems to lose his temper more when you're not around."

Wanda's fungus had still not cleared up, so I got the bottle of purple ointment and held out my hand, a signal for her to rise up out of the water to shake it with her flipper. As she hovered there on her tail I swabbed the area behind her ear hole. Sammy performed the same maneuver, not wanting to be left out, and I gave him a little token swipe with the applicator brush.

Wanda performed raggedly during the two afternoon shows, but I could sense her earnestness. It was our failure, not hers. There was something she didn't get, something we wanted from her that she did not understand. Since Canales was gone we cut out the Arion bit, but Sammy and Wanda carried Sara around the pool without a hitch. The response from the audience was enthusiastic. Mr. Granger was in the bleachers, as he often was now, his face from my perspective on the pulpit as inexpressive as dough. He came down to the pool after the performance, bent down stiffly, and gave Sammy an affectionate cuff on the beak. Sammy opened his jaws, hoping for a fish, throwing his head back so that the roof of his mouth was visible, pink and speckled like an old man's skin.

"You know that girl?" I said to Mr. Granger. "The one who wrote the letter to the editor? I've been seeing her."

"Socially?"

"I guess. I think she's kind of sorry about what she wrote about you."

"That's good to hear, Jeff. Is she pretty?"

Life could be so simple. "Yeah."

"What's her name again?"

"Mary Katherine."

"Mary Katherine." He pondered a moment, his hands deep in his suit pockets. "I'll tell you what, Jeff. Why don't I take the two of you into Corpus and take you to dinner at the

Petroleum Club? How would that be? That's something nice I could do for you two."

"I don't know, Mr. Granger."

"Aw hell, you'll have a good time. And I won't get in your way. When are you going to see her again?"

"Tomorrow night."

"Well, let's us just go tomorrow night. I'll make the reservations right now."

"I'll have to check with her."

"No, no," he said, growing excited. "You leave that to me. I'll give her a call tonight. The old ogre calling her up. You just give me her phone number and I'll set it all up."

"I should call her first, though."

"Naw, surprise her."

Why not, I thought. Let her have it. I gave him the number, told him what time she would be back from Molly's. He copied it down on a little gilt-edged notebook which he put back into one of his many upper pockets and patted with satisfaction.

"This'll be a real treat," he said.

Chapter 8

"I don't believe this guy," Mary Katherine told me over the phone late that night. "Did you know about this? Why didn't you tell me he was calling?"

"He wanted it to be a surprise."

"God. At first I thought he was some sort of pervert. He sounded like some goosy high-school kid asking me out to the prom."

"Did you accept?"

"Of course I accepted. He's your friend, isn't he? And it should be fun, I suppose. I don't know what to wear, though, I mean for the Pe*tro*leum Club! Molly has a dress I can borrow. I think she was married in it or something."

I told her I thought that would be fine. The next day I left my corduroy pants at the cleaners, and went on my lunch hour to the Dad and Lad store and bought a drab sport coat and tie and a pair of wing-tip shoes that made my feet feel as if they had weights attached. It all cost about a hundred dollars, but Mr. Granger was paying me two hundred and fifty a week, plus my free room at the Salt Sea, and the indulgence itself was somewhat therapeutic.

When I put my dry-cleaned pants on that night they felt wonderful against my sunburned skin, like fresh linen. I jiggled the battery cables on my old Chevy when it wouldn't start and drove the few blocks to Mary Katherine's beach house, feeling all the way quaint and dignified, in line with some order of behavior I had barely known existed. Here I was, an adult, going on a date.

She opened her door. She was wearing a dress whose color reminded me of litmus paper, as if her tanned skin had caused a reaction that turned the material a faint blue. The dress left the cool planking of her shoulders bare. The muscles of her calves twitched as she teetered down the stairs in her high heels.

"Do you think this is all right?" she asked.

"Of course it is. You look lovely."

"So do you. You really went whole hog. A tie and everything."

"You kids have a good time on your big date," Molly said from the top of the stairs. Nat leaned against the rail and looked down at me resentfully.

When she got into the car Mary Katherine sat close to me at once, and I was grateful for that. I kissed her before I started the ignition.

"Let's go in by the causeway," she said. "Then we can come back by the ferry."

I drove south along Padre Island and then turned onto the causeway. On the way to Corpus Christi neither of us said much. Mary Katherine kept smoothing her dress and picking off lint. Through the open window we could hear the rumble of the car, perfectly pitched to the sound of the smooth passage of the salt breeze. When we reached the top of the causeway bridge (it was lower than the harbor bridge on the opposite side of the bay, but the sensation of height was greater) she slipped away from me to the passenger window and put her head outside. It was still twilight and we could see for miles up and down the Laguna Madre. A few boats plied through the intracoastal canal. Padre Island, the spoilbanks that lay behind it, the mainland itself all seemed part of the same unpatterned fabric: a mixture of water, land, and sky, all on the same level, all resting on the same still surface. It was the flat unmarked interface of sea and land I remembered from my childhood.

We passed a bait stand I used to visit with my father, and I wondered if the painting I had marveled at as a boy was still there, a painting of a fisherman standing knee deep in the surf coaxing a naked woman from the waves. The woman, I remembered, was trying to cover herself with her hands, and looked at the dry land as if it was something she had never seen before.

It was almost dark by the time we reached Ocean Drive. The lights had come on on the T-heads, illuminating the white hulls of the sailboats docked there. In the failing light the water of the bay was taut and shimmering, and the skyline, with its prim, even buildings, gleamed like a toy city.

The Petroleum Club was on the top floor of an old office building that rose above the bluff separating "downtown" from "uptown." We parked near the cathedral and stood for a moment at the top of the bluff, looking over the downtown rooftops at the manicured bayfront.

"I wish I'd been born here," she told me. "Like you. I think that would have helped me in my work."

"How?"

"It would feel more ordained or something. Sometimes I feel like I'm trespassing, or like I used to feel when we'd come down here from Oklahoma on vacation. About the time we hit Dallas Mother would start babbling about how wonderful the ocean was and by the time we got here and I actually saw it I was kind of disappointed. The Gulf of Mexico seemed like a bargain-basement ocean. And then I'd get stung by a man-of-war, and of course not know what it was and think I'd been attacked by ants, and then my mother would say, 'Honey, there are no *ants* on the beach.' I hated it."

"You seem to have gotten over that."

"I *had* to get over that, because I knew that salt water was what mattered to me. Now of course I can't stand the thought of being landlocked. I don't even *like* fresh water. Oh, sure, a babbling mountain stream is *pretty*, but there's nothing there. Salt water, though, you can sense it right off—gravity. I don't see why you ever left."

"I suppose when my parents died I felt I'd had too big a dose of that gravity."

"I'm sorry," she said. "I didn't mean to sound so self-right-eous."

"I didn't mean to sound solemn, either," I said.

In the lobby of the building we boarded an old-fashioned elevator that had been designed for an operator but converted to self-service. A brass grating closed automatically when I pushed the button for our floor, and when the doors opened again we were met by a maitre d'. I mentioned Mr. Granger's name and he escorted us to a table in front of a picture window where Mr. Granger was standing with his hands out for us. He was wearing a carnation in his lapel and his face was so pink it looked as if he had scrubbed several layers of skin from it.

Mr. Granger took Mary Katherine's hand into both his own and stood there simply admiring her. She blushed, charmed.

"I was so happy when you agreed to join me," he said. "I'm just a lonesome old man, and you don't know how it cheers me up to have a pretty girl like you at my table."

"I can't believe you're *that* lonesome," she said, in a mock flirtatious voice I hadn't heard before. "You look pretty dashing tonight."

Mr. Granger had us sit down. A young man my age in a white jacket reverently set three menus before us. I noticed there were no prices on them.

"Would you like drinks, Mr. Granger?" he asked.

He ordered us all False Dawns, another drink he had invented.

"It's the opposite of a Tequila Sunrise," he explained. "Now I want you two to get the lobster. Or a good steak. Or both. You look like you could use a decent meal, you're both so skinny. Hell, yes, you get the steak and the lobster both. It's got protein.

"That's what we'll have," he said to the waiter, "and then we're all going to want a great big piece of chocolate cake."

When the waiter left Mr. Granger played with his napkin

and looked out the window at the dark bay, which seemed like a vast pit into which the center of the city had fallen.

"So what do you think of our porpoises?" he asked Mary Katherine.

"They're very nice," she said. "Of course you know I'd rather see them free."

"Well, honey, you just keep thinking that way. You may convince me yet. I'm willing to admit I've got some mixed feelings."

Mary Katherine took a sip of the False Dawn the waiter brought her and ran her finger around the rim of the glass.

"It's a very simple process," she said, "just opening the gate."

Mr. Granger put his hand on her forearm and winked at her. "We'll talk about it sometime."

I wondered how serious he was. Setting the porpoises free was an idea that he kept suggesting but would never develop. I think he was as tied to them as I was, that he wanted to keep them, that by having them around some channel was open that would otherwise be closed.

The lobsters came, looking like nightmarish insects.

"I've never had a lobster before," Mary Katherine said. "How do you eat it? What is there to eat on it?"

"You eat the tail and the claws," Mr. Granger explained. "You take this little nutcracker thing here and just go after it. Jeff, you help her out."

"All right," I said. "But I've never done this either."

"What's the matter with you two? Never had a lobster!"

Mary Katherine poked around the carapace until she found the meat in the tail.

"It's wonderful," she said, tasting it. To me the lobster tasted springy and insubstantial, and I cut into the rib eye sitting next to it.

"It's a strange animal," Mr. Granger said. "I don't know whoever got the idea you could eat it. You know, I've been in some parts of the world, in restaurants, where they had porpoise on the menu. Supposed to be a delicacy. I would never try it, though. I just didn't want to."

"There are lots of places where people still hunt them," Mary Katherine said. "In the Azores the kids practice their harpooning on them, and then when they grow up they go after sperm whales. Then of course there's the tuna industry."

"They're just not safe anywhere, are they?" Mr. Granger said.

I saw Mary Katherine look frankly into his face. I knew she was looking for something there, a trace of irony or guile, but there was nothing, just the smooth, uncomplicated, swollen face, the thick glasses, the slick hair.

"I'm very sorry about that letter," she told him. "I mean the part about you. I didn't know you."

Mr. Granger blushed and pushed his half-eaten lobster across the table toward us.

"You two finish this," he said. "I can't eat another bite."

We both protested, but there was no point. He had apparently had a few False Dawns before we arrived, and he was slightly drunk and feeling too much like a master of ceremonies. We picked at the remains of his lobster. Under the table she slid the edge of her shoe up and down my shin. Mr. Granger leaned back in his chair, beaming at us. Ricky Nolan and the Stargazers took their places on the bandstand and after tuning up for a while began to play a brassy version of "The Girl from Ipanema." The Stargazers all wore red blazers with a shooting star on the pocket, and between riffs they would hold their instruments in the crooks of their arms and wag their heads and smile. A few couples stood up and began to dance, big beef-faced oilmen and their wives. Mr. Granger insisted that Mary Katherine and I join them.

"I don't know how to dance," I said.

"Neither do I," said Mary Katherine. "Not that way. I had ballroom in the eighth grade but I'm sure I've forgotten everything."

"That's no excuse. There's nothing to it. You just go out there and shuffle around a little. It's good for you."

The music stopped but Mr. Granger went on in a loud voice exhorting us to dance. The whole restaurant was listening.

"Dance with her!" Ricky Nolan said into the microphone. Everyone applauded.

"Well, I guess that's our cue," Mary Katherine said. I stood and held out my hand as I had seen people do in movies and led her to the dance floor.

"A lovely young couple," Ricky Nolan said. Everybody applauded again. Mary Katherine hid her face in my shoulder.

"A-one, a-two," the bandleader said, leading his group into "Feelings."

A few other couples came onto the floor to take the pressure off us.

"Okay," I said, "give me some sort of hint."

"Just move your feet in time with the music."

We leaned back and forth, like dancing robots. It seemed to me the other dancers were actually gliding by us, as if they were on roller skates.

"This isn't so bad," I conceded.

"Look at him looking at us." She was pointing with her eyes toward Mr. Granger, who was staring at us, drunk and happy.

"Everybody else is looking at us, too," I said.

"Why not? We're a lovely young couple. Do you mind?"

"Not really." I ran my hand up her spinal column and then slid it back down to rest on the small of her back. We danced jerkily to the other side of the floor.

"You know what this reminds me of?" Mary Katherine said. "Did you ever stand on top of your father's shoes while he walked around? I think we've got the same effect going here."

When the song was over there were a few drunken yelps and sporadic applause that I realized was meant for us. We turned to go back to the table but Mr. Granger was waving us back onto the floor. We danced through two more songs. I set my eyes over Mary Katherine's head and looked out the wraparound window at the lights of the city and the abrupt chasm of the bay where they disappeared, listened to the *ta-shew, ta-shew* of the snare drum, played by a man with long sideburns and slicked-down back hair. We began to move rhythmically, to anticipate one another's direction, to adjust ourselves to it the way Wanda and Sammy silently aligned themselves for their tandem high jump, gauging speed and distance and height with a perfection that had always mystified me, even though I knew I had taught it to them.

During the third song—some movie theme I half-recognized—I looked over and saw Mr. Granger at the table gesturing to us, his face even more flushed than before. First I thought he wanted us to come over, then for us to hold back and keep dancing. The signs he was making seemed frantic, discordant. I couldn't understand what he wanted, and my helplessness was aggravated by the momentum of the dance, which seemed to hold me from him, to keep me from understanding.

Finally Mary Katherine saw and took her hands from my shoulders.

"Is he all right?"

I saw the sweat on Mr. Granger's forehead, the skin prickling on his scalp where the hair had thinned out. I reached him just as he lurched forward from his chair onto the floor. He was looking up at me, his face bloated, unrecognizable.

"Somebody please call an ambulance," Ricky Nolan said calmly into the microphone.

I loosened Mr. Granger's bow tie and then the collar of his silk Taiwanese shirt. He was breathing, he was licking his lips with his tongue.

"What went wrong?" he said very slowly. "Did I have a stroke?"

"I think you may have had a little heart attack," Mary Katherine told him. "Just lie still now and wait for the ambulance."

"Did the band stop playing because of me?"

"They'll start again in a minute," I said.

"I feel silly just lying here."

"It doesn't bother anybody."

Ricky Nolan came over, took off his red blazer, and tucked it under Mr. Granger's head.

"How you doin', Dude? For a minute there I thought I'd lost my biggest fan."

"Ricky," he said, "why don't you play something so all these folks can dance instead of just standing around?"

The bandleader nodded and left. In a moment the Stargazers were playing "Three Coins in the Fountain." Mr. Granger lay very still, blinking his eyes, not speaking. Two ambulance attendants arrived and eased him onto a stretcher, then wheeled him through the crowd and onto the elevator.

"I feel like I'm floating," he said as the elevator descended. "Like this place is underwater and I'm just swimming through it."

"Is that right?" one of the attendants said.

"You ride with him in the ambulance," Mary Katherine said to me. "Give me your keys and I'll meet you at the hospital with your car."

Mr. Granger said nothing in the ambulance. He was very calm and looked about in wonderment, as if he had just opened his eyes on the world for the first time. He was hooked up to a portable EKG machine. The attendant gave him an injection of something.

"Yeah, you'll be fine," he said without much interest. "Having a night on the town, huh?"

Mr. Granger nodded. The attendant looked over at me.

"How you doin'?"

"Fine."

The ambulance hit a rut in the road, and Mr. Granger's bulk pitched a little on the stretcher. He seemed to have relinquished control of his body, he was so passive.

I found Mary Katherine in the lobby of the hospital. She was talking to Nat on the phone.

"I can't, honey," she was saying. "A friend of Jeff's is very sick and we have to help out. I'll be home before you wake up. We'll go out and have some doughnuts for breakfast, okay? Now let me speak to Molly again."

Across the lobby was a large mosaic mural. A fragmented Christ gathered sheep into his lap, holding his hand above them in the sign of blessing, the sheep and the man-god all wearing the same simpering expression on their faces. I remembered the mural—I had stared at it for a long time before each of my parents had died.

Mary Katherine hung up the phone and took my hand.

"How is he?"

"I don't know. He seemed pretty listless in the ambulance. Listen, you can take the car back if you want to get home. I may be here all night. I don't think he'd expect you to wait around."

"Don't be silly. Molly loves staying at my house. She plays all my records."

"The doctor's on the way here," I said. "As soon as they know something they're supposed to tell us. I told them we'd be in the coffee shop."

"Let's wait there then, come on."

We took a booth and drank two cups of coffee each without saying anything.

"You're pretty upset, aren't you?" she said finally.

I nodded.

"I wasn't sure exactly what he means to you."

"I'm not either. He was a good friend of my parents'. I guess he's the closest thing to family I have left."

"He's a sweet man."

Dr. Rush came into the coffee shop a half hour later. He had not changed much since the day eleven years ago he had told me of my mother's death. If anything he looked younger, his hair fuller and his face thinner and tanned.

"How have you been, Jeff?" he asked, taking my hand. "Son of a gun. I think it must be ten years."

"About that," I said. "This is Mary Katherine Severin."

Rush took her hand and gripped her elbow with that same cool professionalism that had taken me in so long ago, making me feel relieved at even his most tragic news, flattered, a colleague.

"Well," he said, "Dude is just fine. I'll tell you what, let's go into the conference room and I'll fill you in there."

The conference room was the size of a large closet. There was another picture of Jesus there, pointing at his swollen, radiant heart.

We sat down on a kind of pew affixed to the wall; Rush leaned back against the opposite wall and crossed his arms.

"He's doing fine," he repeated. "He's had a coronary occlusion, a fairly serious one. He's in intensive care where we can keep an eye on him."

Mary Katherine and I nodded our heads dumbly. Already I felt the crisis leaving us, receding before this solemn shoptalk.

"He knows you can't go in to see him for a few days yet, but he's concerned about you and told me to tell you to go back to Port Aransas tonight and look in on the porpoises.

"Now what the hell"—he laughed—"are you doing with porpoises?"

"He's got a porpoise show over there."

"The hell he does? Ol' Dude. You know, I never knew porpoises were as smart as you hear about them being today. I used to see them in the bay, try to catch them with a rod and reel, but I guess they were just too smart to go for it. Now everybody's got them doing tricks."

I looked up at the picture of Christ, pointing to his heart. It seemed in bad taste, like LBJ displaying his gall bladder scar. The image came back, the porpoise hung by its flukes from the post.

Rush unfolded his arms now and rubbed his hands together.

"Jeff," he said, "this is not a good thing for a man Dude's age, and he's not in particularly good health, so I don't want to give you a pie-in-the-sky prognosis. His condition is stable right now, he's doing fine, like I said, but he's still very critical.

"I want to get him up to Houston as soon as he's a little better, have Cooley look at him. The best thing in his case might be a bypass, I don't know. Right now we just have to wait it out. You go back to those porpoises like he said, and I promise I'll call you if there's any change at all."

I gave him my number, and the number at the compound, and Mary Katherine gave him hers as well.

"When will he be out of intensive care?" she asked.

"We'll keep him in there for three or four days. Now don't worry anymore. Go home and get a good night's sleep."

We obeyed. The hospital parking lot had been full when Mary Katherine drove up, so she had parked the car illegally on Ocean Drive. There was a two-dollar ticket under the wiper blade.

"Sorry," she said.

"That's all right."

"Do you want me to drive home? You look so tense."

But I felt like driving. I steered the car north toward the harbor bridge, and we climbed high above the bay, which was as dark as the moonless sky above us.

When I was in high school I dove once on the wreck of an oil tanker that had sunk long before in a hundred feet of water. At that depth it was very dark, even in the clear water of the Gulf. I had been swimming along a kind of spar, thinking I was heading toward the surface and confused by the gloom that huddled closer about me with every stroke of my fins. Someone grabbed me, pointed toward the surface and shook his head, then pointed downward and made an okay sign with his fingers. It took a few seconds of agonized, slow-witted thought for me to understand that we were hanging upside down in the water, that I had been swimming down into the blackness rather than up from it as I had thought.

Nearing the summit of the bridge I remembered that feeling, an absence of gravity and bearings that made it seem possible that the car would keep ascending, soaring away from the water below us and into the corresponding darkness of the sky.

But we were soon back down at sea level, following the curve of the bay. We recognized the land only by the lights set down upon it by humankind, but I could sense the desolate reach of it, the great smooth brow of land shelving off into the dirty waters. Near Aransas Pass a barn owl swung down across our headlights. We saw its blanched, startled face.

Ours was the only car on the ferry. Mary Katherine and I both got out and sat on the hood during the brief crossing.

"I'm going to check on the porpoises," I said. "I'll take you home first, if you'd like."

"Would you rather I went home?"

"No."

"Okay then."

The porpoises greeted us in a lunatic manner, walking on their tails, waving with their fins, leaping so high and so recklessly I was afraid they would miss the water altogether and land on the dock.

"They're glad to see us," I said.

In a few moments they calmed down and swam over to us, resting their chins side by side on the dock. Mary Katherine bent down and stroked Wanda's beak. The porpoise rolled over on her side and made her contented clicking sound.

"Let's get in with them," Mary Katherine said. "That's what they want."

I looked at her as she crouched on the dock in her blue dress and high thick heels. She was staring at me.

"Okay?" she said.

I nodded. She began to take off her clothes with an affected casualness. Standing in her underwear, she laid the borrowed dress along the bleachers with a prim, embarrassed attention to detail. She put her shoes there too, and then her underwear, and walked unhurriedly to the edge of the pool and slid into the water with more grace than I was able at that moment to absorb. I followed her, taking off the formal clothes, feeling the salt breeze on my skin. The water was warm, a well-drawn saline bath that lulled rather than excited us. Wanda passed in front of me and I grabbed her dorsal and took a ride across the pool, letting go when we came to the place where Mary Katherine treaded water, her shoulders just above the waterline. Two rows of teeth began gently raking up and down my leg.

"They did it to me, too." Mary Katherine laughed. "That's mating behavior. They want to make love with us."

"I don't think I'm ready for that," I said.

She leaned back and floated for a moment, her breasts rising out of the dark water.

"I don't know," she considered. "I can see it. Maybe if you weren't here with me I'd give it some serious thought. I don't think it's so disgraceful."

Sammy breached very close to our faces, spraying us with vapor and with exhausted air that smelled close but not foul. The porpoises were growing calm again, either from our discouragement of their advances or from an increasing interest in one another. For a while we swam with them chastely, grabbing them by the dorsals and running our hands across their backs, or holding them by the pectoral fins in the parody of dancing that was part of their performance. Letting go of one of the porpoises, I would turn to Mary Katherine and touch her bare skin, not really registering the difference, not knowing which smooth body belonged to which species.

We came out of the water to make love. I spread my sleeping bag out by the side of the pool, unzipping it all the way so that it was twice as wide, and we lay down together on the printed pattern of a hunter taking aim at a deer. Our bodies retained a brittle layer of salt, which did not interfere. It had been a long time since the Seamstress' last grudging tenderness. We listened to the porpoises beside us and to those in the channel, slapping their tails, exhaling with all the power of their lungs into the night air. I moved in and with Mary Katherine, thinking of that feral reach of dark, muddy water just beyond us, greater than any continent, unpeopled, waiting for us.

We could see Sammy and Wanda entwined (as much as their blunt bodies would allow them to be) in the pool beside us, Sammy rolling out of the water, his odd penis exposed, their quick, fervent face-to-face coupling.

"All this time," I said, "and I've never seen them do that."

"We set them off." She was beginning to shiver a little. I brought a towel from the shed and we dried off and dressed. Then we drove to my room at the Salt Sea and stood together in the tiny shower stall, beneath a stream of fresh water.

"I love this place," she said, crawling naked into the sheets I had washed that morning, in hope. "It's so bare."

I turned off the light and got into bed too, putting my glasses on the nightstand. She reached over me and turned the light back on.

"What?" I asked. She was looking into my face.

"I just wanted to see. You have nice eyes."

"They don't do me much good. You'll be a blur if you move away."

She moved even closer, and though we were both exhausted we began all over again.

I fell asleep worrying about Mr. Granger, and dreamed that he and I were clumsy slithering beasts lying on the beach of Corpus Christi Bay. We were dragging our bellies along the oyster shell, about to enter the water, knowing that there we would be buoyant and swift. We saw Wanda out in the bay, hovering in the air, desperate for us to leave the shore.

It was one of several dreams I had that night, for I woke half a dozen times from a need to assure myself that Mary Katherine was beside me. Each time she was asleep, perfectly asleep in the same position all night, her head on a corner of the pillow we were sharing, her mouth slightly open but still. Her whole body rose and fell with her breathing, but the stillness was dominant, like the hidden, changeless ocean bottom far beneath the surface swells.

The last time I woke I reflexively reached out for the alarm clock and shut it off before it rang. It took me a few moments to wake her, and I was afraid that when she did wake she would not remember me, would not know where she was.

But she smiled from her sleep and without opening her eyes cupped her hands around the back of my neck.

"What time is it?"

"Six thirty. You have to pick Nat up for breakfast."

"Hmmmm. Are you coming?"

"If I'm invited."

"Of course."

"What time does he get up?"

"Seven. He watches *Captain Kangaroo*. Did you know they still have Mr. Greenjeans? And that dancing bear."

"That's reassuring. You get dressed. I'm going to call the hospital."

Over the phone a terse voice told me that Mr. Granger was resting comfortably. There had been no change in his condition.

No change. I had longed once to hear those words. Even when my father had been in his coma and I had been told he would not break through it, "no change" filled me with a strange, static hope. It was not yet necessary to grieve or despair, I could be happy and secure a little longer.

"I suppose that's good, isn't it?" Mary Katherine said as she pulled her dress over her head.

"It's okay. I'd rather hear he was doing better, but at least he's still alive."

"Of course he's still alive. Don't be such a pessimist."

I put on my cutoffs and my Bigfoot T-shirt, which made it necessary to explain my brief career as a *bête noire*. Mary Katherine laughed and looked at me in wonder.

"I can't imagine it," she said.

Nat was watching television when we arrived. I doubt that he was glad to see me, but his mother's good humor won him over. We went to a little bakery, a carry-out place with only a few tables.

"Can I have chocolate doughnuts?" Nat asked his mother, staring at them in the bakery case.

"Not this early," she said.

We sat down at one of the tables. I watched Nat raise his doughnut to his mouth with his thumb and forefinger, looking at it the way a predator regards an unfamiliar victim, searching for the place it was most vulnerable. He was a quiet child, at least in my presence. After each bite he held his doughnut in front of his eyes, as if to measure any changes he had caused in its form. He took half an hour to finish his two doughnuts.

Mary Katherine and I sat with our coffee and waited patiently for him, our legs grazing against each other beneath the table.

Nat looked like his mother. He had the same eyes, spaced rather far apart above his broad cheekbones. His nose was unformed yet, but it would be hers too—straight, with a faint cleft at its base. I was glad he looked like her and not like his father.

"Hurry up, honey," Mary Katherine had to say at last. "Jeff has to go to work."

"I don't have to be there for a while," I said.

"Are you going on the boat today, Mommy?" Nat asked her.

"Not today. What would you like to do?"

"Can we see Jeff's dolphins again?"

"I don't know," she said.

"Let him," I said. "Come to the one o'clock show. I'll tell whoever's at the gate to let you in."

"I'd rather pay, Jeff."

"I understand."

"It doesn't bother you?"

"No. I'll pay for breakfast."

I drove them home and kissed her reservedly at the bottom of the stairwell outside her house. Nat watched us without emotion.

"I'll see you later," I said to him. He grinned and ran up the stairs.

"He likes you," Mary Katherine told me. "I could see you were worried he might not."

She shifted away from me and leaned back against one of the pilings that held up the house.

"One thing. Please don't start acting paternal around him unless you're very serious. That's happened to him before, and I don't want to explain it to him again. You can be like some jolly uncle who's always playing practical jokes, pulling quarters out of his ears, things like that. He won't miss you half as much."

I started to say something, but she held her hand up. "I'm

sorry. I'm already backing you into a corner. But I really care for you, Jeff. If it's going to be casual, fine. I can handle that. I just have to have certain ground rules because of Nat."

"I love you," I said.

"No. Let's be calm."

She looked at me steadily, and I was calmed and sure. She put her arms around my waist and grabbed my empty belt loops familiarly, and I laid my face into the wide berth of her shoulder.

Chapter 9

Canales and Sara drove up as I was unlocking the gate, but they sat for a long time in the cab of his pickup, not speaking. I went in alone and began the day's chores while they had it out. While I cut up the fish, set out the props, and went over yesterday's charts, the porpoises followed me with their eyes just above the waterline, like crocodiles.

Canales finally came in alone.

"Forget about Sara for today," he said, putting his whistle lanyard on over his shark's necklace. "She's on strike. We'll cut her part." We heard the truck peel out on the oyster shell road.

"Bitch!" Canales said under his breath.

I didn't ask him for any details.

"Mr. Granger's in the hospital," I said.

Canales looked up from the chart he was studying. "No shit?" he said gravely.

"He had a heart attack last night in Corpus. Mary Katherine and I were with him."

"What sort of shape is he in?"

"I'm not sure. He's stable right now. But he's pretty old."

"He'll hang in there."

"I suppose."

Canales sat down on the dock. Sammy leapt out of the water and splashed him, but he did not react.

"Guess who I talked to on the phone last night?" he asked.

"Who?"

"Bill Mason."

"What did he want?"

"He was basically just checking out the scene down here. He needs some new stock for Sea Park. He says the porpoises in Florida are getting too wary, so he's going to bring his catch boat to Texas. But here's the big news: I told him about Sammy, what a great porpoise he is, and he wants to come down and check him out."

"Why?"

"Because he's a talent scout. He's making a porpoise movie. He thinks the time is ripe for a new Flipper."

"You think he'd want Sammy?"

"No question. The animal is perfect. He's adaptable, he's sharp as a whip—a hell of a lot smarter than that porpoise they used for Flipper—and he doesn't have a scar on his body. Mason said the only other porpoise he's found that was worth considering was chewed all to hell around the flukes. Anyway, he's flying in tomorrow afternoon. He's bringing his boat up too."

"What about Wanda?"

"He'd probably take her off our hands at the same time. Farm her out to the petting pool at Sea Park. Or maybe some zoo where they just keep porpoises as exhibits, where she wouldn't have to do any tricks."

"I don't know if Mr. Granger would want to sell them."

"Yeah, well, that's the thing. Mason's buddies at the Marine Mammal Commission told him there's going to be another barrage of bureaucratic bullshit. New minimum standards. Larger pools, holding tanks, salinity standards, resident vets. They're trying to shut down the small businessman. They'll send some asshole inspector out here who doesn't know the difference between a porpoise and a jellyfish, and he'll take one look at our pool and ask us how we control the water temperature and we're finished."

"But this is seawater. It doesn't need to be controlled."

"These are *bureaucrats!*"

"Maybe we can convince Mr. Granger to meet the new standards."

"Come on, Jeff, we're talking about very big bucks here. Maybe Dude could get the money up, but I don't think the whole project excites him much anymore. Besides, there's a lot more in it for you and me if we just let the thing die peacefully. Sammy's going to need trainers, we're the logical choices. We can write that into the deal with no trouble at all.

"Listen," he went on. "If and when Mason makes an offer, it'll make a difference if we present it to Dude together. I think I can jew Mason up pretty high—my theory is that Sammy would be like a movie star, a hot property, right? And what do movie stars get paid? Millions of dollars. Robert Redford, that guy lifts his little finger he gets seven figures. It shouldn't be any different with Sammy. Dude could stand to make a lot of money on this, but he's going to want your opinion."

"Let's wait till he's better," I said.

"All right, but these deals can move fast."

I nodded, but some part of me was already beginning to panic. Whatever happened it seemed that I would lose them.

We did the first show of the day, rearranging the behaviors to cover for Sara's absence. Wanda did a backward rather than a forward flip, a deviation the audience was not aware of. But I saw Canales at the pulpit, fuming, plotting revenge. I told him after the show that he had made his hand signal in such a vague manner that it was impossible for Wanda to know which behavior it meant, especially when we were working out of sequence. He cooled down a little, but was a long way from taking the blame.

A half hour before the one o'clock show the phone in the shed rang. I answered it—it was Sara, in tears, asking for Canales.

"Can you take the next show by yourself?" he asked me when he had hung up.

"Sure."

"She's playing suicide threat again. I have to pretend she's serious and talk her out of it."

"You're sure she's not?"

"Someday she might be, but it's sure as hell not going to be over me. Listen, just do the tricks, just your basic behaviors. I'll be back as soon as I can."

"Don't worry," I said. "I'll handle it."

Mary Katherine and Nat took their seats on the bleachers without coming up to say hello. The one o'clock performance was the best attended of the day—the bleachers were filled with middle-aged women from Corpus, children with their mothers, a few surfers and junkies trying to give off an impression of superiority.

At one o'clock, as usual, I picked up a bucket of fish in each hand and walked to the end of the pulpit and set them down. I took the microphone and clipped it around my neck. Below me the two porpoises kept their eyes fixed on my hands.

I opened my mouth to say "Ladies and gentlemen . . ." but as it turned out I did not speak. Instead I stood there for a moment enjoying the silence from the bleachers. I looked at Mary Katherine, at the eager confusion in her eyes, and then took off the microphone and tossed it back onto the dock.

When I let my hands drop to my sides the porpoises positioned themselves beneath them, the tips of their beaks on a direct line with the tips of my index fingers. I felt their presence there as a power, a stored-up power I had never before thought to use, but when I looked down into the water, at their blunt faces staring back at me, I saw they thought of themselves as accomplices. My silence and the stillness of my hands stirred their imaginations, and they waited with conspiratorial patience for me to direct them.

Not saying a word to the audience, I sent Wanda and Sammy into their opening leap. Without human patter behind it the leap seemed to unfold slowly, lyrically. The audience sat there with their cameras half-raised as the two beasts crossed at the apex of their jump, their pectoral fins seeming to support them for a moment like two sets of stubby, primitive wings.

When the animals returned to the water (with the splashless precision of human divers) the audience did not applaud, no more than they would have applauded a creature they had surprised in the woods. Still, I felt that I had them, that I had caught their attention.

I gave Sammy and Wanda their fish openly, twice as much as they usually received. Wanda rolled over and looked up at me, and I saw myself, the pulpit, and a great arc of blue sky reflected in her eye. I made another sign and the two porpoises lunged forward, dropped beneath the surface, and rose up at opposite corners of the pool, balancing on their tails. I heard a slight gasp from the audience as the porpoises walked backward across the pool, their bodies shivering with the effort of balance. At the end of the behavior I did not even bother to blow my whistle. They knew they had earned their fish, and they understood what I wanted from them—precision, silence, grace.

I worked them in sequence so that they could anticipate me, be confident about what was coming next. My hands moved through the air, the animals took off through the water leaping, waving their fins, beaching themselves, moving to the progression they followed three times a day, the progression that was the only thing they knew anymore, the only hold they had secured in the world of their captors. But now for the first time I felt they *believed* in their behaviors, that their training had superseded their awareness, and that they were approaching the semiconscious realm of human art.

We entered that realm together. The three of us knew something the audience did not. At the end of the show— though properly speaking there had been no show and it had not ended, since Wanda and Sammy continued to run through their behaviors, and I simply left the pulpit—a few of the spectators asked for their money back at the ticket booth. None of them came up to me, none of the women who usually wanted to know where they could get a porpoise—"Well, do pet stores carry them, or what?"—as a gag gift for their husband, none of the kids with their endless questions about sharks or their pleas that I take them on as apprentices.

But one kid did come down to the pool. He gazed at the porpoises with a blank, flushed look and then simply dived into the water.

"*Stevie!*" his mother screamed. She stood quaking at the edge of the pool, convinced that the porpoises would eat her son.

Sammy and Wanda huddled on the far side of the pool, their eyes above the water, watching the boy swim toward them in a good, even crawl despite the weight of his clothes. For the mother's benefit I jumped in and grabbed him by the waist before he reached them. This did not seem to interrupt his stroke—he kept swimming as if I were a temporary obstacle he could simply shake off. Then suddenly he went limp and let me pull him out of the water. He sat on the dock, his eyes still on the porpoises. He was shaking.

"I'm sorry," he told me.

"Don't worry about it," I said. His mother led him away, both of them dazed.

Mary Katherine came over, holding Nat by the shoulders.

"Poor kid," she said.

She went into the shed and brought me a towel. By this time most of the audience was gone, except for a few people who lingered around the ticket booth, trying to understand what had just taken place.

"That was a lovely performance," Mary Katherine said. "Was that for our benefit?"

"For mine."

"Maybe I love you."

"Sure you do."

Sammy and Wanda were watching us. Nat squatted down and put his hand on Wanda's beak, then Sammy nosed her out of the way and rose a little out of the water.

"He wants you to pet him," I told Nat. "On his head."

"He feels funny."

Sammy opened his mouth and Nat ran his fingers fearlessly along the teeth.

"Jeff?" Mary Katherine said.

"He won't bite him."

The two animals spun vertically in the water, their eyes closed, languishing in Nat's attention.

"Can you come over tonight?" Mary Katherine asked me.

"I wanted to hang around the phone in case Rush calls. Why don't you come to my place?"

"I'd have to bring you-know-who."

"That's fine," I said. "We'll have a quiet evening at home."

"*Very* quiet."

Rush called me about six. He said that Mr. Granger was still in intensive care but would be moved and allowed visitors the next day.

I lay on the bed and fell asleep as I waited for Mary Katherine. When I opened my eyes I saw Nat looking down into my face, his tiny nostrils almost translucent in the light from the lamp on the nightstand.

"Your door was unlocked," Mary Katherine said, "and you never heard us knock, apparently, so we just came in. Are you sure you're awake?"

"Sure. Hi, Nat."

He turned his face away and smiled.

"How's Mr. Granger?" Mary Katherine asked.

"Better. He can have visitors tomorrow."

"I knew he'd be all right," she said with satisfaction. She was sorting through several white bags she had deposited on the bureau.

"We stopped at Custard's Last Stand. Have you eaten?"

It took me a moment to remember. "No."

"I got you a cheeseburger. With everything?"

"Fine. Thank you."

"And a Dr Pepper."

The three of us sat on the bed eating our hamburgers. I put two quarters into the vibrator to show Nat how it worked, and we sat there with the mattress drumming beneath us.

"You *live* here?" Nat asked.

"Uh-huh."

"But how come you don't live in a house?"

"This is sort of a house," I said. Then, to Mary Katherine, "I heard some news today."

She knew all about Mason.

"He was in the oceanarium thing from the ground floor," she said. "Before that I think he made horror movies. There's no telling how many dolphins that man has killed in the course of his career. Have you ever seen *Adventures with Animals?* Cute, isn't it? He traps these animals in Kuala Lumpur or someplace and flies them to his "studio habitat" in Florida and films the adventures there. God knows what happens to them after he's through."

"How would he treat Sammy?"

"Like a star. But he'd dump Wanda someplace."

"Canales says we're through anyway. The Commission is clamping down on places like ours."

"That's possible. They come out with stricter minimum standards every month. If you get closed down the dolphins'll probably get auctioned off. Guess who'll be top bidder. Either way you lose them."

"Unless we let them go."

"Would you?"

"I'd have to be driven to that."

"We'd need to plan it very carefully. You can't just let them out. They're dependent on us. We'd have to acclimatize them back to the wild."

"I don't want to talk about it right now," I said. "Let's watch TV or something."

Mary Katherine kicked off her sandals and swung her legs onto the bed.

"Fine," she said. "Let's just sit here and watch *Charlie's Angels.* That'll clear our heads."

"I'll turn it on," Nat volunteered.

On one station there was a middle-aged detective, one of those character actors who had paid his dues for so long that he had finally been given a toupee and a show of his own. I had Nat change the channel. Starsky and Hutch were questioning a hooker. Their jacket collars were turned up; in the next scene they had changed into different jackets, but their collars were still turned up. On the third channel a disco band was lip-syncing its latest twelve-minute hit.

"Enough?" Mary Katherine asked.

"Enough?" Nat echoed, his hand on the knob.

"Go ahead," I said. He pressed the button and the picture fell away into the vortex.

And so we whiled away the evening, as a family might. Nat had brought a few storybooks, and I held him in my lap and listened as he read. They were old dog-eared 25¢ Golden Books—Mary Katherine's—and I remembered one of them from my own childhood, a grumpy beaver's surprise birthday party, at which he discovered his woodland friends truly loved him. Nat ran his finger along each sentence, but it was clear he was not so much reading as reciting. He had committed the story to memory long before. I looked down at the myopic beaver about to blow out the candles on his cake and remembered the mystical resonance of my own childhood, the shimmy and shake of possibility, my mother bustling around the house singing

> *You'll find that you're*
> *In the Ro-to-gra-vure*

and every perception of mine rallying around the words, investing them with the deepest secrets of existence.

Later we walked back up to Custard's Last Stand for some ice cream. We sat in the little dining room, vaguely aware of the languid, self-absorbed Jackson Browne music that seeped out of the p.a. system.

Mary Katherine looked up at me. "I called David today. He has a good-sized boat. I thought someday this week we could borrow it and go out into the Gulf."

"I'd feel funny about borrowing his boat."

"It used to be half mine. As far as he's concerned it still is. He doesn't get jealous. We could fish. When was the last time you went fishing?"

"In high school."

"It's a good boat. There's no radio or anything, but if it's a nice day we could go out a couple of miles without worrying."

I felt secure enough in her affections to agree. I thought how good barbecued kingfish would taste. "The king of fish, the kingfish," Mr. Granger used to say.

We agreed to go out the day after tomorrow. Canales owed me a day off.

"Would you like to do that, Nat?" Mary Katherine asked. The boy nodded as he revolved his ice cream cone around his tongue.

"Would you like to stay at Jeff's tonight?"

"I guess so," he said warily.

Nat went to sleep early, instantly, and we put him in the center of the double bed and got in on either side of him—leaving our underwear on—and kissed each other good night across his body.

"Do you mind this?" she whispered. "Should we have stayed home?"

"I'm glad you came," I said, and fell asleep with the boy's light snoring in my ear.

"I really appreciate you covering for me," Canales told me the next morning. Sara was with him. They treated each other with icy courtesy and me with elaborate warmth.

"You look nice today," Sara said. "Did you get a haircut or something?"

"No," I said.

"Well, you look nice anyway."

It was a normal day. I climbed the pulpit when it was my turn to m.c. and did the routine straight. The porpoises responded well enough—no doubt to the audience they seemed joyful and impulsive, but to my eye they were solemn, formal, their gestures as practiced and dispassionate as those of a priest at daily mass. I knew they had been expecting something from me today, more wild improvisation, but I simply loomed above them and sent them on their errands.

Bill Mason was there for the last show. He stood with two

of his assistants by the ticket booth, dressed in his tailored jeans outfit. He was a bigger man than he seemed on TV, his bald head neat and evenly tanned, his beard sun-bleached. A few people recognized him on the way out, and it was a while before he could extract himself from their attentions and come over. When Canales introduced us, Mason put his hand out resolutely, but the shake itself was limp; it suggested a moody, reserved power.

"Goddamn, you boys have done good with that porpoise," he said. "You weren't fooling me, were you, Mando?" He went over to the side of the pool and bent down. Sammy presented his pectoral fin to be scratched. Wanda stayed away.

"Any health problems?" Mason asked.

"Not so far," Canales said. "Of course we shot them up with antibiotics as soon as we caught them. Wanda has a mild case of rot over by her right ear but Sammy hasn't caught it."

Mason stood up. "That's a fine animal. There's not a mark on him. You can barely even see the waterlines."

"He's about the best I've seen," Canales agreed. "A joy to work with."

"Well, let's all go run up my expense account," Mason said. "You fellas know a good restaurant in this Corpus Christi place?"

"I'm afraid I'll have to bow out," I said. "I've got to go by the hospital to see Mr. Granger."

"That's the man who owns this animal?"

"That's right."

"He coming along okay?"

"I think so. He's still pretty sick."

"You tell him to get well. I might want to be doing some horse-trading with him."

"I'll tell him," I said.

"Well, Jeff," Mason said, "I'm sure sorry you can't come along, but I'll catch up to you later. We're going to be here awhile rounding up a few porpi in some of these bays you got here."

I shook his hand again and drove to the ferry, not bothering to get out of my car as it crossed the channel. Looking out through the window, I was relieved for some reason that no "porpi" were visible in the water. When the ferry landed I was not aware of it until a man in a Day-Glo orange hat leaned across the hood and clapped his hands sharply in front of my windshield, then held up for my inspection the wooden wedges he had pulled from beneath my tires.

The hospital elevator that took me to Mr. Granger's floor let me out at a panoramic window that looked out over the bay. It was dusk. The T-heads rested placidly on the water, gleaming with the white and orange excursion boats and the big sloops tied up to the yacht club docks. The water supported it all, a liquid plain. Above the seawall, along the curve of the bay, the office buildings rose above the bluffs. Once it had all been a sandbar where the Karankawas gathered to dig roots and hunt game in their ignorant, indolent, starving way. I asked myself, when I saw a fin break water at the bow of one of the excursion boats (lit up now against the dusk, with a few couples dancing on the upper deck), if none of this were here, if I were standing now on a sandbar starving and naked, what creature I might invoke to help stave off the special loneliness of my race. Surely *that*, that thing so far out in the water that showed nothing of itself except for that one fin, but whose benevolence was an innate belief in my savage mind, a constant like the warmth of the sun.

That would have been my totem. It *had* been my totem, until I dragged it ashore and demanded that it recognize me. I did not believe Freud. Totemism was not patricide, it was the opposite: a way I thought I could invoke my dead father, a way to put myself again into the range of his influence. But I had not been abiding by the spirit of the covenant; I had been using the porpoises, trying to force information from them. It seemed necessary now to restore them to what they had been before: powerful, shapeless specks on the water.

A man and a woman were just leaving Mr. Granger's room as I approached it. We passed in the hall, and the woman gave me a slight nod, as if she thought she should know me. They were no more than a year or two older than me, but they were both dressed very tastefully and maturely.

"Did you meet the Dawsons?" Mr. Granger asked me. "They were just here. They're a fine young couple. Brad and Ella."

"Who are they?" I asked.

"Brad's my lawyer now, ever since his father died. Crabmeat Dawson. Famous criminal lawyer."

I saw that other people besides the Dawsons had come to see him. The windowsill of the hospital room was covered with cards and flowers. Mr. Granger was reclined in the bed, and he was wearing one of his peculiar sport coats over the pale green hospital gown. His face was bloated—the cortisone, I guessed—so that his features were even more indefinite than usual. The only remaining reference point was the thick glasses whose unornamented wire frames cut into the swollen bridge of his nose.

"You shouldn't have come all this way to see me, Jeff," he said. His speech was a little slurred. I could see he was doped up. "I'd have been coming to see you in another couple days. Damn, I'm so embarrassed about this whole thing."

"You look good," I said.

"Well, I feel fine, especially now that I can see people. I tell you, I'm an old man and I should have been prepared for something like this, but I was scared when it happened, I don't mind telling you. It felt like I was already dead. I just lay there on the floor and looked up at all y'all people, and it was like I was trying to talk and you couldn't understand a thing I was saying. Like a bad dream."

"You were very calm. I was impressed with how calm you were."

"It was probably because I was trying to think of my last words. Maybe I won't need to for a while yet.

"You know, Jeff," he said, slurring his speech a little more than he had, "you were one of the reasons I was afraid to die. I would've felt like I'd abandoned you. I know I probably never meant all that much to you, but I always felt you'd sort of be like an orphan without me around."

"I've felt that way too," I said.

Mr. Granger pointed to the shelf. "See that card there? The one with the porpoise on it? See if you can guess who that's from."

I took the card down and looked at the engraved picture on the front.

"Go on and read it."

Inside there was a typeset notation—"Atlantic Bottle-nosed Dolphin (*Tursiops truncatus*)"—and beneath that a note from Mary Katherine in a neat, ornate handwriting I realized I had not yet encountered.

> I'm sorry our evening together was cut short by your illness. I truly enjoyed your company and hope we can resume our friendship when you're feeling better. Please take care of yourself and do everything the doctor tells you.
>
> Mary Katherine Severin

"Isn't that sweet?" Mr. Granger said. "She didn't have to do that."

I put the card back on the sill. "She likes you."

"I also got a card from our friend Mando. Read that one too, see what you think of it."

He indicated a bright yellow oversized card with a cartoon of a man sitting on the edge of the bed with his feet in a tub, a thermometer in his mouth, and a rain cloud over his head. "A little under the weather?" it read. I opened it, not bothering to read the punch line. The note was in a cramped, backward-slanting hand.

> Dude,
>   Sorry to hear you're not well. Hope this cheers you up. When you're back on your feet let's talk some business.
>
> Mando

"What do you suppose he means by 'business,' Jeff?"

"You know who Bill Mason is?"

"The TV star?"

"Uh-huh. He wants to buy Sammy. He was down at the

pool today. He and Mando are having dinner right now, trying to put a deal together."

"Why does he want Sammy?"

"To put him in the movies."

He chuckled a little until he saw I was serious. I told him about how we might be shut down.

"What do you think about all this?" he asked me. He seemed very confused.

"You'll get a good price for Sammy. Enough to make a profit, probably, on the whole operation. He'll give you something for Wanda too."

"That's not what you think."

"No, I think we should let them go."

Mr. Granger laid his head back on his pillow.

"None of this has worked out very well, has it?" he asked.

"It's nobody's fault."

"Look, I'll be out of here in a week or so, and then you and I'll straighten this mess out."

"I imagine Mando will bring Mason to see you tomorrow. He'll probably have an offer."

"I won't take it. We'll decide about it later. Right now I'm so doped up it hurts my head to think about it. I just feel bad about the whole damn thing."

I looked out the window. The excursion boat I had seen before was passing beneath the harbor bridge.

"I should have stayed in New Mexico," I said.

A nurse came in without knocking, placed a paper cup filled to the brim with pills on Mr. Granger's bed table and stood over him impatiently as he began to swallow them.

"Take three or four together," she said. "You don't have to take them one at a time."

"Miss," he said, "I have a very small gullet."

The nurse looked away as Mr. Granger continued with the pills. He lifted each one in his stubby fingers, inspected it, then finally washed it down.

"Visiting hours are now over," she said to me as if she were announcing the fact over the p.a. system. She seemed to take pleasure in being disagreeably efficient.

"I'll come back tomorrow night," I told Mr. Granger. "Don't worry about anything."

"Don't you bother, Jeff," he said, suddenly very drowsy. "That's a long drive for you and I'll be home soon anyway. You just take care of the porpoises."

Chapter 10

David's boat was a broad, heavyset Arkansas Traveler, with a homemade cabin and a red fiberglass deck that had faded to a rose color.

"It's a little old but it's a good boat," he said, helping me hook the trailer up to the hitch. "Keep it as long as you want. All weekend if you need it."

"Thanks," I said. We shook hands. David was obviously enjoying the whole scene, conferring upon me the mantle of responsibility both for his boat and for his ex-wife.

It was a calm day and we took the boat about a mile out into the Gulf. We caught three kingfish. We saw them writhing forty feet below the surface, gleaming in the steely blue water like creatures trapped in ice. When they were on the deck I dispatched them with a short club from David's tackle box and then cleaned them as we came back in. The entrails came out in one long neat train. I tossed them overboard along with the heads and then washed the split carcass in seawater. Nat stood in the center of the boat, wearing his lifejacket, watching in silence until I noticed that the swells were up and that he was seasick.

He recovered once we were within the protection of the jetties, and fell asleep as soon as he was home. I built a fire in a little grill below the house, filleted one of the kingfish, and cooked half of it over a piece of aluminum foil. We ate with our fingers directly from the grill. It was as I remembered it: firm, a little dry.

"Do you like it?" I asked Mary Katherine.

She nodded, her mouth full.

I left her early in the evening. I wanted to check on the porpoises and then drive into Corpus to see Mr. Granger. When they saw me come through the gate Wanda and Sammy rose up from the water like missiles, and I felt a great relief I had not been expecting, as if I were a parent who had seen a child hit by a car and had come home to his own children to find them safe.

Canales had left a note. Both animals had botched the last show and so were four pounds short for their feeding, which I was to make up. And I was to treat Wanda's fungus, which had reoccurred in an isolated patch on her gums.

I had her open her mouth and swabbed the purple ointment inside. Sammy tried to grab the applicator and managed to spill half the bottle of medicine into the water. I fed them their fish, throwing whole smelt into their open mouths and rubbing their ventral sides with my feet while they made their clicking sounds and blew bubbles with their spiracles. When I left they began their usual commotion, leaping high into the air and landing on their backs.

But I locked the gate between us and drove into Corpus. Mr. Granger had regained some of his color. He was still pale, but diffused beneath his skin there was a faint rosy tincture of health. Someone had brought him a tiny glass seashell, a paperweight, that Mr. Granger glanced at as he talked to me. It caught the fading light like a prism.

"Mando came by with that Bill Mason today," he said. "Hell of a nice fella."

"Did he make you an offer?"

"Roundabout. He said he didn't think it was appropriate to discuss business while I was sick, but that he wanted me to think about fifty thousand dollars. We've got ourselves a valuable property there, Jeff. I told him I'd give him an answer in a week, after I'd talked to you. You still against it?"

"Yes."

"He as much as offered you a job, too, working with Sammy. You and Mando. Training him for the movie. I told him you had some acting experience."

"Thanks." I laughed. "Really, thank you for not selling right away."

"Well, I won't pretend I'm not tempted to take him up on it. But I'm with you—I'd just rather get out of the whole thing. It was a mistake, that's all there is to it. Just a mistake."

I sat with him for another half hour. He didn't seem to want to talk much.

"Should I turn on the TV?" I asked him.

He shook his head and looked out the window.

"I always thought the bayfront was so pretty," he said. "You wouldn't believe how it's changed since I first came here. The water used to be clearer. I think all that dredging muddied it up."

He was silent for a long time. "I'm not much company," he said. He started to cry a little.

"It's all right."

"I'm just an old blabberpuss."

"No, you're not. You're tired. And you're doped up."

"Maybe that's it," he said. "I *do* feel like I'm dragging a little."

"Once you're out of here you'll be back to normal," I said. "You're just worn out."

He fell asleep like a child. I tiptoed out of his room and drove back to Port Aransas. At Mary Katherine's house Nat answered the door in his pajamas.

"I've got to go to bed," he told me.

I stood outside his room while Mary Katherine tucked him in. I could hear them whispering to each other.

"He wants to say good night to you," she said when she came out of the room. I went in and sat on the edge of Nat's bed.

"Good night," I said, not knowing what I was supposed to do or say.

"Are you going to be here all night?"

"Yeah. Is that okay?"

"I guess so," he said.

"How are you feeling? You're not still sick at your stomach, are you?"

"No," he said, "I'm all right now." He looked up at me, wanting something.

I did not know what to say to him. I kissed him good night.

"When I was Nat's age," I told Mary Katherine after he had gone to sleep, "I thought that I could change into anybody I wanted. I could become Donald Duck if I wanted to, actually *be* Donald Duck. I'd walk down the street with my mother, holding her hand, and tell myself, 'I have the power to become Donald Duck!' "

"Did you ever try it?"

"No."

"Why not?"

"Knowing I had the power seemed enough."

"That's the first secret thing about yourself you've ever told me," she said.

I spent the rest of the evening skimming through her cetacean books, coming again and again to the grisly whaling pictures, the mass strandings, the dolphins in coffin-sized Plexiglas tanks with electrodes implanted into their brains. Mary Katherine sat on the other side of the room, watching Jacques Cousteau.

When it was late we walked out onto the porch. Mary Katherine wriggled out of her corduroy jeans and the blouse she was wearing. She stood there, naked, leaning against the rail.

I touched her skin, the salt rime that covered it.

"Donald Duck." She laughed. "What is that called, the transmigration of souls?"

"Something like that," I said. We made love and slept and dreamt, and though I forgot my dreams they were with me all the next day, sweet and unapproachable. It was a good day: the porpoises performed well, we ate another kingfish, and the drive into Corpus was smooth and relaxing.

I took a child's pleasure in riding the hospital elevator, an amazing conveyance I resolved to appreciate more in the future. I passed the nurses' station on my way down to Mr. Granger's room, and immediately one of the nurses came running down the corridor after me. She touched me on the arm and told me Mr. Granger was dead.

She used the word "expired." "Mr. Granger expired a little while ago."

"Oh," I said. I looked at her. She was young, with a puffy face and a bad complexion. I had the strangest urge to comfort her.

"You may go in if you like."

"Okay," I said. I didn't want to go in but I didn't know what else to do. The glass seashell was still on the windowsill. Some of the cards had fallen to the floor. His arm must have flung spasmodically across the sill and then dropped to the side of the bed, where it rested now, or rather lay with its inert weight, the fingers of the hand gnarled like a root system.

Dr. Rush was there, speaking to an intern in a very low, casual tone.

"They shouldn't have let you in yet," he said. "I thought they knew better." He put his hand on my shoulder, a touch so familiar and dreadful a chill dappled my spine.

"He had a massive coronary. Just a few minutes ago. It's something that happens."

The intern looked at me sorrowfully. He was younger than I was, with big basset-hound eyes and a full beard.

I looked down at Mr. Granger, thinking of those words, "massive coronary," and almost felt the force that had thrown him back onto the bed where he lay now as still as the heavy air outside. I saw the teeth in his open mouth, where all the life that had been in his body seemed compacted, waiting for final release. No breath came or went, nothing hovered there. The stillness frightened me, that and the blue, the actual blue of the skin. How would they get that out?

"Why don't you go sit down in the waiting room?" Rush said to me. "You really shouldn't be here now, they shouldn't have let you in. Wait around for a while and we'll have a talk."

I wandered down to the lounge at the end of the hall and sat on an overplush institutional sofa. A spasmodic charge of grief took hold of my body, forcing open my tear ducts and causing me to cramp forward on the couch. Then, abruptly, I had control again.

The same nurse came up to me, sounding very contrite.

"Would you like a cup of coffee? I could get you some coffee."

"I don't think so. Thank you."

"I'm very sorry. I thought he was . . . prepared. I shouldn't have let you go in."

"Don't worry about it," I said. "It doesn't make any difference."

There was a pay phone on the opposite wall. I put in some change and dialed Mary Katherine's number. The operator came on and told me it was long distance, even though I could look out the window across the dark empty bay and almost see the lights of Port Aransas. I put in my quarters and Molly answered the phone. Mary Katherine was working at school, she said, transcribing a backlog of data. "You can probably call her there."

"No, I'll see her at home in the morning."

But I was desperate to talk to someone, to *move*, to shake off the still, infected air that seemed to cling to me. I went down to the lobby, changed a dollar, and came back up and called Canales.

"Oh, Jesus," he said. "Well . . . shit, I don't know what to say, man."

"It was a massive coronary," I said, using the words that Rush had given me.

"Look, is there anything I should do?"

"I don't think so. I haven't had much of a chance to think yet. I might not be in tomorrow."

"Sure thing. And don't worry about the animals. I'll take good care of them."

When I hung up the phone and turned around I saw Miles Randolph, the columnist, sitting on the couch, his shoulders hunched forward so that the collar of his shapeless gray suit rode high on the back of his neck. He was slung so low in the couch it looked as if he would never be able to get up, but he sprang to his feet as soon as he saw me.

"Hell of a thing," he said, shaking my hand. "Dude was an old friend of mine, you know."

"You told me," I said.

"I'll give him one hell of an obit."

"That's good."

"Still got that porpoise thing over there?"

"Uh-huh."

"I sure liked those porpoises. They're almost human, aren't they?"

He went on with his hard-bitten, cheery nonsense. He was one of those people who are energized by death. He began a string of anecdotes about Mr. Granger that Rush mercifully cut short when he joined us. Randolph shook his hand, called him "Doc."

"Well, it's a sad thing," Rush said. "But I'd say he lived a pretty full life."

"That's the truth," Randolph said.

The elevator doors opened. The couple I had seen earlier, the Dawsons, came out and walked up urgently to Rush. It was the wife who spoke. The husband stood behind her, mute and unreadable.

"Can we see him?" she asked.

"In a minute," Rush said.

"Was anyone with him?"

"Not at the time, no." She looked down and then directly up at me. She had a pretty, edgy face, discreetly made up.

"You're Jeff?"

"Yes."

"I'm Ella." She offered her hand forthrightly and then introduced her husband, Brad, who leaned forward from behind her and gave me a firm, fleshy handshake.

"We're the Dawsons," Ella added.

"He told me about you," I said. I introduced them to Randolph, simply out of form, and he began a monologue about how "newspapermen" see a lot of death. Rush went back down to the room and returned a few moments later.

"You can go in now if you want," he said.

Ella looked at me. "Are you coming?"

"Not right now."

"Will you wait for us?"

"Of course."

Randolph went with them uninvited into the room. Rush stayed with me.

"Jeff," he said, "I've got to be going. I'm damn sorry. I think you and I have seen a little too much of each other under these circumstances."

"Thank you," I said.

"You go home and get some sleep. Will you be able to? I could get you something."

"No, I'm fine. I feel all right."

The Dawsons came out, Ella unabashedly in tears, her husband's face red and puffy.

"Shall we have a cup of coffee?" she suggested.

"Thank you," Randolph said, including himself in the invitation, "but I've got to go write this up."

The three of us went down to the coffee shop. Instead of a cup of coffee, I ordered a hamburger and a chocolate malt.

"That sounds good," Brad said. "I'll have that too."

Ella, through her sorrow, gave a little conspiratorial smile and ordered a hamburger for herself.

"How are your porpoises?" she asked me.

"Fine."

"He talked so much about them. And about you."

I smiled and looked at the two of them sitting together on the other side of the booth, their faces flushed with grief. I liked them very much and saw how Mr. Granger had been drawn to them. They must have filled the same role for him that my parents had.

"He was so sweet to us," Ella said. "We didn't really know him that well until a few years ago; he was just a client that Brad had sort of inherited from his father. Then our baby boy died. The infant death syndrome. Dude just appeared one day and asked if there was anything he could do and wouldn't take no for an answer. He helped us through the worst part. He kept us together really, individually and as a marriage."

Brad nodded and looked away toward the grill where our hamburgers were cooking.

"I'm sorry," I said, not sure exactly what I was sorry about.

"We all have our crosses," she said.

"Do you mind," she asked, "I don't want to sound presumptuous, but would you mind if Brad and I handled the funeral? Apparently there's no one except for the three of us to be consulted, and we owe him so much."

"I don't mind at all. I could help out with expenses."

"That's not necessary."

"I'd like to, though. A little, anyway."

When the food came Brad picked up his hamburger but could not seem to take a bite of it. He put it back down on his plate and started to cry.

"I just wish somebody could have been with him," he said.

Ella put her hand on his thigh.

"Please, eat," he told me.

I did as he said. I could have eaten two more hamburgers, but I got up to leave instead.

"Leave us your number," Ella said. "We'll call you tomorrow about the funeral."

Brad took a notebook out of the inside pocket of his sport coat. It was the same sort of gilt-edged notebook that Mr. Granger had carried. He wrote the number down and then stood to shake my hand.

"I'm glad we finally met you," Ella said.

I drove back to Port Aransas, easing out of the shock and into the warm hold of pure sorrow. I had to stop at the office of the Salt Sea and tell Lois. She turned the sound off the TV but left the picture on, so that while she cried silently and ground her teeth I watched a harsh, no-nonsense announcer standing by a mountain of tires, and then a woman singer on the *Tonight Show* prancing about absurdly, in silence, with her dress slit up to her thigh.

I waited a long time, listening to Lois cry, not knowing what to do.

"Will you be all right?" I asked finally.

"Oh, sure, honey. Don't you worry about me. I was just so sure he was going to get well, is all."

The phone was ringing when I got back to my room.

"I've been calling you," Mary Katherine said. "Molly said you sounded upset."

"Mr. Granger died."

"Oh, darling. I'll come over. Do you want me to?"

"Yes."

She showed up twenty minutes later with a bottle of wine and a little baggie of marijuana.

"I'm here all night," she said. "Molly's going to stay over with Nat."

"You don't have to do that. Besides, you need to get up early."

"I can take a day off," she said.

We sat on the floor and drank the wine. It was some sort of expensive wine. The marijuana was prime too—David had given it to her. It formed a hazy corolla around my skull, a new layer of brain.

"I don't know what to say about it," she said.

"Whatever comes into your head."

"I guess I'm upset too."

I sat back against the wall and rested my hand on a gas jet. Mary Katherine got up to open the window. As she sat on the floor opposite me I saw her as a porpoise might have, as an impulse felt deep in the body, at that place below the abdomen that a Taos guru had once pointed out to me as the stable center of the body. I felt her there, and it seemed almost pointless to reach out and touch her, but I did anyway.

"Let's go to sleep," she said. "You need to."

"I don't know if I can."

"You're almost out as it is. Come on, get up."

"They had to sedate me when my parents died," I said. "Both times. I wouldn't let myself go to sleep. I didn't want to wake up in the morning thinking everything was all right."

"Hey. You're grown up now, remember?"

Chapter 11

Mr. Granger's obituary was on the second page of the next morning's paper. LONGTIME COASTAL BEND BUSINESSMAN DIES. Randolph had sketched in some of Mr. Granger's biography—his years in South America, his early purchase of a great deal of land in Port Aransas, his lifelong belief that Corpus Christi and vicinity would be "the country's next Miami Beach."

It was a standard obit. The picture they had dug out of the files was twenty years old. Mr. Granger's face had a glossy, retouched look.

At the rosary in Corpus two days later Mr. Granger's face looked remarkably like that old photograph. It looked younger and stranger than I had ever known it. The Dawsons had managed to find a somewhat tasteful casket, but it was upholstered with an obscene, silky fullness, like the inside of a snake's mouth. The body lay there as if that was where it belonged, and when a funeral director in a clip-on bow tie closed the lid I could hear the soft rustle of the material meeting itself.

The funeral was held in the cathedral. Several hundred people were there. A monsignor talked in vague terms about eternal life, and then Brad Dawson and I and four older men wheeled the coffin down the aisle to the hearse.

Mary Katherine and I rode in a limousine with the Dawsons.

"What did you think?" Ella asked, turning toward us from the fold-down seat.

"It was fine," Mary Katherine said.

"Yeah, that was a fine funeral," the driver said. "Must have been quite a guy." He and the funeral director sitting beside him began to talk about the limousine's fuel economy. The four of us kept quiet. Finally the funeral director realized we were listening to them.

"Hey, I'm sorry," he said. "If you'd rather we didn't talk, no problem."

"I think I would," I said.

"Fine. Sorry."

At the cemetery we stood beneath the awning as the monsignor struggled to hold the pages of his missal down in the wind. To the east a line of high-rise apartments hogged the horizon, but in the gaps between them I could see Corpus Christi Bay, penetrated by private motel piers.

Canales stood on the far side of the grave, dressed in a three-piece charcoal suit, his head bowed, his hands clasped together over his groin. Sara stood beside him, holding his arm. When it was over Canales came up to me and put his hand on my shoulder.

"See you back in Port A," he said.

"Yeah."

After the limo had dropped us off at the cathedral Mary Katherine and I got into my car and drove to the Dawsons' house, where there was to be what Ella had referred to as "a sort of memorial brunch."

"Do you like them?" I asked Mary Katherine on the way.

"Yes, I do. They're pretty well-bred, aren't they? But they're very nice."

The Dawsons lived in a sprawling one-story house on Ocean Drive. There was a large window on the east wall of the living room that looked down a slope to a swimming pool and, beyond that, the open bay with a private dock. In front of the

window the caterers had set up a buffet of chicken wings, dev-
iled eggs, ham, and coffee cake, all of it served by black teenagers in red jackets. At the far end of the big room was an open
bar.

Perhaps a hundred people were there. Most of them were
middle-aged or older. They held Bloody Marys and laughed
heartily as they told one another stories about Mr. Granger.

"It sure is a jolly affair," Mary Katherine whispered to me.

I recognized a few of the guests, people who had come
over to my parents' house occasionally with Mr. Granger.
None of them seemed to remember me.

"Would you like to be introduced around?" Ella asked me.

"Frankly, no," I said. "We can't stay that long."

"Get something to eat at least. Jeff, I think Brad wants to
talk to you. He's around here somewhere. There he is."

She waved him over.

"Why don't we go back to my office?" he said.

"I'll take care of Mary Katherine," Ella volunteered.

Brad led me down a long hallway and into a room paneled
in dark wood that matched the leather bindings of the law vol-
umes in his bookcase. On another wall, in glass cases, were other books, first editions, and on a broad coffee table beneath the
window a collection of paperweights. The seashell that had
been in Mr. Granger's room was sitting on Brad's desk, away
from the other paperweights, as if he was reluctant to add it to
his collection.

"Did you get something to eat?" he asked, wheeling a
plush leather chair out from behind his desk and indicating I
should sit there.

"I'll get something in a minute," I said, taking the chair
while Brad hitched up his pants—I hadn't seen that gesture in
a long time—and sat on the edge of the desk. He rubbed his
hands together sluggishly and looked out the window at the
swath of lawn and the bright turquoise pool sitting by the bay.

"I wanted to let you know that you've been named as an
heir in his will," he said. "I talked to the executor today, he's a
good friend of mine. You and I are both included, as a matter

of fact. We won't know what or how much until the formal reading. That'll probably be in a month or two.

"Frankly, I wouldn't expect a great deal. From what I understand, his affairs are a mess. It seemed for most of his life he couldn't miss, and then he just overextended himself toward the end without anybody noticing much. I think—myself—that he was just a little early with all this development. Five years or so might have made a difference. It's inevitable, the boom he kept talking about, but I'm afraid he missed it."

"What'll happen to the Porpoise Circus?"

"Who knows? He may have owned it outright, but most likely it's a corporate holding like some of these other things, the condominium or the restaurant. It'll be up to the shareholders, in that case. I'll try to find out what the deal is for you."

"I'd appreciate it," I said.

"I'll call around and get back to you," he said, making a note to do so.

"I'll tell you," he said, sliding off the desk onto his feet. "He was sure good to us. A lot of people were kind of embarrassed by him, but not us. We went through a pretty hairy time—what Ella told you about the other night—and goddamn he was there every day, rain or shine."

"I think he got something in return," I said.

"Jesus, I hope so. Well, look, let's get back to this party—whatever you call it. I just wanted you to have some idea of your prospects."

We shook hands again. He was one of those people who shake hands at the conclusion of each stage of a discussion, but it was learned behavior with him. I could tell he found it almost distasteful. There was a basic shyness about him that I liked.

I had a brief image of the two of them looking into the crib that morning, Brad howling perhaps like an animal, Ella standing there silently, something inside her drawing tighter and tighter until at last there was a deep, implosive scream.

In the living room an old man was playing the piano very

softly and very badly. It was a song I didn't know. Mary Katherine was standing in the corner holding a Bloody Mary, speaking politely to the monsignor, who was dressed in black now, his wild vestments stowed in the trunk of his car. He was about forty, with a thin flushed face and small teeth.

"We were arguing about whether animals have souls," Mary Katherine explained to me. "Apparently they don't, according to the Church."

"No, now, that's not what I said." He wagged a finger at her good-naturedly. The monsignor was trying to flirt but he did not know how—his voice was too high, and he could not keep still. "They have some sort of soul. What do you call it?" He snapped his fingers. "*Animus!* But they don't have a *divine* soul, because that is the direct result of God's intervention. Human beings are made in God's image. Now, I grant you that that could be interpreted loosely, but come on, a *pig* made in God's image?"

He began giggling.

"See?" Mary Katherine said to me. She looked flushed and radiant, and the monsignor and I were both charmed.

"Well," he said, gaining control of himself, "a lot of people are questioning a lot of things we once thought of as fundamental." He spread his hands in a gesture I remembered from long ago—*Oremus*—and said, "Who knows?"

We drifted away from him.

"Are you ready to go?" I asked Mary Katherine.

"If you are. What did Brad want?"

"I'm mentioned in the will."

"What do you get?"

"I won't know for a while. Come on, let's go."

We said our good-bys to Ella. She introduced us to the man she was talking to.

"Christ Almighty!" he said. "You're Joe Dowling's boy. You've sure grown up some, haven't you."

"I guess so," I said. "Nice to see you again."

"You had a chance to talk with Brad?" Ella asked me at the door.

"Yes," I said. "And thank you. This was a nice . . . brunch."

"We felt the need to do something," she said, "and I just sort of felt that he wouldn't have approved of anything gloomy."

"No, you're right."

"I hope we can get to be friends," she said. "The four of us."

Mary Katherine leaned forward and hugged her. "I hope so too," she said.

"What's going to happen now with the dolphins?" she asked me on the way home.

"There's no telling. Brad's going to find out for me."

"Mason's going to get them, you know. Sammy'll be a star and Wanda'll probably end up in some research lab someplace."

I said nothing. She slid across the seat to me.

"Jeff, let's try to think of something."

"I'm trying."

At the ferry we both got out of the car, but neither of us saw any porpoises.

"It's too late in the afternoon," Mary Katherine said. "They'll be up in Aransas Bay now."

I looked up the channel toward Aransas Bay, at the empty water. The seascape had changed, some force was being withheld from it, its "animus."

Far away in the channel I saw a fin break water, despite Mary Katherine's dictum. I held her hand, conscious of a desire to dive off the ferry and swim with all my strength toward that wild creature I could barely imagine.

"It looks like Mason's got your porpoises," Brad told me on the phone a few days later. "He moves fast, I'll say that for him. I had no idea how screwed up Dude's assets were. Apparently he didn't even have a majrrity of the shares for the Porpoise Circus, so all Mason had to do was wine and dine the board of directors, tell them the place was about to be closed down anyway, and offer them the money for the porpoises. Fifty-two thousand was what it came to.

"Does this interfere with some plans you had? The facility itself is still unsold. Maybe you could convince them to fix it up so it would conform to whatever these standards are, then you could catch a few more porpoises. . . ."

"That's not what I had in mind," I said.

"Well, if there's any way I can help."

"You've done a lot," I said. "Thank you."

"Let's get together for dinner soon. Ella wanted to know if you and Mary Katherine play bridge."

"No. Maybe we could learn."

"I'll give you a call," he said.

I went to work. Sara was there on the pulpit with a fish in each hand, offering them to the porpoises and then drawing them back.

"You're teasing them, Sara," I said. "Don't."

"I'm just playing with them." She threw them the fish.

"Where's Mando?" I asked.

"In the shed."

"Hey," he said. He was thawing fish.

"You didn't waste any time, did you?"

"You already heard about that, huh? Yeah, Mason was anxious to close the deal. He had to get back to Florida. He's holding a job open for you."

"I don't want a job."

"Well what, then?"

I started to tell him what Mr. Granger had said about letting the porpoises go, but I decided against it.

"I just think it was in bad taste."

"Maybe," he said. "I don't know. I'm not in a position to worry about that. This is my *chance*, man. I've been in this fucking business twelve, thirteen years and I've never come across an animal like Sammy, never had a break like that. Yeah, maybe it would have been better if we'd waited till the body was cold, but what can I say, the guy moves fast, he's an operator."

"When are they taking them to Florida?"

"Mason's coming back up next week. He'll hang around a few days and then fly back with them. I figure we close down this weekend and let them rest up all next week till he comes. You want the first show today?"

"I don't care."

"Look, I'm sorry if this upsets you. You better get on the phone today and tell Mason you want that job. I don't know how long he'll hold it open."

"I don't want the job," I said.

"Think about it, man. That's my advice to you."

During the first show Sammy was marvelous. He knew something. He was keyed up, and I could sense the even release of tension that was the essence of athletic form and grace. Wanda was sluggish, unconcerned. She broke speed twice during the buildup for her high leap, so that I had to stall at the mike, looking down at the shadow of her submerged body.

"She's circling now ... she's picking up speed ... she's really wound up ... here she comes ... she's about to jump ... almost here...."

Finally her form burst free from the water, the hard beak sailing upward like the nose cone of a rocket, the eyes on the sides of her head swiveling forward, toward me, locking me into the field of their stereoscopic vision. At the crest of her leap she accepted the fish from my hand, her teeth closing gently around it in that split second before gravity pulled her down again.

This was the part of her performance that always touched me the most—the clumsy buildup, and the redeeming delicacy of her flight. The delicacy existed only in my mind. I knew the audience saw only a great mass of scarred blubber exploding into the air. But I knew that behind the power, buried deep inside that blank hulk, there was some incomprehensibly strange awareness.

After work Lois stopped me on my way to my room and handed me a postcard, the only piece of mail I had received in months. She hung around the door for a while, talking about Mr. Granger, and her husband, and how at her age she was all alone.

"Would you like to come in and sit down?" I asked.

"Oh no, I don't expect I'd better. You've got things to do. I just need to let off a little steam now and then."

The postcard was from the Seamstress. The picture on the front was of a miniature golf course in some town in northern California.

"Here's where I ended up," she wrote. "I'm getting my certification as a Rolfe therapist. Still with the porpoises? I miss you sometimes. Come up and see me if you want."

I threw the postcard on the bed and stared at it, at the goony-looking golfer with a crewcut and baggy pants, his knees together as if he were trying to keep from wetting his pants, about to knock the ball between the legs of a giant chipmunk. For a moment I could smell the pine needles, the exalted air of the Sierras. I thought of what it would be like to sit before a fire again, the Seamstress Rolfing my back while our granola cookies browned in the oven.

I walked to Mary Katherine's house and stood for a moment in her unpaved driveway, looking up at the kitchen window where I could see her washing dishes in a brilliant frame of yellow light. She moved fluidly, almost as if she were conscious of impressing me, her arms drifting softly in the light from sink to dish drainer.

When she opened the door she wiped her soapy hands on her hips.

"I'm making gumbo," she said. "Have you eaten?"

"Not yet."

"Good. And I'm going to make a cake later. Tomorrow's Nat's birthday."

"Why didn't you tell me?"

"It slipped my mind," she said rather brusquely.

"I'll drive into Corpus after dinner and get him something."

"That's crazy. You don't have to do that."

"What do you mean? I want to."

"Okay," she said, and went into the kitchen and shifted the magnets around on the refrigerator.

"What's the matter?" I asked.

"Nothing. Here, dinner's ready." She handed me a bowl of gumbo and got one for herself. It was dark and slick, with an occasional bright pink shrimp drifting up through the slimy film of okra on top.

"It tastes like shit, doesn't it?" she asked.

"What's wrong?"

"I'm just upset. Number one, I'm a lousy cook. All day long I've been thinking about the Dawsons and their baby. And guess what I saw this morning? I passed Mason's catch boat in Lydia Ann. They'd just caught two dolphins. They were lying on the deck. I didn't know what to do. I just shot them the finger.

"And then you walk in here like you're Nat's father, which you're not, like you have every right in the world to drive sixty miles to buy him a birthday present. Do you have any idea how many guys there are out there who really get off on giving some poor kid a birthday present and then just dropping out of his life; trying to impress you about how kindhearted they are, how much they love children, but they just can't get tied down, baby. And you know what they get him, every time? War toys. I mean like plastic M-*Sixteens!*"

"I'm not like that," I said.

"I know," she said. "I know you're not." She left the spoon in her gumbo and sat back in her chair. "How did it go today? How are Wanda and Sammy?"

"More bad news. Mason's bought them."

"Oh no," she said. "Already? But they're not gone yet?"

"No, he's gone to Florida. He's coming back for them late next week."

"Then there's still time."

"For what?"

"You know what, Jeff. For us to let them go."

I didn't answer her.

"That's what Mr. Granger wanted," she said.

"He's dead now."

"But that's what he *wanted!* You know that!"

"Yes, but what you're talking about now is a major theft. Besides, how do we know they won't be better off with Mason?"

"Christ!" she said. She picked up our half-eaten bowls of gumbo and dropped them into the leftover suds in the sink. The water turned dark.

"Tell me," I said. "How do we know?"

"That's just something you and I know," she said patiently. She opened the refrigerator, pulled out the vegetable tray, and pretended to look for something there.

"You'll catch cold," I told her.

"I don't care," she said, crying now.

I put my hands on her shoulders and drew her away from the cold air. She fell back onto my chest.

"You know I'm thinking about it," I said.

I drove into Corpus, thinking about it, thinking how it might be done, but the act did not seem as pure to me as it did to Mary Katherine. I was not sure about my motives, whether it might not be an act of cruelty to the porpoises to cast them out now from our company, which they had come to love and even to understand a little.

The only place open in Corpus that sold toys was an all-night drugstore, and they seemed to specialize in various weapons tied in with TV cop shows. I found a benign counterpart of GI Joe among the SWAT arsenals and handcuffs, a figure called Big Bert, whose ankles and wrists swiveled and whose joints moved stiffly back and forth like those of a man crippled with arthritis. On the box it said "Big Bert's Deep Sea Adventure," and the package included a diving bell, a giant squid, and a rubber dolphin named Chubby whose job it was, according to the scenario laid out on the side of the box, to deliver Bert's messages to the surface and to help him out in case of trouble from the giant squid.

I brought it back.

"He'll love it," Mary Katherine said. "I'm sorry for what I said before. I can't believe I said that to you, of all people.

"I decided to shoot for a three-layer cake. It may be a little too ambitious, after the gumbo debacle."

Three round cake pans were already cooling on the porch. She was working on the frosting now, beating it with a portable electric mixer.

An abrupt thought came to me. "I want to get married," I said.

She didn't answer or look up, but concentrated her attention on the cake. She stacked the layers on top of one another, bonding them together with the frosting. All three layers were lopsided, but by fitting the angles together she was able to make the cake reasonably even. When it was completely frosted she took a green aerosol cake-decorating can and wrote "Happy Birthday, Nat" in large droopy letters across the surface, then trimmed the circumference with an uneven hedge of green icing.

"If that doesn't rot his teeth, nothing will," she said.

When the cake was finished we went to bed and lay there without speaking.

"I'm thinking," she said.

"I know you are."

I fell asleep and did not stir until she woke me in the morning.

"I've got to get up," she said. "I've missed too many days lately. You want some breakfast?"

"Sure."

"Why don't you wake Nat up?"

"It's so early."

"It's his birthday. He won't sleep much longer anyway. Besides, I like for you to wake him."

I went into Nat's room and whispered "Happy Birthday" softly into his ear.

"Is it time to get up?" he said.

"It's a little early."

"Today's my birthday."

"I know."

He stretched, overcome with some sedate joy I could remember feeling a long time ago. The three of us ate breakfast at the little dining-room table. Mary Katherine had bought birthday napkins. Nat kept smiling to himself and covering his mouth with his hand so we wouldn't see.

"When can I open my presents?"

"This evening, when Jeff comes back from work."

He looked up at me, wondering who I was now that he had to wait all day for my return.

For most of the day I kept my distance from Canales, and he didn't seem eager to fall into conversation with me. It was almost over, the whole thing was almost over. We worked the porpoises for form's sake, to give them something to do.

"We're almost out of fish," Canales said. "You want to go into Corpus tomorrow for some more or shall I?"

"I don't care," I said.

"You go. If I go I'll have to take Sara, and she'll have a list of errands a mile long. Just get the regular amount—if we don't use it all up before Mason comes he can take it with him. Oh, and stop at the vet and get Wanda some more medicine. I'll call the prescription in. Take the whole day if you want. There won't be much happening here."

After work I went immediately to Mary Katherine's house. Nat's birthday cake was on display on a card table, and Molly and Joshua were there, along with a boy from down the street Nat didn't like but whom Mary Katherine had invited anyway. The two boys were playing with an expensive, nearly full-sized pinball machine Nat's father had dropped off earlier in the day.

After the cake and ice cream Nat opened his presents. His grandparents had sent him a blackboard and a little desk that I had to assemble. Molly gave him a plain wooden armadillo she had bought in Austin that rolled around on wheels. From his mother he got a set of plastic farm animals and three T-shirts.

"Oh boy, Big Bert!" Nat said when he opened my package.

"Let me see!" the neighbor kid said. He snatched Chubby the Dolphin and ran around the room guiding it through the air and making airplane sounds under his breath. Nat watched him anxiously, exercising a touching forbearance. When the kid finally brought Chubby back and picked up the giant squid instead, Nat slyly hid the rubber dolphin in his pocket. Molly set Joshua down on the pile of wrapping paper, where he rustled about and babbled to himself.

The next morning I drove into Corpus to get the fish. Mary Katherine decided at the last moment to come along, forsaking her work for the day. We dropped Nat off at Molly's house and then drove to the ferry. There was a long line of cars waiting to get across and we had to wait for almost an hour, inching along behind a carload of hungover surfers who kept leaning their heads out the windows and throwing up on the pavement and then waving to us, thanking us for our indulgence.

Once we were across we made good time. We crossed the harbor bridge and then drove down to a dockside warehouse on the ship channel, where we loaded frozen blocks of herring and smelt and cod—the combination of fish that Canales considered a balanced porpoise diet—into a big cooler in the bed of the pickup.

The veterinarian's office was a few blocks inland from the bay in a prosperous neighborhood. The waiting room was filled with women holding quivering poodles with long painted nails.

The vet invited us into the back while he dispensed Wanda's medicine. He was a small, brisk, immaculately groomed man who smelled strongly of flea powder.

"That porpoise doing okay?" he asked me.

"I think so. The fungus seems to be clearing up a little."

"I'd like to get down there and look her over sometime. I've never seen one close up, really, but that's one animal I'd like to study. They've got more than one stomach, did you know that?"

"That's what I read."

"And that sonar business is interesting as hell."

He handed me the medicine. One of the assistants brought in a Pekingese and set it on the examining table. The vet looked into its ears.

"To tell you the truth," he said, "I'm getting a little tired of these goddamn snothounds."

We fooled around the rest of the day, went to an afternoon movie and then to the art museum, which featured an exhibit of black canvases that had been contorted in various ways, and groups of geometrical figures sculpted in chocolate and displayed in refrigerated glass cases.

Afterward we sat on the seawall, watching the tiny sailboats shuttling back and forth to the spoil islands, the barren land forms that had been deposited there when the ship channel was dredged. Children in ski belts hiked out over the boats, reining them tightly into the breeze. The water was uncharacteristically luminous.

I was feeling peaceful, far removed from that tortured personality who was trying to decide whether or not to let the porpoises free. I melded into the mood; all I wanted was to be calm, to go about my life in an orderly and reasonable fashion.

"What are we going to do about them?" Mary Katherine asked me.

"I'm giving it a lot of thought."

"If we did it right, really planned it and did it so that we always had Sammy and Wanda's interests at heart, we could get so much popular support you wouldn't believe it. The Sierra Club, Defenders of Wildlife, Friends of the Earth."

"Is that what we want? Would we be doing it to impress those people?"

"Not to impress them, Jeff, to involve them! This is an *issue!*"

"It's not an issue," I said. "Not for me."

We had an early dinner at an oyster bar, both of us sulking a little, and then drove back to Port Aransas. It was nearly dusk when we got back to the ferry. I got out of the car and looked down into the water and saw the change and was unaccountably scared. I could see all the way to the bottom of the channel; I could see stingrays twenty feet below the surface. The water was nearly as clear as a Caribbean lagoon.

"What happened?" Mary Katherine asked me.

"I'm not sure," I said. "It's like a weather inversion or

something. I've heard of it happening before. It lasts a few days and then muddies up again."

There were divers' flags all up and down the length of the channel, and as the ferry came in to dock I saw a great shadow pass beneath the boat: a manta ray, drawn inland by the confusion.

As soon as the wedges were pulled from my tires I drove to the Porpoise Circus, picking up speed along the way, not knowing why. Mary Katherine looked at me strangely but did not speak. She felt it too.

For a moment after I unlocked the gate and entered the compound I thought everything was fine. I saw Sammy's fin break the clear water and then Sammy himself leaping clear, higher up into the air than I had ever seen him go. I went up to the edge of the pool. I could see all the way to the bottom, could see the submerged chain-link fence beneath the dock. But it was all wrong.

"Where's Wanda?" I shouted.

"Oh, God!" Mary Katherine said.

I went into the shed and dialed Canales' number.

"Will you promise me one thing, Jeff?" he said. "Will you take it easy?"

"What happened to her, Mando?"

"We don't know. It was very sudden. It could have been the fungus. That can go to the lungs. It could have been a heart attack. It's impossible to say. I'm going to do an autopsy."

"Where is she?"

"Over here."

"I'm coming over there."

"Fine. Come on."

I hung up the phone and looked around at Mary Katherine, who stood in the doorway, watching my face. I wanted to move toward her, but I didn't know what to do with my body. My arms, that could have held her, all at once seemed absurd, uncontrollable appendages that were of no use in this element.

"I'm going over there," I said finally. "To Canales' house."

She came along silently. It was dark by the time we

reached the house. Sara opened the door. Her face was swollen, and there was a newly formed bruise on her cheek. Canales walked in from the kitchen, wearing his disco shirt and the shark's-tooth necklace.

"Sit down," he said. "Why don't I get you a beer or something?"

We sat down together on the couch, beneath a pair of shark jaws he had hung on the wall. I saw him leave and go into the kitchen and bring us two beers. I saw him put the beers down on the coffee table in front of us. I wanted to grab the shark's tooth and rip it off his neck.

"Okay," he said, sitting down. "About one o'clock this afternoon, right after the water began to clear, I was taking them through their behaviors, just to keep them from getting bored. Her breathing was a little labored, but slight, you know? Nothing bad. Then it got worse, like she wasn't breathing at all. So I winched up the false bottom. That took awhile. Okay, she's up there, I thought she'd swallowed something, that there was an obstruction. But I couldn't find anything. I didn't know what to do, all of a sudden she starts to breathe again, very painful breathing but at least she's getting air, right? So I figured I had a little time. I called this vet I know in Miami. He wasn't home. I went back out to check on her. She just lay there and sort of gasped, and that was it."

He leaned back in his chair and made a gesture of resignation with his hands.

"I'm sorry, Jeff, I really am, man. I'll do the autopsy tonight. We'll find out what it was. Maybe she caught some sort of weird virus, maybe it has something to do with the clear water, some parasite came in."

I noticed Sara staring hatefully at him from the kitchen bar, fingering the bruise on her cheek.

Canales stood up. "She's out here," he said softly.

I followed him out through the kitchen door and into the garage. He reached up in the darkness and pulled the cord on a bare yellow light bulb. Wanda was lying on a blanket in the center of the concrete floor. I didn't recognize her—she was twice the girth she had been, all that unsupported weight bearing down on her. Her eyes were open, and I saw the whites, still and swollen, crowding the lifeless iris. There was the hole in her fin, and the propeller scar, and the uncured fungus at the side of her head.

Canales held back reverently and didn't speak. I looked at the shark's tooth at his throat and was suddenly no longer able to control myself. I sent my fist flying toward his nose, remembering that other night when I had done the same thing in Wanda's defense and heard the bone snap beneath my hand.

He ducked the fist easily enough, but slipped in the process and hit his head on a vise. It didn't hurt him much.

"What sort of piddly shit is this?" he said.

"I'm sorry. I apologize."

"This is not like you, man."

"I realize that."

"Why don't you just go home now. I'm sorry about your porpoise. I realize you're completely innocent, of course. The whole thing is my fault."

Mary Katherine came out now for the first time. She looked down at Wanda and took my hand.

"Jeff?" I heard her say. "Honey?"

"I want to bury her," I said. "I don't want her in this garage. It smells like turpentine."

"It's dark," Canales said. "Besides, we have to find out what killed her."

"We killed her," I said. "Now let's bury her."

"All right," Canales said. "I'll put down heart attack on the forms."

We took her to one of Mr. Granger's undeveloped subdivision sites on the far side of the island, and the four of us worked for two hours digging a hole deep enough. Then we dragged Wanda's body from the back of Canales' pickup, wrapped it in several blankets, and lowered it as gently as possible into the hole. It was unbearable, the thought of Wanda undergoing a terrestrial burial, but it would have been worse to think that she might wash up one day on the beach. We shoveled the sand back on top of her, and stood there awhile with nothing to say, then drove away in our separate cars. "I'm going to the pool," I told Mary Katherine when we reached her house.

"Will you come back later?" she asked. "I don't particularly want to be by myself tonight."

"I'll be there in a little while," I said.

"You know how Sara got that bruise?" she asked after a moment.

"I can guess."

"He threw a bottle of beer at her. That's what she told me while you were out in the garage. He's such a jerk."

I didn't want to argue with her, knowing I was as much a jerk as Canales. Looking at her, I felt a nagging loss, the realization that something was gone from our life together.

At the pool I stood and watched Sammy swim in circles, his eyes always above the waterline, watching me. He needed something from me, but I didn't know what it was or how I could give it to him.

I closed my eyes and imagined the sorrow that grew like a tumor deep in Sammy's body, a growth that could not be dissolved or dislodged. I could see his fear too, understanding that the fear had no focus, that the malevolence it tried to grapple with was as diffuse as the clear water that had invaded his environment.

I tossed a fish out to him. He regarded it with curiosity and left it alone. But I called him over and placed another fish gently in his mouth, like a priest dispensing a host. He reared his head back, holding the fish by its tail, then let it go down into his throat.

Thank God, I thought, at least he'll eat.

"You were walking in your sleep last night," Mary Katherine said, "did you know?"

I thought for a moment, and had a dim recollection of cruising around in the darkness on some strange errand.

"You went into Nat's room," she said, unplugging the coffee pot and sitting down. Her face was puffy and haggard. "He said you just went in there and sat on his bed and babbled nonsense syllables."

"Did I scare him?"

"No. I don't think so. I told him about Wanda. He knows we're both upset."

"What time is it?"

"Eleven. I slept late too."

We could hear Nat beneath the house, playing with his birthday toys, trying to guard them from the boy down the street.

"How was Sammy?"

"He's functioning," I said. "I got him to eat."

"The poor thing."

"I'm ready to do it," I told her.

She looked at me solemnly. "You're sure?"

"We don't have that much time," I said, not feeling it was necessary to answer her. "We'll have to readapt him somehow."

"You don't mind committing grand theft or whatever it will be?"

"No."

"All right. Let's talk about what we'll do."

"I don't think you should be involved. It isn't necessary."

"I'm involved, okay? How will we do it?"

"First we'll get him used to live fish again. Then one night this week we'll get David's boat and let him follow us. We'll go way down into Laguna Madre. There are a lot of vacant spoil islands down there; we'll just pitch camp and stay until he feels secure enough to leave us. Of course he may swim off as soon as we let him out of the pool. If that's the case, fine."

"He won't want to leave us," Mary Katherine said. "There've been cases of dolphins who were released going out of their way to jump back into the nets of the capture boats."

"At least then it'll be up to him," I said.

"How will we get him out of the pool? The two of us can't lift him over by ourselves."

"I can unhook the chain-link below the dock and close it back again after he's out."

She nodded silently. "What about the other thing? Do you still want to marry me?"

"Of course I do."

"Let's do it before we let him go."

"Okay," I said, and then mouthed the word again. Okay.

Chapter 12

We called her parents in Oklahoma City.

"Who are you, exactly?" her father asked me.

"Nobody you have to worry about," I said.

"I don't know that that's very reassuring," her mother said from the extension. "Now I'm going to fly there this minute and meet you face to face, young man. I have a grandson to think about, you know."

"I know, and I think you're taking this whole thing very calmly."

"But what's the hurry if she's not pregnant?" the father asked.

What could I say: We're young and in love?

"I'll put Mary Katherine on again," I said.

"Trust me," she told them, and they did.

"Okay," her mother said. "We welcome you with open arms, sort of, because Mary Katherine says you're all right. But we want to inspect you. We're coming down there or you're coming up here no more than two weeks after the wedding. You understand? Two weeks."

"I should have waited until afterward," Mary Katherine said when we'd hung up, "but I just couldn't do that to them. They're good parents. You'll like them."

Nat took the news—"Honey, would you like Jeff to come live with us?"—with a good-natured shrug. I was in. We went that afternoon to get our blood test, and then picked up a seine at the marine science building and drove down to the beach and pulled the net through the breakers. The water was still clear, and I could see the mullet suspended in the waves, riding them without effort. When we dragged the net onto the sand we found we had caught six or eight of them, as well as a small sand shark, which I prodded back into the surf with my foot. I threw the mullet into a plastic garbage can half-filled with seawater, put the lid on tight, and set it in the passenger seat of my car. We made another pass with the net and took a few more mullet, and decided for the time being that that was enough.

We stood on the beach for a moment when we were through, overcome by sadness, promise. A frigate bird flew along the shoreline, then a flock of pelicans, finally a series of nondescript shorebirds.

"Omens," Mary Katherine said. "The sky is full of omens."

With the barrel of live mullet sloshing in the front seat we drove to the compound. Canales' pickup was parked outside.

"Shit," I said. "I didn't think he'd be here this late."

"We'd better go in and talk to him. He might have heard us drive up."

We took the trash can out of the car and hid it on the far side of the compound. Inside Canales was feeding Sammy a large amount of dead fish all at once, occasionally making a signal with his hand and putting the animal through a routine that was half-hearted on both sides.

"I didn't know if you were coming or not," Canales said.

"How's the back of your head?"

"Better than the front would've been if you'd connected."

"I'm sorry, Mando."

"Listen, Mason's going to be here soon. You want that job or don't you?"

"No."

"You're crazy."

"Mary Katherine and I are getting married. Then we'll probably move to New Mexico."

He turned around to look at Mary Katherine. She glared at him.

"You really hate me, don't you?" he asked her.

"I haven't thought about it much."

"Well, shit," he said. "All's well that ends well."

He threw a handful of smelt into Sammy's open mouth. They landed together, like a bunch of rotten bananas. Sammy sprung up out of the water and walked across the pool on his tail just for the hell of it. His form was perfect, and for a moment Canales and I were allied in our appreciation of it.

Canales blew his whistle and threw Sammy an extra fish.

"When is Mason going to take him?" I asked.

"He'll be up here sometime tomorrow. I think he's planning on flying him back in his plane on Friday."

Friday was three days away. We could do it in that time. No problem.

We left and came back when Canales was gone. I dragged the garbage can out of its hiding place and chased one of the mullet around inside until I had a grip, then slung it into the pool, where in its disorientation it leaped straight into Sammy's forehead. The living fish scared him, and he retreated to the other side of the pool and stayed there while the mullet slipped in and out of the water over and over.

"It's been a long time," Mary Katherine said. "Still, I would've thought he'd take it right away."

"He's terrified," I said. "He doesn't know what's happening to him." I took another fish from the can and held it by its tail over the side of the pool. It was hard to keep my grip, but I managed to hold on until Sammy came over, as I directed him, and surfaced beneath the fish. He rolled over on his side, looking at it, puzzled. I put the fish in front of his beak and blew the whistle. He took the fish in his mouth and threw it high into the air, catching it again but not swallowing it.

"He has no idea what to do with it," Mary Katherine said.

"It may be because he's not hungry. I'll throw the rest in and maybe he'll eat them later."

But once the mullet were in the pool Sammy seemed to remember what they had once meant for him. He herded them together and began chasing them into a tight circle. They leaped out of the water four or five at a time, but very soon they had disappeared. In the dark clear water I could see the bright silver fish being overtaken by Sammy's dull gray shadow. He was eating them.

When all the mullet were gone I went out to the car and got my mask and the underwater light I'd bought for night diving in Belize. Jumping into the pool, I was startled all over again by the clarity of the water. Sammy swam toward me immediately and tried to take me upon his back, but I discouraged him, giving him instead a few strokes along his side.

The light, swinging from a lanyard around my neck, illuminated almost the whole bottom of the pool. Something was moving across the bottom—the shell of a hermit crab making its rickety way across the great submerged plain of the pool. It reminded me of an old man in an overcoat shambling across a desert.

Sammy's face was just behind my shoulder, watching me with frankness and curiosity. Looking up through the surface of the water, I could see the outline of Mary Katherine crouching on the dock, gazing down at me. I rose up toward her and took a breath, and when I submerged again I saw that Sammy had the shell in his mouth and was offering it to me. I took it and set it back down on the floor, then swam to an outside corner of the pool.

I was trying to discover how the chain-link was put together. It was simple: the fence was joined by detachable bands to the main support pole. It wouldn't be much trouble to take the bands off with a Crescent wrench, pull the chain-link back, escort Sammy through, then put it all together again. They would, of course, know who it was who had let Sammy go, but there was no sense going out of my way to leave clues. Perhaps they might even think that Sammy, stricken with remorse, had dared to leap over the dock and into the open water outside.

"We should be able to do it," I said, surfacing. "I don't see any problem."

"I feel very light-headed," Mary Katherine said. "And cold-footed."

"I can do it by myself."

"Maybe I haven't been objective enough," she said. "We've both been running on emotion. Maybe it's not as wonderful to be free as we think. Look at him," she said, indicating Sammy, who was looking up at us expectantly. "I'm not sure he wants to go. Maybe we're just being knee-jerk ecologists."

We went home and tried to discuss it soberly.

It would not bear discussion.

"Don't think about being a criminal," I said to Mary Katherine.

"Why not?"

"Then let me do it on my own."

"No."

As we lay in bed I could not keep a firm grip on my motives. It seemed like an act of petty vengeance or sentimentality until the conviction returned that it was neither of those things, that it was central and pivotal.

The next morning I drove into Corpus and stopped at a dive shop. I rented a tank and regulator for a week.

"It's just about the last one we have," the guy said, hooking the tank up to the compressor. "They really came out of the woodwork for this clear water."

While he was filling the tank I looked up at the posters on the walls—Cozumel, Grand Cayman, Bermuda—that showed divers hovering above coral reefs, the water so pure it seemed a photographic illusion.

Passing the compound on my way back to Mary Katherine's, I saw Mason's baby blue Scout parked outside. I went in to say hello, to remain above suspicion.

Two of Mason's employees were playing volleyball absently with Sammy. They were swarthy and well formed, like the extras in beach-party movies. The hair on their chests was bleached by the sun.

"If you're looking for Bill, he's in the shed," one of them said to me, throwing the ball to Sammy, who caught it in his mouth and tossed it to me with a spasmodic jerk of his head.

I threw it back to him and went into the shed. Canales was there with Mason, leaning back against the wall with his arms folded. I guessed they were discussing his job.

"Good to see you again," Mason greeted me. "I was expecting a call from you last week. Like you to come work for us."

"I appreciate it," I said. "I'm getting married, though."

"Aw hell, bring her along."

"We'll be going to the mountains."

"Well, you just give it some more thought. Mando tells me you have some acting experience. I'm about to hold auditions for a new co-star on *Adventures with Animals.* You might want to consider that. All you'd have to do is wear a bush jacket and keep your mouth shut. It's all voice-over."

"That sounds tempting," I said.

"Give it some thought, like I said. I'll be around a day or two longer. We want to catch a couple more porpi and then we'll take ol' Sam back. You let me know before then.

"By the way, I was sorry to hear about your other animal. She wasn't much, I know, but you can get attached to them even if they're not so bright. I had a beluga once down at Sea Park—dumbest son of a bitch you ever saw—but when he died I just sat down and cried like a baby. I don't care who knows it."

He put a hand on my shoulder, as if in consolation. He looked me in the eye. I could use a man like you, his clear blue eyes were telling me. I could use a sentimental dupe.

"I suppose you'll want to be here when we take Sammy back in the plane," he said. "So you can say good-by and everything. I was just telling Mando here about all the specialized equipment we've got in that machine. I had them rip out all the seats first off, then we put in these permanent fiberglass troughs, six of them, all with their own automatic sprinkler systems. Then we've got a portable EKG, plus a gadget that controls the water temperature. We've got everything in that plane except for a place for the porpi to perform. Got the same setup in the catch boat."

He fixed his eyes on me severely. "It may seem elaborate,

but it's just good business. I've got a lot invested in that animal and, by God, I'm going to see that he's fit and healthy."

I nodded, more than superficially in agreement with his good sense. His tone was so logical, so kind really, that I had to remind myself that I could not take his job and appear on TV every week with a lion cub or wombat while his voice-over warned, "Watch out, Jeff, those little fellas can be pretty feisty!"

We could throw it all off; everything could be all right now. Sammy would be happy, Mary Katherine and I would marry and relocate to Florida and have access to a delightful pet. Or we could escape it all; add a quart of oil to my car and aim it toward New Mexico after all, sit naked in the hot springs or by the fireplace of an adobe house with exposed beams, maybe buy a little piece of land with a tiny stream in which nothing lived but an occasional crayfish.

That afternoon we stood in the office of the justice of the peace, a surprisingly young man, not much older than me, with a soft hill-country voice that suggested flawless breeding. Mary Katherine stood beside me in a new dress she had bought the day before, her chin high, her eyes clear and calm. I felt safe with her.

The ceremony went by smoothly, the JP's mellifluous voice covering for the jarringly secular tract he read to us.

Onto each other's finger we slid our twelve-dollar silver rings, as plain and featureless as the state of love itself. I touched Mary Katherine's hand and stroked her ring, feeling the cool hard surface.

When it was over Mary Katherine turned toward me slowly. Her chin was still high, her throat taut, her gray eyes looking slightly upward at mine, an even, loving stare charged with purpose. I kissed her and shook hands with the judge. He wished us well, remembering to call us by our first names, and graciously accepted my fifty-dollar check for his trouble.

We turned to face the congregation. There was Molly with Joshua squirming in her arms, the pulse on the top of his head beating steadily; beside Molly stood Nat with his hands in his pockets and his hair parted neatly in the center and brushed to either side. I crouched down beside him and touched his shoulder, not knowing what to say to him. I felt like a hoary, overbearing adult who had come to violate his happiness.

Mary Katherine kissed him. He shrugged it off, but did not seem to mind. He simply recognized that he was out of his depth.

"You go home with Molly, okay?" his mother told him. "And Jeff and I will be back a little later."

We took a walk on the beach. I was wearing the clothes I had bought for our night out with Mr. Granger. Despite the wind, the humidity was nearly unbearable, and I took my sport coat off and carried it over my shoulder. The wind blew our hair over to one side; I could feel the grit of sand against my scalp. It was not a pleasant day, but we did our best not to notice. We walked along holding one another through the layers of unfamiliar fabric.

Neither of us spoke. The wedding, the act of marriage, had changed us. I had not been prepared for how overpowering and intangible the change would be. It was as if I had moved a notch up some evolutionary scale I hadn't even known existed. We had advanced, and yet the first act of our advanced state would be to teach a fellow creature to regress.

"I wish it weren't necessary," Mary Katherine said. "It would be so lovely if it weren't necessary."

Exhausted from the wind and the soft sand and the weight of our good clothes we left the beach and drove to the Marlin Spike.

"At least we can have a good lunch," Mary Katherine said.

In the restaurant the hostess said "Ahoy" to us and I said it back. The same man who had been playing the piano when Mr. Granger had taken Canales and me here on the day we had caught the porpoises was still there, playing in a trance. Easy listening.

"Did you like the wedding?" Mary Katherine asked me, as if we were discussing someone else's marriage.

"I was a little out of it."

She shuffled her salad around with her fork. "When I married David it was a hippie wedding, in the park. A friend of his played the recorder. David wore his fruity Elizabethan special occasion shirt, and the minister read from Kahlil Gibran. The whole trip. God, I think he may have even read that Fritz Perls thing!"

"Were your parents there?"

"Oh, yes. With tears in their eyes. They hated David; of course, he hated them too. But everybody's mellowed now, as they say. Except for us. We're radicals."

Our red snapper came, broiled whole, the eyes staring upward with an old man's expression of disgust. Mary Katherine adjusted the garnish to one end of her plate so that the fish's head was hidden beneath it. As we ate our feet touched beneath the table.

The room at the Salt Sea seemed much shabbier and emptier than it ever had before. It did not take me long to pack. I had only to gather up my clothes and put them into my backpack, stuff my diving equipment into my gear bag, and stack my long overdue library books on the dresser. In a drawer of the nightstand I found the little packets of lens-cleaning paper that Mr. Granger had given me and that I had never used. I threw them into the backpack.

"I'll go tell Lois I'm leaving," I said when I was finished.

"Wait a minute." She kissed me, hard enough that I felt the barrier of her teeth against mine. A simple adjustment she made to each shoulder strap caused her dress to fall to the floor, leaving her there in the pantyhose that rose to the bottom of her rib cage, making her look like a manikin that was meant to swivel on its thorax. She took those off, too, and sank onto the bedsprings, watching me. I had spent so much time in the last year trying to read the subtle shifts of expression in a dolphin's eyes that the jumble of emotions I saw in Mary Katherine's was nearly an overload, though I knew clearly enough what was there.

It seemed I was half asleep when we made love. I heard my name rolling along above the water, coming in from the Gulf and drifting along the shore and settling like a fog upon the shore: "Jeff. Jeff, I love you." I was back with her then, holding her, feeling her shiver. She fell forward onto me, and I felt the heat draining away from us, leaving the pleasant cool emptiness of our bodies.

Mary Katherine fell asleep. I left her for a moment to tell Lois I was leaving. She was sitting behind the counter by the postcard rack, watching a game show on which the celebrity contestants wore headphones.

"Lois," I said, "I'm going to be moving out. I just got married."

She looked at me severely and turned the sound off the television.

"I never knew you was engaged," she scolded.

"It was just a civil ceremony. You see, Mary Katherine's been married before, and she would have been embarrassed to go through another wedding. Otherwise, of course, we would have wanted you there."

"Bless her heart, I don't blame her a bit. Mary Katherine, now that's the little girl you've brought around to meet me once or twice? She's a doll. Where are you two going on your honeymoon?"

"We haven't decided yet. For the time being I'll be moving to her house, over by the beach. Then we might go to New Mexico."

Lois nodded. From time to time she glanced nervously at the TV screen.

"So I guess I'll be moving out this afternoon," I said. "I hope that won't cause you any problems."

"No, honey, there's no problem at all. I was glad to have you here for so long, and I'm so happy for you getting married. That's just so nice."

"Can I pay you something for the room?"

She shook her head sweetly. "That was always Dude's treat, you know that."

"But you've gone to so much trouble."

"Not a bit. Not one bit. Now I want to give y'all a wedding present. Do you know your pattern? I could call Lichtenstein's and they could send something to you in New Mexico."

"I think Mary Katherine already has all of that. From her first wedding."

"Jeff, you don't want to eat off the same plates that other boy did, do you?"

"I guess not," I said. "We'll talk it over and choose a new pattern and let you know."

"You do that." She hugged me, lightly at first, then for a moment drew me against her bony chest with some force. The hair that brushed against my cheek was as dry as tinder.

"I'm so glad something worked out for you here," she said when she released me. "I only wish poor Dude could have stayed around to see it."

"I do too," I said. "I'll see you soon. And thanks."

Back in the room Mary Katherine was still asleep, lying on her back, naked on the worn tufted bedspread. I sat down beside her, rocking the bed. She opened her eyes and looked up at me with alarm.

"What time is it?"

"Two."

She turned over and studied the bare wall for a moment, then jumped to her feet and began to dress. "I'll miss this place," she said.

We filled the backseat of my car with my belongings and drove them to her house. When we had unloaded them we sat for a moment on the bed.

"Is it time to get ready?" she asked me.

"I think so," I said.

We moved sluggishly in gathering up what we would need. Neither of us wanted to go; our reluctance bordered on dread. But we kept at it, and in an hour everything we needed was in a pile on the living-room floor: Mary Katherine's old canvas Baker tent, our sleeping bags, a lantern, clothes, four bags of groceries we'd bought the day before, cooking utensils, the seine we'd taken from the marine science building, a dozen gallon jugs of store-bought spring water, a radio.

At five o'clock Molly brought Nat home. He stared with concern at the pile of equipment in the middle of the floor.

"Nat," Mary Katherine said. "Remember what I told you, about a honeymoon?"

"Uh-huh."

"Well, Jeff and I are going to go on one for a few days. Is that all right with you? Can you stay with Molly?"

He was beginning to cry, picking up on our tension.

"Here, Nat," his mother said, "come on back into the bedroom with me."

She led him off and closed the door, leaving me alone with Molly and Joshua, who was on the floor, chewing on the tent.

"I took Nat to *Fantasia*," Molly said. "It was showing in Corpus. He really got off on the part where Mickey Mouse has all those brooms dancing."

I could hear Mary Katherine whispering from the bedroom. Molly leaned down and pulled Joshua away from the tent and went to the refrigerator to get him an ice cube.

"Mary Katherine told me what you guys are going to do," she ventured. "I think it's really great. It takes a lot of courage. Are you nervous?"

"Yeah," I said. "I'm not used to stuff like this."

"I had a boyfriend once who needed a battery for his car. He talked me into going with him to this parking lot and helping him steal one. He just lifted the hood and took it out. It was creepy, but it was kind of fun, too, getting so wired up. Of course it's not the same thing."

"Same effect, maybe."

"Just take a lot of deep breaths. Rhythmic breaths. Even criminals should take deep breaths." She laughed. "Seriously, it helps you to think clearly, and you can regulate your energy that way."

I took a couple of deep breaths.

"That's right. Fill your lungs from the bottom."

Mary Katherine and Nat came out of the bedroom. Nat's face was red from crying, and he was holding onto one of his mother's knees. Molly bent down to him.

"Like to spend a couple days with me, Nat? We can go up to Rockport and see the alligator farm, okay?"

The boy nodded solemnly. Mary Katherine hugged Molly. "I really appreciate it."

"Nothing to it."

Then Molly hugged me. She was crying, too. "Good luck," she said. "*Vaya con queso.*"

I bent down to talk to Nat.

"When we come back what would you like to do?" I asked him.

"I don't know. Eat at the Dairy Queen, I guess."

"Okay, that's what we'll do." I lowered my voice a little. "I love you, Nat. Okay?"

He nodded, then walked bravely out of the room, holding Molly's hand. He even turned around and managed a cheerful "Bye."

"Oh, God," Mary Katherine said when they were gone. "That poor little boy. God knows what he thinks we're up to."

"Why don't you go with him? There's really nothing I can't do by myself."

"No. Don't pay any attention to me. I believe in what we're doing. I just have trouble believing that we're actually doing it."

She moved slowly around the house, locking the sliding glass door to the porch, turning off the air conditioner, sweeping up crumbs with her hand, all the while looking about sadly, as if she never expected to return.

"Do you think," she asked, "that it's abnormal or peculiar or anything, the way I feel about dolphins?"

"Probably," I said.

"No, really."

"Let's get to work. Let's commit the crime."

Mary Katherine had called David the day before to ask if we could borrow his boat to take it up the channel for a long weekend. He had agreed easily enough, but had sounded hurt when we hadn't invited him along. Mary Katherine called him now to tell him we were coming for the boat.

"There's something else," I heard her tell him. "Jeff and I got married."

She cried a little after she hung up.

"He acted like my older brother," she told me on the way to his house. "He wanted to know how good a job you had, if I was pregnant. I think he's pretty hurt without knowing it. Poor David. I doubt if he's even realized yet that you'll be raising Nat."

"Let's at least go get some champagne," David said when we arrived at his house. "You two have got to celebrate."

"Actually we're a little worn out," I said.

"Look, I've got a little coke. Why don't we snort that? After all, you're married! We've got to consume *something!*"

The only way we could get him to sit still was to let him draw out the coke lines. He held his knees close together, balancing a mirror on them, and separated the cocaine with miserly finesse, using a double-edged razor.

He left six lines on the mirror, and we passed it around twice, using a little sterling silver coke spoon that he produced. Neither Mary Katherine nor I wanted any, but out of courtesy we sucked a line of powder into each of our nostrils, feeling the numbness, the mild inconsequential high that flagged our purpose briefly and left us sitting there with David.

"Man, I just cannot believe this! Don't you feel great?" he asked me. "I mean, don't you?"

"Yes, I do."

"I love you both."

Oh please, I thought, give us your boat.

"So where are you headed?"

"Up toward Copano Bay," I said, though we were going south, down the lagoon.

"Man," he said, shaking his head, "I still can't believe it. I've got to give you some kind of wedding present."

"No, David," Mary Katherine said, and I heard their old intimacy in her voice. "I'd rather you didn't."

"Yeah," he said, "I can understand that."

We sat around for a long time, listening to the dreadful music that played incessantly from David's elaborate stereo. It was dark when we pulled away with his boat. We bought two extra gas cans at the marina and filled them at the pump, then drove to the slip, backed the trailer in, and began unwinching the boat. The prow loomed above us as it slipped down the ramp, the fiberglass underside standing out in the darkness as a pale, fishbelly white.

I stayed with the boat while Mary Katherine drove the car back to her house, leaving the trailer by the slip so its connection with my car would be no easier to make than it had to be. She was going to walk back, so I had a half hour or so to myself. I tied the boat to a cleat and jumped inside, then rearranged the gas cans along the side of the deck and squeezed the rubber bulb on the fuel line until it was hard. I sat on the gunwale and looked up at the moonless sky. It seemed to hang low over me, and gazing at the stars, I lost my perception of up and down. It seemed that by the slightest act of imagination I could fall into that sky and land in a net of stars.

Far up the channel I could see the lights of the shrimp boats that were coming home after long runs in Campeche or Yucatán. The mournful sound of their engines traveled unimpeded over the water. I could hear very faint snatches of music and dialogue from the Crow's Nest and tried to calm myself by shutting out every thought and extraneous sensation so that I could deduce what the movie was. There was a lot of screaming and heavy breathing. A monster of some sort, gargantuan and irradiated.

Mary Katherine came up the road. She was barely visible, but I recognized her slow, even pace. When she was closer I watched the cuffs of her bell-bottoms swaying above the ground, like waves breaking peacefully over her feet. Watching her, I almost held my breath.

She was carrying a paper bag. "Hamburgers," she said. "I remembered we hadn't eaten. I don't know if I *can* eat, but I got them anyway."

We were both much hungrier than we realized, and sat in the cabin of the boat eating the hamburgers.

"Did you happen to notice what was showing at the Crow's Nest?" I asked her.

"Let me think. *Grizzly*. Why? You thinking of going to the movie?"

"Just curiosity," I said. "You can hear some of it from here."

"I hadn't noticed. Wait . . . yeah, I hear something growling now."

When she had finished eating I drew her over and kissed her, tasting mustard. It seemed a preposterous intimacy. She put her hand on my thigh and dug in hard with her fingers.

"Ready?" I whispered.

Deep in the hollow of my shoulder I felt her nod. I turned on the running lights, then the motor. Mary Katherine cast us off, and we backed out of the slip, immediately picking up a cool westerly breeze. We were in the main channel soon, heading away from the jetties and the Gulf toward the ferry crossing, and beyond that the broad shallow waters of Corpus Christi Bay. The compound was only a few hundred yards away. I kept the throttle low as we approached it. The arc lamp at the front of the gate was lit, but the pool itself was in darkness.

"We'll make a pass first," I said. "If somebody's there I don't want them to hear the boat stopping."

We saw no one as we drifted by, and after a hundred yards or so I turned the boat around and went back up the channel, setting the shift into idle about fifty yards offshore.

"Listen," Mary Katherine said. "I can hear somebody."

We listened. Unmistakably, voices were coming from the front of the compound.

"What do you think?" she whispered.

"I think Mason's being cautious. But they're outside, it shouldn't matter."

I set the regulator onto the tank, opened the valve, then took off my T-shirt and pulled the tank on. Over that I put on my weight belt, then hung the light by its lanyard around my neck.

"I'll flash the light once when I'm about to come back," I told her. "If something goes wrong I'll flash it twice. Then you take off back to the slip, all right?"

"All right."

"Count on about twenty minutes."

I spit into my mask, washed it out, and pulled it over my face. I grabbed the Crescent wrench, hooked the lanyard clip through the hole in its handle, then pulled on my fins and rolled over the side on my back. In the second before I hit the water I felt a surge of absolute panic, but the cold shock that followed dispelled it. The water was murky again. I knew that in the dark, in dirty water, I could be turned around within ten feet, so I swam toward the pool along the surface, using my snorkel instead of the regulator. It was not an easy swim: the water seemed stiff and abrasive, and there was an overpowering sense of loneliness in that short distance between Mary Katherine and Sammy. I understood a little how it must have been for my father, adrift at night on the surface of the open ocean. I kicked harder and looked back at the boat, a black cut-out against a black sky, with Mary Katherine's figure at the gunwale.

As I came closer to the pool I heard a series of splashes and saw Sammy jumping repeatedly in the pool, arcing high over the dock. I swam away from the compound to a little remnant of beach off to the side, taking off my fins so they would not be lost in the deep mud, and hauled myself up among the oyster shells and beer cans. I wanted to make sure the two voices we had heard were still outside the gate and not in the pool. They had not moved. I listened to them talk and recognized the voices of Mason's two assistants I had met earlier. They were talking about Jimmy Buffett and some bar in Key West where they had heard him.

I sat in the mud and breathed deeply a few times as Molly had recommended. I was exhausted by the swim, by the weight of the tank, and by my own trepidation. I could hear the motor idling very softly out in the channel, a comforting murmur. There was no reason now not to go through with the plan. I entered the water, replaced my fins as soon as I was clear of the sludge, put the regulator into my mouth, and submerged. I did not yet dare to turn on the light. It was perfectly dark, no visibility whatsoever, and for a moment my head spun, trying to seize upon some kind of bearing. Until I was stabilized mentally I took deep wasteful breaths, the compressed air rushing insistently into my lungs. I had to remember to expel it. With my right hand I kept feeling for the fence and finally touched the hard diamond pattern covered with slime and corrosion. I grabbed the fence with my other hand and swung my face close. I could see it now, not clearly, but it was the only reference point in the void and I was grateful to have it. I worked my way along the chain-link until I came to the corner pole where it was attached. Sammy's beak appeared from the darkness on the other side of the fence, then his right eye as he turned to look at me. He knew who I was. When he put his beak right up against the fence fabric I could see him a little. He was calm, fascinated.

Starting at the bottom, using the light cautiously, I unfastened each band and hooked them into my weight belt. The fence curled back like a stiff curtain, and I swam through the gap into the pool. Sammy's face drifted close to mine. I put my hand out and touched his beak. He opened his mouth and I ran my hand along two rows of even teeth, then withdrew and swam backward, hoping to coax him out through the gap in the fence which he had surely perceived through echo location. But Sammy grabbed my leg and began to stroke it with his teeth. Then he bolted out of the water above me, sending a shock wave through the pool. He did this repeatedly, until the surface was a pale froth.

When he stopped and the water calmed, I saw a light trail across the surface. I slid over to the side of the pool and up the mesh to the cramped breathing space between the fence and the dock. I took the regulator out of my mouth and held it above the waterline so there would be no bubbles.

They were up there, directly above my head. I could look up through the spaces between the planking and see their pants cuffs. The flashlight was still on, but was pointed absently down now, a few feet away from me. They would not be able to see the rolled-away fence through the murky water.

Sammy was leaping again.

"Crazy fucker," one of them said. "I wonder if he's trying to impress us or what."

"Probably just wants some company."

"Let's give him some fish. Maybe he'll calm down."

They threw a handful into the center of the pool. Sammy ignored them.

"Tough shit then, buddy. We've got better things to do than watch you jump up and down in the water. Save it for the movie, okay?"

They walked along the dock and, I assumed, out the gate. I put the regulator back in my mouth and swam to the center of the pool, where the dolphin met me. Then I passed through the gap, uncertain in the darkness whether Sammy had followed me or not. I risked the light and saw his bulbous, shining head staring out warily through the opening. I swam further out; he followed this time and stayed behind me as I tried to pull the mesh back. I could barely move it; I had to hook my leg around the pole and use it as a brace while I pulled with all my strength to get the chain-link back where I could replace the bands. That had to be done under tension, and it was some time before I got the first one on. The rest were easier. All the time I was working I prayed that I was blocking the gap well enough with my body so that Sammy could not slip undetected back into the pool. When I was finished he was still behind me, hovering very close. The refastened section of fence was not as taut as it had been, but I thought it looked reasonably untampered with. It was a good piece of work, and I was proud. In the morning, when they discovered Sammy missing, it would seem as if he had simply gone out with the tide. Of course I knew that we would be immediately suspect, but it gave me a craftsman's pleasure to have erased the most immediate evidence.

I surfaced and flashed the light once. The running lights on the boat flashed in response. Sammy stayed very close as I snorkeled out to the boat, his breaths exploding next to my ear. Once or twice he stopped and swam back a little way in the opposite direction, toward the pool, but I kept on and he came back each time, nearly ramming me with his beak in his need for contact. He was scared now. What he had first thought was a game had become very serious.

The open water terrified him, much more than it did me, for his senses drew in every whisper of movement and predation in the dark channel. The safe parameter of his home no longer existed; I had led him into a chasm of sensation, fear, opportunity.

When we reached the boat Mary Katherine had David's little ski ladder over the side. I handed her the fins and the tank and hauled myself up to the first rung with some difficulty, then collapsed onto the deck, utterly exhausted. I could hear Sammy's confused squeaks at the waterline.

"It's all right, Sammy," Mary Katherine was saying to him in a soothing, urgent voice. "It's all right, baby."

"How did it go?" she asked me.

"Not too bad. Those guys were in front, but they came back once. They didn't see me. I got the gate closed."

Sammy jumped high out of the water.

"We'd better get moving," I said. "They might hear all the racket he's making."

But Mary Katherine stood there without moving, looking down at the confused and frightened animal in the water.

"Look," I said. "If he won't follow us, if he swims back to the pool, I'll go back with him and let him in again. Then we'll go home, okay?"

"That's not what I was thinking," she said. "I'll take us out."

She picked up the ladder, walked into the cabin, and sat behind the steering wheel with fatalistic resolve. When we pulled out, Sammy leaped clear of the water, startled, then immediately followed us, keeping close to the side of the boat where he could see me. His anxious breathing rose above the sound of the motor.

"Come on, Sammy," I shouted, as if I were urging on a dog.

We followed the ship channel around to the lee side of the

island, then broke off and headed south across the bay. Around us the lights of the city, of isolated refineries, buoys, villages, bay shrimpers, glowed steadily or blinked softly on and off. We took the boat into that section of the horizon where there were no lights, into a corridor of darkness and open water.

In an hour we had crossed the bay and passed beneath the causeway bridge that led to the narrower waters of the Laguna Madre. I sat all that time on a lawn chair on the deck, listening to Sammy's breathing at the side of the boat. A few miles into the lagoon we pulled away from the main channel and stopped to give the dolphin a rest. He swam around the boat in slow circles, his breathing still irregular and frightened.

Mary Katherine leaned over the side of the boat and splashed her hand in the water. Instantly Sammy's beak was beneath it, pressing her palm upward.

"He wants to play his game." She shoved him down by the beak as we had done before in the pool, and each time she shoved he rose back like an inflated beach toy. She played with him for fifteen minutes, calming him, and then in the firm, patient voice of a parent said, "That's enough now."

"In about an hour," I said, "we can start looking for a spoil island where we can set up camp. Down past Baffin Bay there are lots of them."

"It seems so far," she said, looking south into the darkness.

"Maybe thirty miles."

"Let's get started then. I'll feel better when we're settled somewhere."

The concentration of lights that circled the bay grew more and more diffuse as we proceeded down the channel that had been dredged from the center of the lagoon. We were far down into the national seashore now, and on the mainland was the northern frontier of the King Ranch, unmarked except for the lights on an occasional windmill or stock tank.

I was driving now. Mary Katherine sat in the stern watching out for Sammy. Once she thought he had strayed and left us, but he had only taken up a new position at the bow, riding the slight waves there.

"How would you have felt if he *had* left?" she asked me.

I continued to steer with one finger on the wheel, like a casual driver, keeping the boat on course between the channel markers.

"I would have felt good," I said. "It would have meant that he was ready to go back, that he had made his choice. So I would have felt good."

"I'm not ready for him to do that yet," she admitted. "A part of me still wants him to be dependent on us. I don't want to give him up. I don't think it's as wonderful for them in the wild as we want to believe."

"What's your point?"

"I'm just sleepy. I always want to argue when I'm sleepy."

Spoil islands bordered each side of the channel now. Most of them were no longer than a hundred yards, with little huts made from driftwood or prefabricated tool sheds set down upon them.

"Are there people living in those?" Mary Katherine asked me.

"Some. Most of them are just fishing shacks. The people who built them come down on weekends. Further down they should thin out."

It seemed we were very far now from Port Aransas. I thought of Pineda, sailing in this direction in the Gulf, arriving finally in the Aztec empire, another planet. We would not go that far—it was impossible these days to travel that far, beyond imagination.

We drank coffee from a thermos. The cocaine had long since worn off, but my tongue was still numb and the bitter aspirin taste of the drug still clung to the roof of my mouth. When the caffeine kicked in I felt much less somber, even cheerful.

In another hour we found a deserted island between the channel and the mainland a few miles past the southern margin of Baffin Bay. There were few lights around, just a lantern a few hundred yards down the channel and the glow from an illuminated stock tank on the mainland. The island was about twenty-five yards off the channel, and I let the boat drift into the mud shelf that began a short distance from the shore. Sammy hung back by the stern where the water was still deep enough to support him. He held his head above the surface, turning around slowly, a variation on his dancing behavior.

With flashlights we explored the surface of the island. Above the mud the spoilbank had a crust of broken shell, with occasional stubby oases of dune grass. The island was perfectly flat and only about fifty yards in diameter, bordered on all sides by thick fetid water.

As we stood on the far side shining our flashlights over to the mainland, we heard Sammy calling to us from near the boat, an eerie sound in that silence. Mary Katherine put her arm around my waist and twisted my empty belt loops around her fingers as if she were rooting herself, preparing for some incredible gust that might blow her away.

"God," she said, "this is terrifying."

I didn't bother to disagree. We pitched the tent near the channel shore, so that Sammy could see us there when daylight came. For now we simply called to him, letting him know we were still around. It took us an hour to set up the tent in the wind. It was a big awkward tent that Mary Katherine had bought long ago at a scout troop's garage sale, and it really required three people to set it up—two to hold the ridgepoles and one to drive in the stakes. But we managed, and when at last it was standing free, its faded green canvas glowing in our lantern light, it looked like the tent of some polar explorer set up on the trackless ice pack.

When we had moved all the equipment inside Mary Katherine collapsed onto her sleeping bag.

"I know it's our wedding night," she said, "but I'm going to conk out anyway."

"Go ahead," I told her. "I'll check on Sammy."

The dolphin was swimming up and down the length of the island, as close inshore as he could come without beaching himself. I walked through the mud and reached the waist-deep water where he hovered. Excited, he swam all around me, handing me a piece of shell, which I threw out for him and which he returned, prodding my palm with his beak.

We played that game awhile and then I took six pounds of dead fish from the boat and fed them to Sammy one at a time. He took each one from my hand with a casual, conniving look. When he had eaten them all I turned around to leave, but the dolphin grabbed the back of my leg with his open mouth, applying more pressure than he ever had before, as if he were really planning to bite me if I tried to leave him.

"No!" I said firmly, and shoved him away. He lolled there in the dark water watching me as I walked back to the tent, and was silent until I had crawled into my sleeping bag. Then he began splashing wildly, whistling, clicking, calling me back. I stayed where I was, feeling the sand crabs crawling over my body. Beside me Mary Katherine was already asleep, with one arm reached tentatively out in my direction. I lay with my head flat against the shell floor, wishing I had brought a pillow, wishing Sammy could understand what it was we wanted from him and would swim out into the channel tonight feeling liberated, unafraid, grateful to us. In the morning then the whole affair would be ended.

I never quite went to sleep, but in an hour or so Sammy's calling was simply a sound that I assimilated into the rhythm of my breathing. At the slightest suggestion of dawn I climbed out of my sleeping bag, removing Mary Katherine's arm, which during the night had worked itself across my chest. Outside the sun was rising over the national seashore, and in the early light the chain of spoil islands flanking the channel blended together into one long pale strip. There were few structures on these islands—the remnants of huts and driftwood campfires—but I could see one free-standing shack several hundred yards away on my side of the channel. It was made of lumber scraps and set upon pilings cut from telephone poles. The two front pilings were in the water—the beach had eroded past them—and the entire structure leaned forward a little. It would collapse one day into the channel.

If Sammy had done any exploring during the night there

was no way that I could have known it. He was swimming in the same place I had left him the night before. When he saw me he rose out of the water and balanced on his tail, his body shuddering with the effort. I walked out to him and stroked him along the beak and forehead, tracing the faint waterlines that showed the history of his movement through the sea. The dolphin rolled over on his side, presenting his pectoral fins, and I stroked him there as well, on the pale pinkish flesh that had surprised me so much the morning we had captured him.

Mary Katherine came out of the tent, wearing only her underpants and a T-shirt. She walked barefoot toward us, picking her way painfully across the shell floor, and then sat down next to me in the water. Sammy put his head into her lap.

"Still with us, I see," she said to him, yawning, and then fell back wantonly into the water.

"I suppose they're about to make the discovery," she said. "What do you think they'll do?"

"Go looking for me. Then you."

"How long do you think it'll be before they find us?"

"We probably have a few days."

"What if Sammy won't leave in that time?"

"I was thinking," I said, ignoring her question. "It'll probably take them a day or so to make the connection between us and David's boat. When they do that, it's only a matter of time. They'll just fly up and down the coast till they spot the boat. But if you took it back today, gave it back to David, they wouldn't know what to look for. I could probably stay here indefinitely. At least until Sammy was confident enough to leave me."

"But you'd be alone."

"I could handle it."

She stood up in her wet clothes and pulled them off with a casual, absentminded motion. Up to her knees in water and mud, she bent over and kissed me.

"I'll think about it," she said, and walked back over the shell to the tent, holding her wet clothes in one hand.

I did not think I could do without her. When she was inside the tent I turned to watch the miniature waves lapping against the shore. The water constantly undermined the mud and ate away parts of the shoreline. It would not be long until the whole island was reclaimed.

When Mary Katherine came out of the tent she was dressed and carrying the Coleman stove. She set it up near the water, lighted it, and started a pot of coffee. For breakfast we ate granola and oranges. We sat on the beach in lawn chairs, a fun-loving couple honeymooning on the beautiful Laguna Madre with their pet dolphin.

"My father used to bring me down here fishing," I told her. "Or sometimes we'd take the jeep and drive down to Little Shell to surf fish."

"How old were you when he died?"

"Seven."

"Did he look like you?"

"A little."

"I'd like to see a picture of your parents sometime. Then if we decided to have a baby I'd have some idea what it might look like. Fortunately with Nat I managed to hog all the genes—that's all I'd need, for him to look like David. With you, though, it'd be different."

Sammy cruised back and forth before us in the still water, a leviathan in that tiny seascape.

"Jeff," she said. "What are we going to do? He's not going to leave us."

"We have to teach him. No more dead fish. I'll seine for live ones and gradually cut down on the amount I give him. Then he'll start feeding on his own. Once he does that I think he'll stray off."

She lay back in the lawn chair. A thin line of sweat ran from her forehead to the bridge of her nose.

"So you think I should abandon you?" she said.

"Not exactly. You can come back down in a few days and let me know what's going on."

"I suppose I could take the skiff from the school. They won't miss it anyway. I'm the only one who uses it."

"What's today?" I asked her. "Thursday? You can come back Saturday. Something will have happened by then. Sammy will be out cruising on his own and I'll be sitting here waiting to be rescued."

"Then what? We flee to Mexico?"

"Then I throw myself on the mercy of the court. Tell them how, completely on my own, with a few things I borrowed from my wife, I let Sammy go."

"It wasn't on your own."

"We can make a very feasible case that it was. Especially if you show up in town this morning and I'm still gone. We might as well be sensible."

"If I do go back, it's to buy us time. After all, I want my share of the martyrdom."

We sat there for a while longer, then I got up and began taking Mary Katherine's gear out of the tent and stuffing it into the well of the boat.

"Hide that stuff as soon as you get home," I told her. "Put it back in your closet. Also it might be better to put in at a slip in Corpus and then call Molly. Tell her to pick up the trailer in her car and then drive over to get you. Tell David we decided to come home early. The fish weren't biting."

She nodded dutifully. From her backpack she pulled out a notebook, a laboratory notebook with graph-ruled paper on which she had drawn sketches of individual dorsal fins. Beneath each sketch there was a paragraph of data.

"All right," she said, sitting down on the paltry beach and studying the notebook. "This is not scientific at all; you can't count on it. But it seems likely to me that Sammy's old herd will be passing through here tomorrow or the next day, probably—let me see—probably late in the afternoon. I haven't seen them in Lydia Ann for two weeks, and I know they go south because I once had a girl down at Baffin Bay to watch for me.

"Okay. You need to look for Triangle Fin, the big bull. He's the harem keeper. I'm sure Wanda came from that herd. It's harder to tell with Sammy because he doesn't have any markings, but if you caught them together I think it's a good bet Sammy came from it too. Anyway, watch for that low fin. If Sammy won't join up with them, I doubt there's any chance. He's housebroken for good, and the kindest thing would just be to let Mason have him."

She climbed into the boat and sat in the cabin behind the steering wheel. I shoved the bow away from the mud shelf and held onto it as she leaned down to kiss me.

"You have the binoculars?" she asked.

"Yes."

"You might start looking tomorrow afternoon. Of course Sammy'll know when they're coming long before you do. I love you. I'll be back. Be careful."

"Stay out of sight," I told her. "Don't let anybody threaten you. Call somebody—Brad Dawson. He'll be all right."

She looked down in tears from the window as she started the motor. I sat in the water and held Sammy as the boat backed off into the channel. He did not try to follow, seeming content to rock lightly in my arms with his spiracle just above the waterline. Watching her go, I unthinkingly pulled the dolphin closer.

Chapter 13

Not long after Mary Katherine had left a bass boat came down the channel. Three grizzled men in jumpsuits sat in the swivel seats and nodded curtly in my direction. I saw them looking around for my boat.

"Any luck?" I called, wanting to be as aboveboard as possible. One of the men held up a stringer of drum and redfish, several dozen of them hung gill-to-gill, swaying like a feather duster.

"How about yourself?"

"Not yet," I said.

"You got a boat?"

"Down the channel. A friend has it."

The man waved, reassured, and swiveled his seat around so that he was facing the bow again. Sammy followed them for perhaps a hundred yards, but they never saw him.

When he came back he rose up on his tail, bobbed his head up and down insistently, and made his impatient clicking sounds. He was hungry.

I brought the seine out from the tent, tied one end to an isolated piling, the remains of someone's primitive dock, and swung the other end around in the water, using the piling for a pivot. There was nothing on the first few passes, but soon I had three mullet and a small six-inch flounder. I fed two of the mullet and the flounder to Sammy, holding them in midair by the rear fins and then setting them loose in the water by his beak. He almost let the first one get away, but gulped down the other two as soon as I released them. He looked at me, still hungry, and then slid back into the channel on his own, where I saw him descend deep into the water and rise in the same spot with that familiar rocking motion I was afraid we had bred out of him. Perhaps he was even foraging on his own now.

I used the other mullet for cut bait and by midmorning had caught myself a decent redfish, along with two hardheads, which I tossed to Sammy, carefully avoiding the sharp dorsal spines that he simply tore off with his teeth. I cleaned the redfish and fried it for lunch on the stove. Then I sat down near the water and waved at the boats passing down the channel, barges loaded with landfill or more fishermen heading for their spoil islands.

"Hey," one of the fishermen called. "They's a big porpoise right next to you. I'd stay out of the water if I was you, just to be safe."

"Thanks," I said. "I'll sure do that."

In the afternoon I scanned the southern horizon with the binoculars but did not see a single wild dolphin. After supper— a can of chili, an apple, and a little container of chocolate pudding with a list of additives two inches long—I went inside the tent and, with the sun still up, tried for two hours to fall asleep. It was dark when I gave up. Sammy was calling for me. Finally I dragged my sleeping bag out onto the beach, far enough away from the crumbling littoral to be safe from the tide if not from the sand crabs, whose journeys left a delicate tracery on my face.

For another hour Sammy tried to lure me into the water with him. He lunged forth into the night sky, a dense black shape against the star field, and as soon as he dropped back into the water, he cartwheeled below the surface and sprang out again. It was a rhythmic pattern, like the obsessive motion of a big cat in a cage or that of an insane man pounding his head against the wall. But Sammy was not a neurotic captive, he was *free* now, in open water, a fact he seemed to refuse to recognize.

Finally he stopped and settled into the water like a small mammal snuggling into its burrow for the night. As he slept I could hear the steady, regular expulsion of his breath every time he rose to the surface.

The rhythm of his sleeping lulled me, and I fell asleep too. When I woke the water was near the edge of my sleeping bag, having consumed a foot of solid shoreline during the night. Something else was wrong. Sammy was gone. I looked out into the water, waiting for him to surface, but he never did. I called him, wishing I had remembered to bring my whistle, but the dolphin did not answer.

That was it, then. He had returned to the wild, simply and quietly, and my work was finished. I had a moment of sickening loneliness, feeling his absence as a physical cratering deep in my body. It passed. I ate breakfast. Then I sat on the beach and waited for Mary Katherine. She would come tomorrow, and I would go back with her to Port Aransas and deal with my crime.

But he came back. His fin broke water across the channel, and I did not see it again until he burst into the air twenty feet away from me, spinning backward and slamming his body down onto the surface.

I went out to him, my heart pounding with a relief I did not want to feel, and swam with him in the deep water of the channel. A school of cabbageheads floated by just below the surface, but I did not mind them, and with their dim perceptions they did their best to avoid me. I took Sammy's fin and crossed the channel, and crossed again riding on his back, my feet locked beneath him. I held on with the skill of a brahma bull rider as he plowed across the unruffled surface. A mullet jumped from the water, its body rigid as a bar of soap someone had shot out of a tub, and Sammy leaped forward, dunking me, and caught the fish in midair between his teeth. He sent it down his throat with a convulsive toss of his head.

But after lunch he left again, swimming away from me deliberately and steadily up the channel until I lost sight of him. He might or might not be back this time, I decided. I settled in the lawn chair, took off my shirt, and sat in the sun in my faded cutoffs. Mary Katherine had thought to bring along her radio and I tuned the FM band until I picked up a weak signal. Some headshop was advertising backgammon sets. When the commercial was over, there was an uninterrupted stretch of Austin music—steel guitars and pretentious lyrics sung by women I imagined as gorgeous. When I was tired of it, I turned the radio off and fell asleep in the sun.

Sammy woke me. He was close to shore, up to something. In his teeth he held a plastic bleach bottle that he slapped repeatedly on the surface. Then he rose vertically from the water and balanced on his tail, still shaking the bottle in the air. It seemed, with the fine tuning of distance burnt out by the sunlight, that Sammy had risen only an inch or two out from the shoreline. The encrusted silver of the shell beach merged with no real demarcation into the opaque blue-green of the water. Indeed, I entered that water not fully aware that I had left the land at all.

I reached Sammy and extended my hand to take the bottle, as I'd assumed he wanted me to do, but he drew back with it still in his jaws and then submerged, reappearing a short distance farther out in the channel. I followed, and he let me touch him, but when I tried to take the bleach bottle away and play the game he seemed to be suggesting, he ducked underwater and emerged still farther away. He was luring me out.

Coming back onto the land, I saw a figure emerge from the shack down the channel and walk slowly across the island to the narrow backwater that separated it from the mainland. The figure entered the water there and bent over. Through the binoculars I could see it was an old woman, holding a bucket in one hand and trailing the other through the knee-deep water. Occasionally the hand came up with an object, a shell I supposed, or a piece of glass.

I trained the binoculars down the channel, looking for Triangle Fin and his herd. I saw nothing, but I turned my chair in that direction and watched the water casually for the rest of the afternoon. Sammy swam lazily in the water before me, pushing the bleach bottle around with his beak, submerging it, casting it adrift and then seeming to pounce on it.

Near dusk I noticed he had disappeared, and when I looked down the channel for him I caught a glimpse of something moving through the water. Through the binoculars I saw it was a group of ten or twelve dolphins swimming slowly in my direction, one of them with the low stunted dorsal that I recognized as the field mark of Triangle Fin. They moved up the channel in close ranks. I was so used to the trained leaping of Sammy and Wanda that the wild dolphins seemed secretive and reserved. They moved with purpose, like a convoy drifting into battle. When they passed me, navigating squarely within the channel, I looked through the binoculars for Sammy and thought I saw his perfect dorsal glide out of the water close to the tattered fin of one of the other dolphins. I wondered just what was going on below the surface. The group seemed tighter now, breaching in twos and threes as if engaged in some sort of council. I could hear their weary exhalations.

Though I kept my binoculars trained at the place I thought Sammy might surface again I did not see him. By ten o'clock that night he had not returned, and I felt that this time he had left for good. Now all I had to do was get off this island. I lit the lantern and sat on the beach in the circle of light it cast. Sand crabs swarmed at the base of my chair. I heard mullet leaping from the water and the deep bullfrog sound of beating gills. The lagoon was alive, but knowing Sammy was no longer out there made it seem inert to me, a solution in which all living molecules had been neutralized.

There was nothing else to do. Mary Katherine would be here tomorrow, maybe tomorrow morning. I turned off the lantern and gave my eyes time to adjust to the darkness before I went inside and fell down onto my sleeping bag. I could not sleep, had not even thought I could. The afternoon had been still and had brought with it a plague of mosquitoes which droned now around my head and covered my body with bites. I pulled on my long pants and long-sleeved shirt, choosing the heat over the insects. We had considered bringing repellent, but I could not remember now if we had actually brought it, and I was not excited about smearing oil over my body anyway. I closed my eyes and felt the mosquito welts and the ticklish, intolerable current above them, like a mountain breeze.

In New Mexico autumn would not be far off now. People would be laying out their flannel shirts and down vests and walking about charged by the first gusts of fall weather. I remembered the fragrance of piñon, a nearly insupportable memory here in the salt air, and mingled with it the fainter fragrance of loss. I could have had some sort of life there. Perhaps I might have still had the Seamstress to burrow down with before the fireplace, a human redoubt against the gorgeous winter.

I fell asleep and slept without interruption until late the next morning, when I woke clear-headed, remembering that this was the day Mary Katherine was to come back. I ran outside, cutting my bare feet on the shell topsoil, and stood on the crumbling, pitiful beach looking for Sammy. He had not come back. It had worked.

Mary Katherine did not come that day. I heated up a can of stew in the darkness, worried and disappointed. She would have come if she could. Something was wrong at her end.

After dinner I listened to the radio. There was nothing on the local news about Sammy. That was either a good or a bad sign.

During the night Sammy came back. When I came out of the tent in the morning he shot out of the water and did a beautiful somersault, much more accomplished than any he had done in performance. I was glad to see him. I threw off my shirt and swam out to where he was. He prodded me beneath the arm with his beak, towed me into the deep water, and swam around me in circles. Treading water, I passed my hand along his back, all the way to the firm splayed musculature of his tail flukes.

He left me for a few minutes, and when he came back he had the bleach bottle again. He swam to within a few feet of me and started his routine all over, drawing me out into the water and slapping the bottle angrily when I hesitated to follow him.

I thought I knew now what Sammy wanted of me, and how impossible it was. The dolphin was training me, weaning me away from the land just as I meant to wean him away from the world of men. The bottle was his target, what I must touch to perform the behavior he wanted from me. I don't believe he knew that I could not live with him in the water. It must have seemed such a simple answer to all our troubles.

And part of me was willing to believe it possible, that child who thought he could will himself into other forms. But I was a man now, a surface breather, and I knew I could merge with that lovely beast only by breaking away from it forever.

I came out of the water one last time while Sammy thrashed about in frustration and confusion, and finally let the bottle drift out of his jaws. That night he went away again and by the morning, my fifth day on the island, Mary Katherine had still not come. I had some food left, but very little will to eat it. I ate an orange for breakfast, pudding and a piece of bread for lunch, then sat down on the lawn chair and listened to the radio. A Coast Guard plane flew over very low and made another pass even closer, dropping this time a yellow Styrofoam canister with a long red streamer that fell near the tent. Inside the canister was a message: "If you require assistance wave your hands."

The plane passed by twice more. Each time I looked up sullenly with my hands at my sides. The pilot waved good-by and left.

Late in the afternoon I spotted someone walking through the shallow water between the spoil islands, heading my way. Through the binoculars I saw it was the same woman I had noticed before digging for shells in the wash. She was very tall, I saw as she drew nearer, and wore a broad old-fashioned sunbonnet and rubber wading boots. She crossed another small body of water and set foot on my island, walking past my tent and down to the beach where I was standing by my chair, ready to receive her. Beneath the sunbonnet was a weathered, sharp-featured face with two small black eyes that seemed impervious to light. I could see a few strands of tensile gray hair that the bonnet did not cover. She was also very thin, the wading boots open at her waist like a comical pair of oversize pants.

She stood there and sized me up for a moment. The black eyes were not unfriendly.

"Seems like you're going to be here awhile," she said, "so I came over to invite you to dinner. I live at that house yonder." She pointed to the shack up the channel.

"Thank you," I said, "but I think somebody's—"

"You come on over whenever you're ready. Better wear some shoes. They's stingarees in the water."

"Somebody might be coming to get me. I think I better stay around here."

"You come on over."

"All right," I said. "I have some food. Can I bring something?"

"No, son. I wouldn't have invited you to dinner if I didn't have what I need to feed you. You come on over when you're ready."

She turned around slowly and walked back toward her shack. I held my fishing rod in my hand as I watched her wade through the shallows, and before she was halfway to her shack something took my bait. I could tell by the tenacity with which it fought that it was large and flat, some creature that would have to be pried up from the bottom. I was right, it was a good-sized flounder. When I brought it up onto the beach it flopped over, revealing the viscous flesh of its belly. I thought how good the flounder would taste—I was hungry now and wished I had not accepted the strange invitation that had just come my way. I considered putting the flounder on a stringer and saving it, but the fish's struggles seemed so desperate, the gills heaving behind the misplaced eyes, that I removed the hook and threw the flounder out to the edge of the channel, where it landed broadside.

I let another hour pass, hoping that Mary Katherine would

come, that Sammy would return. Neither did. I wrote a note for Mary Katherine and pinned it to the tent with a fish hook, then set off through the shallow water. In some places the mud sucked my feet in up to the ankles, in others there was a firm base of shell. Both of the islands I crossed to reach the shack were vacant. There were no signs of habitation except for a few bottles, the arm of a doll, and a float or two from somebody's fishing net.

The shack was a much more substantial structure than it had seemed from a distance, and did not lean quite so far forward as I had thought. It looked like a child's clubhouse—a hodgepodge of fiberboard and driftwood, stray planks and sheetrock all dyed over time to a dark dirty gray crusted with salt. I noticed the stairs were sound. They were made of railroad ties, still dark with creosote, and they led to an open doorway covered with a floral-print shower curtain. I knocked on the body of the house and heard the woman say from a distance that could not have been more than ten feet, "Coming," and then heard her shuffling about for a long time, as if she had to cross an immense room to reach the door.

She drew back the curtain and stood before me. She had taken off the waders and was wearing khaki shorts now, though both her legs, as well as one elbow, were completely swathed in dirty Ace bandages. She had taken off her bonnet too, and her hair hung to her shoulders, as bright in the failing light as a pile of steel shavings.

The old woman grinned, showing a complete set of teeth, and motioned me inside the tiny room. It had one window without a pane. There was a lantern, a little propane stove, and a setting for four of cheap battered china on display above the four-by-four house frame. Her canned goods also ran along this makeshift shelf. On the floor there was a bare mattress, and above that her wading boots and a pair of overalls hung on a fishing rod that spanned one end of the house at chest level.

"Sit down," she said, pulling a chair out from a small table.

The legs of the chair were uneven, and it wobbled every time I stirred. Looking down through half-inch gaps in the floorboards, I could see the crumbling edge of the island.

"My name is Jeff Dowling," I decided to say.

"You sit there and I'll get dinner."

She shuffled around the kitchen end of the room, a towering figure from my perspective in the stubby chair. She took down a can of corn, a can of Vienna sausages, which she looked at with real absorption before rejecting, finally went to the door and began pulling on a piece of string. A redfish, still working its gills, rose up into the shack. She cut its head off with a machete and put it into an empty Crisco can.

"Most people don't like the heads," she said. She fell silent again as she gutted and filleted the redfish. She poured the corn in a pot and put it on the stove, then heated up some Crisco for the fish. I did not dare to speak but felt comfortable in a way I had not anticipated. The old woman's long-practiced rhythm calmed me. I could have fallen asleep.

"We're having fish and corn for dinner," she announced, as if I had not spent the last twenty minutes watching her prepare them. She set a plate in front of me, then lowered herself into the other chair.

It was nearly dark now. We ate by lantern light, a mild glow whose intensity seemed keyed to the diminishing sunlight. The fish wasn't bad. She had forgotten to turn the heat on under the corn, but it was still palatable enough.

"I seen you with that porpoise out there," she said. "You teaching it to do tricks?"

"No. I want him to leave."

"Sometimes it's hard to get rid of a porpoise."

"You've had one?" I asked.

She chewed her corn for a long time and seemed to consider an answer.

"They're nuisances sometimes," she said.

I started to repeat my question, but she was already on her feet and wiping our supper dishes with a wet rag.

"I'll help you build your house over there," she said. "You got a permit? You got to have a permit to build a house."

"I'm not going to build a house. I'm going to leave, maybe tomorrow."

"What about the porpoise?"

"He'll stay."

"I thought you come down here to live with that porpoise," she said. "I would have helped you build your house.
Build it back from the water or it'll fall in like mine. No, I
thought you and that porpoise was gonna live here."

"No," I said.

The woman placed the dishes back on the four-by-four
shelf, then stepped back to regard them as if they were pictures she had just hung.

"You haven't told me your name," I said.

"Rosa." She stood above me, hulking.

"You live out here all the time?"

Suddenly she laughed out loud, three or four sharp guf-
faws that seemed to threaten the tiny house.

"No," she said, laughing more reasonably, "I just come
here on my vacation."

All at once she looked remorseful. "No," she said quietly,
"I live here all the time since my husband died in the oil field.
For a while I lived in that city, Corpus Christi, in an apart-
ment. Then I came here. You live where, son?"

"Port Aransas."

She nodded her head knowingly. "The surfing craze."

She sat down again and set her hands on the table as if she
was going to cause it to rise. They were huge hands, well-
formed, with splayed fingertips, and very dark. I stared at
them.

"Are you in trouble?" she asked me.

"Yes. Over the porpoise. He doesn't belong to me."

She offered no advice or words of consolation, but I felt secure sitting with her and must have passed half an hour that
way, feeling the fresh salt breeze that had long since dispelled
the cooking odors from dinner.

"Go back to your tent and sleep now," she said, rising
from the table. "Take this lantern." She pulled one off the shelf
and lit it, nearly blowing us up. "You can bring it back to me
later. Watch for stingarees in the shallow water. Look for a little rise in the mud. It's probably a flounder but it may be one
of them stingarees."

I took the lantern and climbed down the thick stairway, stepping off into ankle-deep water that seemed to grow even murkier with the direct shock of light I carried. I walked to the next spoil island, startling a great population of sand crabs that swept across the shell and sand like a wave. Entering the water again I saw a stingray shaking off a layer of mud and taking wing a foot in front of me. I froze, suddenly terrified, and let the feeling pass like an electric shock through my body, feeling it leave by the soles of my feet. The panic was gone, but in its place came a loneliness that was almost as debilitating. I wished I were home, home somewhere in New Mexico, or in the distant past, sleeping in the hard wooden bunk on my father's shrimp boat.

By lantern light my tent seemed a peculiar outgrowth of the substance of the spoil island, its faded green color lost in the indiscriminate blast of light. The lantern, though, blew out before I reached my camp, and the tent's afterimage lingered for a moment against my retina. I tripped over one of the lines, slackening it, and by the time I had made it taut again I was accustomed enough to the darkness to find my way inside and fall onto my sleeping bag. In my dream Rosa came back across the water; she was naked except for her savage ornaments.

Sammy was there in the morning, calmer and more assured than he had been before he left. I swam with him for a while, and when I left the water this time he did not protest but simply patrolled the beach, hardly lifting himself above the waterline.

At midday I saw a ski boat coming down the channel. It attracted my attention because it was not weather-beaten like most of the boats that passed by. It looked like it had just come out of the showroom.

Brad Dawson was behind the wheel, driving with one elbow resting on the gunwale. When he saw me he waved and swung the boat at almost a ninety-degree angle out of the channel, then killed the engine abruptly and let it glide onto the mud shelf and founder there.

Brad nodded civilly from behind the wheel and stood up. He was wearing a striped terry-cloth shirt with a matching bathing suit. He put one foot on the gunwale and looked down at the mud, searching for a place to set it. Sammy watched him from behind the boat, keeping his head low in the water.

"You might want to take those shoes off," I told Brad as he stood on the boat deliberating.

"No, it's all right. They can get wet."

He jumped into the water, landing on both feet at the same time. The mud pulled off one of his shoes and he spent a moment looking for it before he extracted it from the water draped with slime.

Stepping onto the beach, he offered me his hand.

"Is Mary Katherine all right?" I asked him.

"She's fine. Worried crazy about you. Listen, we need to sit down and talk. I've got an ice chest full of cold beer in the boat. Maybe you can help me with it."

He took his other shoe off before wading back to the boat. The chest he handed down to me was filled with Heinekens.

"I didn't know what kind of beer you'd want," he said. "I've got some other stuff here too." He looked down at Sammy, who had rolled over on his side and was fanning one of his pecs in the air.

"So that's the famous porpoise. Do you mind if we go into the tent? I think I'm getting pretty sunburned."

In the pale green light of the tent Brad sat down, crossing his legs and setting his beer against his crotch. I waited patiently for him to speak.

"I'm here I guess as a kind of mediator," he said. "Mary Katherine got in touch with me yesterday. Up until that time she thought she was going to be able to make it down on her own.

"Basically, the situation is a mess. Mary Katherine got back to Port Aransas about the time Mason discovered the porpoise was missing. Of course they suspected you and wasted a lot of time running round in circles. Mary Katherine had been home for a while when they got to her house, and they decided just to sit around by the phone with her for a few days, hoping you'd call."

"What about the police?"

Brad took a sip of beer and shook his head. "No police. It seems Mason was involved in something like this before. Some janitor or somebody let one of his porpoises go at Sea Park. Mason pressed charges, the guy became a folk hero, Mason became a slave owner, that kind of thing. He's publicity shy. That's why Mary Katherine had to put up with them hanging around the house—there was always the threat that they would bring the police down on you. Basically, though, they want to settle the whole thing out of court, so to speak. All they want is their porpoise back. They don't know where you are yet, and if you've still got him or not. I told them I'd talk to you about it if they'd get off Mary Katherine's back, so she and the boy are in Corpus now with us. It's all very civilized."

He leaned back on an elbow.

"But it might not stay that way," I said.

"I suppose it depends on your attitude. They really are going out of their way. If you return the animal, no problem."

"I don't think so."

"You might want to think about it. It's a peculiar situation."

He pulled two more Heinekens out of the ice chest and opened them with a Swiss army knife.

"I thought I'd have more trouble finding this place than I did," he said. "It's just a straight shot, though, down the lagoon. Mary Katherine drew me a map but I only needed to look at it a few times."

"What do you think will happen if they don't get Sammy back?"

He shrugged. "Well, like I said, Mason is civilized, but he's not going to let you walk all over him. As long as you've got the porpoise and he's got the threat of criminal proceedings, you've got each other over a barrel. When and if the porpoise reverts to the wild, you'll have lost your advantage.

"Look, Jeff, I want you to know I'll try to help you no matter what you decide. I'm not exactly sure what you're up to. Theoretically I understand it, at least enough not to badger you about it. It's your cause, and I respect that. But it's important for you to realize how very serious this whole thing is."

"Thank you. I do."

"Have you had lunch? Ella fried some chicken for us, and there's some potato salad too, I think."

"That was nice of her. Both of you."

"I'll go get it."

He came back in a few minutes with an old-fashioned picnic basket and an envelope.

"This letter is from Mary Katherine," he said. He opened the picnic basket and set two paper plates onto the ground.

Jeff [the letter began. I was strangely touched by the urgency and concern the omission of "Dear" seemed to imply], Brad will tell you everything. I had to call him finally. Mason's two assistants were hanging around the house day and night. They played with Nat. I didn't know what to do. I was so worried about you, knowing you probably thought I'd deserted or betrayed you.

What should we do now? If Sammy has left yet perhaps you should come back with Brad on his boat and we'll face whatever charges they want to file. If he's still around I just don't know; maybe we should give him back. Everyone is so polite it's frightening.

Dear [here the missing word caused me to shudder], I love you, I trust in you. I know I'll see you in the next few days. I almost don't care anymore what the circumstances are, as long as I can be with you. Let Brad know what you plan to do. I love you.

M.K.

Brad waited until I had finished the letter, then handed me a plate filled with chicken and potato salad.

"There's pecan pie too," he said.

After lunch we sat in the tent and reviewed my options.

But I had none. I could hear Sammy splashing around outside the tent and began to wish Brad would leave soon so I could join him in the water.

"Just make sure Mary Katherine and Nat are safe," I said.

"Don't worry. This isn't the Mafia. It's you I'm worried about."

I heard the Coast Guard plane again, passing low over the island.

"I'll leave you the beer and the rest of the chicken," he said.

I shoved his boat out into the water for him, and shook his hand over the gunwale.

"Thank you for coming," I said. "And thank Ella."

Sammy followed the boat a short way up the channel, then broke off and swam back to me, demanding that I enter the water with him. As I did so, I heard the plane again and then saw it passing very low from the south. It was not the Coast Guard plane. Looking up at it as it buzzed the island, I could see the Sea Park logo on its nose, a dolphin jumping through a hoop.

The plane did not come back. It did not need to, since the pilot would have seen Brad's boat on the first pass. Sloppy planning, I thought.

The plane would go back to Port Aransas, and they would send the catch boat down for Sammy. I began kicking up the stakes of the tent, then left off when I saw a group of porpoises moving toward us down the channel. Through the binoculars I saw Triangle Fin leading them.

"Go on!" I yelled at Sammy, pointing toward the water where the herd was. "Go!"

He slapped the water hard with his tail and remained where he was.

The wild dolphins passed by. Sammy made a fierce impatient squeak but still would not go to them.

I hauled everything out of the tent and then collapsed it, letting the whole thing billow to the ground. When I had taken the ridgepoles apart and thrown them on top of the canvas, I had a bundle I could carry, however awkwardly, in my two hands.

Leaving the rest of my equipment for another trip, I carried the tent across the water to Rosa's shack. I called for her at the door but there was no answer, so I left the tent on the steps and went back for my other things, the stove, the lanterns, the ice chest, and sleeping bag. It took me four more trips to transfer the rest of the equipment and provisions. Sammy followed me anxiously offshore, and once tried to swim into a shallow inlet between the islands.

It was nearly dark when I was through. I sat down on the steps of her shack and waited for Rosa, and after a half hour or so saw her walking home from down the channel. The fierce sunset behind her took up half the sky, the great red cloud furrows running parallel with the chain of islands.

She smiled when she saw me and held out the bucket she was carrying for my inspection. It was filled with gray seawater and about a dozen crawling shells propelled by hermit crabs that could not get a purchase on the metal.

"Good shells," she said. "A woman in Corpus Christi comes down here sometimes to buy them from me."

I stood there for a moment admiring the shells.

"Is there any chance," I asked her, "that I could stay here on your island for a day or possibly two?"

She was nodding even before I had the question fully stated.

"Bring your things inside," she said.

I piled them as far away from the center of the room as possible, and then went downstairs to check on Sammy. He was directly under her house, swimming by the front pilings where the sand had been eaten away. Rosa came down and stared at him for a long time, entering the water in her waders but not touching him.

"It's dark enough now to go after a flounder," she said, still looking down at Sammy.

I went with her. She had only one gig, but I waded behind her with a lantern. In the shallow water between the islands the two lantern beams joined together, forming a binocular spotlight that shoved its radiance into the impenetrable water. As we walked slowly through the muck, each step that we took raised clouds of mud that followed behind us. Sammy cruised with us in the deeper water offshore. He was making no noises except for his breathing and an irregular clicking sound that turned into a gurgle as he let his open spiracle beneath the water. He seemed very calm, and I hoped he would leave again before the catch boat reached us.

Rosa's gig stabbed the water a few feet ahead of us. She brought up a flounder, a large one, that flapped violently on the other end. She put the fish on a stringer that was tied to her waist and let it trail through the water as we walked back to her house.

"He'll be big enough for dinner," she said. I followed her dumbly, having lost my bearings in the darkness. I could hear Sammy following behind us, the gentle slap of the water as he sounded and breathed.

When we reached her house I turned to look up the channel and saw the running lights of a large boat. The well-tuned hum of its engines carried without interference across the water.

"That's them," I whispered, fearing my own words might carry as well as the engine sound. I left Rosa and walked out to the shelf of the channel and quietly slapped the water. Sammy came to me, nudging me with his beak, thinking I wanted to play.

I held the dolphin firmly by the pectorals and rocked him in my lap in the shallow water.

The boat slowed down near my old island, and swept the shore with a powerful deck light. My old campsite was illuminated. With the boat idling I could hear voices bickering with one another on the deck. For a moment it looked as if they would turn around and head back up the channel, as I had hoped they would do. But the boat picked up speed and moved south instead, sweeping the shore as it went.

They would surely catch me in the light if I stayed in the

open. I let go of Sammy, coaxed him out into deeper water, and then ran up the heavy stairs. Rosa was standing at the table, looking down at the flounder she had caught.

"They're coming this way," I said. "They may ask you about me."

"I won't tell them anything."

We both stared at the fish for a few moments as the boat drew closer. Through the door I saw the light sweeping the base of the house, then it rose and came in through the window, absorbed into the lantern light. The boat fell back into idle again, and I listened for Sammy, praying that he was out in the channel now, submerged, his lungs full of air.

"Excuse me," Mason called. "Is anybody home?"

Rosa leaned out the window. "You bet," she said.

"I'm sorry to bother you, ma'am," Mason called. "But we're looking for a friend of ours who said he was going to meet us somewhere down here. He's a young man, probably has a green tent set up someplace. And you probably won't believe this, but he's got a pet porpoise with him."

"A porpoise!" Rosa said.

"Yes, ma'am."

"No, I ain't seen nothing like that."

I looked down at the floor. I could hear the water lapping below us, eating away the shore.

"Well," Mason said resignedly, "I thank you for your time."

The boat started up again, its engines as subdued and composed as Mason's voice. It proceeded several hundred yards down the channel, then made a wide arc and turned back north, toward us. I stood with my knuckles tense against the table edge. The boat light began to sweep the shore again. If Sammy would just lie low for one more pass we would be all right.

Then Canales blew his whistle. I ran downstairs and into the water, slapping it. Sammy came to me, but he was agitated, he wanted to get away.

"No!" I whispered, stroking his high forehead, hoping to

calm him. "Stay here." The light was sweeping the other side of the channel now. We had a chance. But each time the whistle sounded it seemed to send a current through Sammy's body. He began to thrash, and finally he broke away and swam toward the boat, which was still a hundred yards below us. I took out after him, running along the shore for a while and then dove into the water. I set out in a racing crawl, thinking I could intercept Sammy before he reached them.

I stopped swimming, lifted my head out of the water, and looked around in the air. I saw the running lights of the boat, heard the hum of its twin inboard-outboard engines, heard Canales' whistle again. Sammy surfaced near me and held his body vertically so that we were on the same keel now. He was waiting for the next blast of the whistle. When it came he rose up and began to walk backward on his tail.

"Christ! There he is!" I heard Canales say. Someone swung the light around and caught the strange gray shape in its beam. I treaded water, not knowing what to do, almost transfixed by Sammy's performance in the spotlight.

I heard the boat slip into gear but did not pay attention. I was thinking it was still possible to swim over to Sammy and convince him to submerge and not come up again until they were far away from us. Then I saw the prow overhead like a shadow.

I took a breath and dove just as the foremost red light passed over me. Even in the dark opaque water I had a clear view of the twin columns of froth gouging the surface. I fought to get down farther. It took a long time to do this, the salt buoying me up. Even so I thought I had made it when I heard a dull, nauseating *thwaaaap* and felt myself being sucked upward. I could see the white wake on the surface of the water toward which I was heading.

Something went wrong, and I did not break through the wake as I would have liked. I was staring into the water, not breathing, descending again. I wanted to breathe air, but could not find my way out of the suffocating, gelatinous element that clung to every pore of my body. Then there was a familiar shape beneath me, prodding me upward. When I reached the surface I was not even aware I was breathing again, simply took comfort in the great exhalation I heard near my face.

Stay on the surface, the shape said. *Stay here and breathe.* I had a vision: I saw into the shape's body, the state of its being. It was the same as my own.

Rest.

I rested on the broad, undulating, uncomfortable thing, sometimes rolling off into the water, gagging on salt, feeling it shove me up again.

Rest.

The pain was growing outward from the precision of the saltwater sting, broadening into a gross, formless presence. I tried to focus it again, but could not, and slid off my support once again, opening my eyes on the muddy water of the channel.

Chapter 14

I was lying on the deck, looking up at the stars, feeling the boat shake beneath me like the vibrator bed in my room at the Salt Sea. The course was remarkably smooth, and I could close my eyes and think with pleasure of the well-formed craft that was rushing me to safety across the placid inland waters.

They had put a pillow beneath my head, and I felt the pressure from a tourniquet just above my knee. Turning my head, I saw Sammy lying next to me on the deck, his mild eye watching me without distress. I heard his clicking sounds and moved my hand across the deck so that I could graze the tip of his pectoral fin with my fingers.

Bill Mason appeared above me, his bald head gleaming in the running lights.

"How do you feel?" he asked, bending down to loosen the tourniquet. I felt the blood in my upper leg sluicing deliriously onto the deck.

"Any pain?"

I shook my head but knew the pain was there, hovering like a cloud above my body, ready to descend.

When Mason was through Canales bent down to take his place.

"You fucked up," he said without malice.

I couldn't answer him.

"You'll be okay," he said. "Just lie back and enjoy the ride."

I took his advice. I looked up at the stars and felt myself passing so swiftly beneath them that the whole panorama of the night sky revolved above me like a planetarium screen. My leg did not begin to hurt until they lifted me onto a stretcher, a dolphin sling. My arms hung down through the holes that had been cut out for pectoral fins. They set me onto a bed, with blazing white stiff sheets. There must have been an ambulance ride then, and an urgent passage into the emergency room, but by that time I was aware of very little.

No one was there when I woke up. I looked down at my right leg. It was still there, something was still there, wrapped in gauze from the knee down to the toes. I pressed the button by my bed. A teenaged boy came in. He was dressed in a green gingham shirt.

"I'm just a Shamrock," he said. "The nurse is coming. Do you want anything? Magazines or something?"

"No, thank you."

The nurse swept in, sent the Shamrock on his way, and opened the blinds. It was afternoon.

"Are you thirsty?" she asked. "Sometimes the medication makes people thirsty."

I nodded. She got me a glass of water from the sink and held my head up while I drank it.

"Your wife and little boy are outside," she said, "but I'm having Dr. Rush paged. He wants to talk to you first, okay?"

I went to sleep again and woke when I heard Rush whispering to the nurse. When I opened my eyes, he shook my hand.

"How are you feeling, Jeff?" he said with great concern.

"Fine," I said.

"You had a water-skiing accident? Is that right?"

"Yes," I said, realizing how smoothly Mason had handled the whole affair. "What do you have to tell me?"

"Good news, I think. We saved your leg, that's the most important thing. There's a damn good vascular man here."

He took out a silver ballpoint pen and began trailing it above the bandaged leg. "What happened is that the boat prop hit you on the right calf. It broke your bone there in about a half-dozen places. The major thing is the tissue loss, that's what we're most concerned about. We'll do some skin grafts, make it look a lot better than it does now, but there's no way we're going to be able to replace the muscle tissue you've lost."

"Okay," I said.

"We'll see how you do, then we'll start some therapy."

I was overcome for a moment. It felt like someone was tightening a screw deep in my bone.

"Discomfort?" Rush asked.

I nodded, unable to speak.

"I'll have the nurse get you something. You tell me if it doesn't do the job. We don't want to start you out on morphine if we don't need to."

"Okay."

"Your wife is outside. Would you rather see her later?"

"No," I said. "Please. Have her come in."

Mary Katherine walked in. She was radiant with worry. She kissed me and wiped her tears away with her palm.

"I didn't know what to do," she said. "I just kept thinking of you there all alone and I couldn't come. Did you know that Sammy kept you from drowning?" she asked.

"Yes," I said.

"I know it's just instinct, but still."

"Where is Sammy?"

"He's in Florida, Jeff. Mason left with him this morning."

She took my hand. "But it's all right. He'll be happy there. Mando said he practically jumped into the boat, wanting to be captured."

She sat and looked at me for a moment. "Did the doctor talk to you? About your leg?"

I nodded.

"You'll still be able to do everything. You'll be able to walk, that's what counts. You almost lost it, you know?"

She tried to embrace me, leaning over the bed with her feet still on the floor. I took hold of her, feeling the fabric of her blouse, the cool skin at the back of her neck.

"I think you're starting to lose your tan," I said, looking into her face.

"It's worry. Nat's worried too. He won't say so, but he missed you so much. They won't let him up because he's under twelve. Oh, honey," she said, breaking into tears again, "we're so lucky. You could have been hurt so much worse."

I had to grip the sides of the bed as hard as I could now, tightening my face so much that tears leaked out of my eyes, but it was not until the pain had subsided that I began to sob.

In a few days I was able to sit in the wheelchair. I met Canales in the lounge by the big picture window.

"God, that was dumb," he said, smiling.

I was still groggy with the Demerol. I was thinking of the metal pins holding together the bone in my atrophied calf.

"I don't really blame you, though," he went on. "You know what Mason told me to say to you?"

"What?"

"No hard feelings."

"He's an asshole."

"Tell me about it. All his trainers have to wear special uniforms, can you believe it? Special swimming suits and these T-shirts that have a picture of Sammy on them and say 'Waldo Is Coming.' That's what his name is in the movie, Waldo. He's supposed to be a screwball porpoise. Zany, that kind of shit."

Canales looked around the room nervously. "So when'll you be walking?"

"A couple months I should be getting around okay. Where's Sara?"

"She went to Austin to seek her fortune."

We didn't speak for a few moments. He walked over and shook hands.

"I'm leaving tomorrow morning for Florida. I'm sorry about everything. But I'll take good care of Sammy, I'll be on his case. Watch for the movie, and don't forget to look for my name in the credits."

. . .

Nat was downstairs waiting with the Dawsons. It was Sunday, and the five of us ate in the coffee shop and read the papers. The sunlight hit the bright mosaic in the lobby with force and clarity. I looked up at the lamb in Christ's lap, at its mild simpering face. A hand was raised above it in blessing, and the yellow light from the halo flooded the innocent flock.

Chapter 15

I was able to book *Bigfoot Stalks!* for the Crow's Nest only a few weeks after its release. Even though we were on the third-run circuit for regular features, we had some muscle with the distributor for exploitation films.

The Dawsons drove over to see it with us, and we all sat anxiously in the open-air theater waiting for dusk.

Then there it was. There I was. Bigfoot leaped from a cliff into a swarm of hand-held camera angles meant to disguise the lack of special effects. I heard a growl I had not made. The girl backpackers whose down sleeping bags I had shredded on the trail held each other and screamed. Bigfoot jumped high in the air and landed on both feet. The ghost tissues in my leg throbbed. That was one stunt I could never do again.

"Is that really you?" Nat asked me.

"Sure it's me," I said, looking at the hulking, furry, terrestrial creature attacking motorists now on the Interstate, pulling skiers out of their lift seats. The animal stormed into the New Mexico state capitol, savaging several senators. Then there he was at the top of the miraculous stairway, shot through the heart by the zoologist hero, staggering downward, then growling piteously and rolling to the bottom. Dead.

We found my name in the credits and applauded. When it was over my leg was hurting more than usual, and I popped a painkiller and limped to the car.

"They should have called it *Bigfoot Sucks*," Mary Katherine said. "That was *terrible*. But I was proud of you."

"Do they really have those?" Nat asked.

"No," I said. "It's like the Loch Ness monster. Mythical."

"Well," Ella said, with rare irony. "We don't know how to thank you for such a delightful evening."

Brad mumbled some pleasantry. He seemed more confused than usual. We stood there for a while in the chilly salt air and made plans to get together again.

"I just had to call you," the Seamstress said over the phone. "Have you seen the movie?"

"I saw it last night, as a matter of fact."

"Wasn't it *great?*"

"Yes," I said. "How have you been?"

"Miserable. I'm back in Santa Fe. Working on another movie. *Harry Truman vs. Godzilla*. I don't know why, but when I saw *Bigfoot* I just started missing you terribly. You were really good, Jeff."

"Thank you. It was the costume."

"How are things?" she asked.

"I'm married."

"That's good. I'm not surprised. I'm happy for you. How are the porpoises?"

"I'm not doing that anymore. I'm running a movie theater now."

"A real businessman. How'd you get into that?"

"Inheritance."

"Someday," she said, "I'll come down to see you. I'm glad that you're married, I think it's the best thing for you. Oh, I'm supposed to ask you if you want to be in the sequel."

I could almost feel the sharp, delirious mountain air coming through the phone with her voice.

. . .

That week I closed down the theater for the winter. In a package of promotional material for upcoming movies there was an announcement for *Waldo the Wacky Porpoise,* "coming this summer to a theater near you."

It was time for Mary Katherine to finish with her research and begin writing her thesis. We went out in the little Boston Whaler one last time, on a November morning with a wind-chill factor of thirty degrees. It was the first time I had noticed that winter had arrived, a soft, even change in the quality of the weather that deepened and darkened the water.

The sky was overcast and close around us. Mary Katherine wore her parka, the hood up around her knit cap, the tan on her face replaced by flushed ruddy skin. Nat sat facing her, trying to keep warm between my knees. She did not speak into the tape recorder, simply piloted the boat up Lydia Ann and into the still, blanketed waters of Aransas Bay.

I could feel the ease and the panic beneath the murky waters, the struggle for sensation among the creatures there, and thought of Sammy's new environment, the Florida lagoon that was as clear as an arctic crevasse. Someday, I thought, it would be pleasant to look into that water, but I knew I wanted this brooding seascape around me for the rest of my life.

My leg ached in the cold wind. The gray water rocked itself smoothly in the inland basin, and I thought of all my dead submerged there, in water nearly as thick and abiding as the earth itself.

Then in the center of Aransas Bay we saw the shapes, after all this time such an unexpected, tantalizing sight. Through my binoculars I could make out Triangle Fin, feeding with his family in the northernmost extent of their range.

A Note on the Type

The text of this book was set, via computer-driven cathode-ray tube, in a film version of Caledonia, a typeface designed by W(illiam) A(ddison) Dwiggins for the Mergenthaler Linotype Company in 1939. Dwiggins chose to call his new face Caledonia, the Roman name for Scotland, because it was inspired by the Scotch types cast about 1833 by Alexander Wilson & Son, Glasgow type founders. However, there is a calligraphic quality about Caledonia that is totally lacking in the Wilson types. Dwiggins referred to an even earlier typeface for this "liveliness of action"—one cut around 1790 by William Martin for the printer William Bulmer. Caledonia has more weight than the Martin letters, and the bottom finishing strokes (serifs) of the letters are cut straight across, without brackets, to make sharp angles with the upright stems, thus giving a "modern face" appearance.

W. A. Dwiggins (1880-1956) began an association with the Mergenthaler Linotype Company in 1929 and over the next twenty-seven years designed a number of book types, the most interesting of which are the Metro series, Electra, Caledonia, Eldorado, and Falcon.

Composed by Publishers Phototype, Inc.,
Carlstadt, New Jersey
Printed and bound by The Haddon Craftsmen, Inc.,
Scranton, Pennsylvania
Typography and binding design by Virginia Tan